Pearl Lake

J D Griesbach

Good Wizard Publishing

* Cover design by Denise Kelly from Tandee Design *

Copyright @ 2014 J D Griesbach

ISBN-13: 978-0-692-31946-8

To
Dad and Mom, who supported me in everything
I ever did, and loved me unconditionally

« Chapter 1 »

I STOOD THERE HELPLESS as Chris ran by me, his eyes opened wide with fear. It was very possible that the big guy chasing him would hurt Chris if he caught him, and there was nothing I could do about it now.

Fourteen-year-old Chris Garrett appeared to be a full foot shorter and fifty pounds lighter than his powerful-looking assailant. Chris looked back over his shoulder just in time to see the attacker's outstretched hands within inches of his body, reaching out to grab him and smash him to the ground. Still sprinting at full speed, Chris planted his left foot and pushed off of it, veering quickly to his right. He narrowly avoided his pursuer's grasp, temporarily throwing him off balance.

It was obvious that the hunter was not going to give up the chase. He swiftly regained his balance, and after a few more steps was right behind Chris again. With a burst of power he leapt into the air with his arms spread wide, ready to pounce on top of Chris like a dominating lion trying to take down a gazelle. Instinctively, Chris immediately swerved sharply back to his left. The attacker flew through the air helplessly and reached out to grab onto Chris' jersey, but it slipped through his fingers as Chris sped away unharmed. The guy crashed to the ground head first, furiously spitting out grass, mud, and a steady stream of profanities.

Chris sprinted straight ahead another twenty yards and calmly set the football down in the end zone.

Following closely behind, the referee blew his whistle and raised his hands upright, signaling and calling out loudly, "Touchdown"!

Chris trotted back to the sidelines with a sheepish smile on his face. It looked like he was almost embarrassed by the attention, but I could tell he was excited about making a terrific play, and he should have been. It was a great run by Chris, and a great play by the entire team.

The rest of the players and coaches were cheering and jumping up and down, patting Chris on his helmet and shoulder pads, and swarming all over him, congratulating him enthusiastically. He walked up to me eagerly as the team surrounded us.

"Matt, Jacob – you both made terrific blocks on that play," I said. I looked around at the rest of the excited players. "Every one of you made your blocks. Good job!"

I looked, finally, at Chris as the excitement continued to build within him. Even with the accolades he received from the other players and coaches, he still craved words of approval from me. In fact, he thrived on them. Maybe it was because as his head coach, I demanded his very best efforts on the football field, and as someone who cared about him as a person, I expected him to be on his best behavior off the field, too, and Chris knew it.

However, it probably had more to do with the horrific car accident that killed both of his parents when he was only six years old. Even though he was taken-in by his grandparents, who continue to raise him in a stable and loving environment, he may have a greater need for praise and acceptance than other kids his age. Not having children of my own, I can't say for sure, but I do know that I care about Chris as though he were my own son.

Looking at him, I was amazed at how much he had grown and matured over the last five years. Chris was of average size compared to the other kids his age. Even though he was unusually quiet and kept to himself, he stood out from the rest not only because of his white-blond hair, but also because of his high level of intelligence. It wasn't only 'book' smarts. He was a straight 'A' student, and his test results showed an exceptionally high *IQ*, but it was more than that. He had common sense and 'street' smarts. Chris seemed to notice things that other kids his age didn't, and tended to have a greater sense of awareness of what was going on around him than most of the other kids, or even adults, for that matter.

Chris used to have a reputation around town of being a troublemaker, but I knew that any trouble he had gotten into was just harmless fun. His bad-guy reputation was also somewhat exacerbated by his quiet demeanor, which some mistakenly took as a sign of guilt. In truth, it was simply a matter of Chris not needing or caring to explain or justify his actions to those who don't even know him. Despite any perceptions others may have of him, right or wrong, Chris has developed into a quiet leader. His teammates and classmates respect and look up to him.

"Are you trying to give me a heart attack?" I asked Chris with as much of a pained expression on my face as I could muster, considering how happy I was for him for making such a great play on his touchdown run. "With all of the terrific blocks you got from your teammates, you should have been able to run into the end zone backwards," I said, giving him a hard time mixed with praise, not wanting him to get a big head. He grinned, not believing me for a moment. "Great play, Chris!" I gave in. "That had to be your best run yet," I added honestly. His smile widened and his face lit up.

I gathered the players and coaches together after the game to celebrate our hard-fought 20-14 victory.

"Jacob, Matt, Brandon – did you notice when we blocked them low," I pointed out, "we got better leverage on them and were able to push them back, even though they were bigger than us?"

They nodded in response, understanding the positive results of executing some of the techniques that we had practiced over the past several weeks.

"Brandon," I continued, "you saw what you made happen in the third quarter when you used the pivot move that you have been working on. You got around the lineman and then hustled to get to the quarterback. I don't think anybody could have stopped you on that play!"

"Yeah!" confirmed Eli, one of the smallest players on our team. "That was an unbelievable move, Brandon!" Eli knew that Brandon hit the quarterback's arm while he was throwing the ball, which sent the ball wobbling high up into the air, enabling Eli to intercept it.

Brandon turned to him and answered, "Eli, you sure made a great interception on that play. It was amazing!"

That's what I liked about these kids. They weren't selfish or self-centered, and really stuck together and complimented each other.

"We beat a team today that was bigger and stronger than us," I said. "We won the game because of your hard work and teamwork!"

The whole team erupted into a loud, deafening cheer. Seeing them enjoy it together reminded me that this close team bonding was one of the best things about playing team sports.

I had coached various little league and grade school teams over the years. After a while, I think some of the other coaches and parents saw that we consistently had successful teams, and the players were having a lot of fun. So they asked if I could help out the Pearl Lake High School coaches. Now here I am nearly eight years later, the head coach of Pearl Lake's freshman football, basketball, and baseball teams.

Coaching ninth-graders may not necessarily be recognized as having reached the pinnacle of all sports jobs, but I really enjoy coaching at this level. I like teaching the fundamentals of the game when the players are still young, knowing that they will utilize what they learn as long as they play football. At their age, most of the kids are very eager to learn and want to do well.

I do this just for fun, though. My real job is Town Sheriff of Pearl Lake. Pearl Lake is located in central Wisconsin, about fifty miles northeast of Madison.

It's not that my job isn't fun, too. For the most part, I like being the town sheriff. It isn't roll over laughing, knee-slapping kind of fun, but it is rewarding work. Pearl Lake is home to me, and I like working for the people in the same town and county where I live.

Ever since I was about ten years old, I can remember my friends and other people in town asking for my assistance in solving one mystery or another. I was often asked to help find lost or stolen items, and even missing children or pets, on occasion. Sometimes I received unusual requests, like one summer when I was asked if I could find out what caused a large number of fish to be found dead, floating on an area lake.

Luckily, every missing child and pet that I was asked to help find over the years was found unharmed, and nearly all of the stolen or lost items were retrieved undamaged. As it turned out, I was able to find evidence that the large fish kill in the area lake was due to a combination of extremely hot temperatures and an accidental fertilizer run-off into the lake that summer. Although some cases were definitely more difficult to solve than others, everyone credited me, often undeservedly, for helping to solve them.

I certainly wasn't *Encyclopedia Brown* or *Danny Dunn* or one of the *Hardy Boys*, who were fictional boyhood geniuses in books that were popular when I was young. Maybe I was just curious, or persistent, but for whatever reason, people from Pearl Lake came to me looking for help. They thought of me as the local *kid sleuth*. It just seemed natural that I ended up here as the town sheriff, continuing to get involved when they needed help as I had always done in the past.

I was born and raised in the Town of Pearl Lake, which is situated directly north of the lake with the same name. The lake is approximately one mile long and nearly one-half mile wide. The Town of Pearl Lake is a small community with around two thousand people, most of whom are hard-working and friendly. Located in Arrowhead County, Pearl Lake is surrounded by plenty of nice-sized lakes, most of which are ideal for fishing, boating, and other water sports.

With their large, sandy beaches, most of the lakes are great for swimming, too.

My name is Jason Avalon. I am thirty-three years old, six feet-two inches tall, and have light brown hair, curly enough to always seem to go in the opposite direction that I comb it. With my job as sheriff, I try to keep in shape by playing various sports like baseball, basketball, and golf, and by working out a few times a week at the local health center.

I am single. It's not that I haven't been looking, but with my workaholic ways and commitment to my job who would want me? Maybe I am too set in my ways. It seems like no woman would tolerate my stubbornness, or my interest in sports, or my other various bad habits like playing cards occasionally with my buddies, or shooting craps in Las Vegas once or twice a year. I guess the odds of throwing three sevens in a row on the craps table are better than the odds of meeting a woman in the Pearl Lake area that would put up with me. I also tend to think that I would score on the *Quasimodo* end of the attractiveness scale, which probably doesn't help my chances.

My parents, now retired, still live happily in Pearl Lake in a house across the lake from mine. My brother, David, who is three years older than me, is married and has two girls, twelve and ten years old, both wise beyond than their years. Both Dave and his wife have professional jobs and live in nearby Madison.

I also have a younger sister, Kimberly. She is a few years younger than me and has an administrative job at the Lakeshore Bank in Pearl Lake. She still lives at home with our parents, which is not that unusual nowadays in small towns like ours. Even though each of us has our own jobs, hobbies, and other things going on in our lives, our family remains very close and we try to spend as much time together as we can.

After I graduated from the University of Wisconsin-Whitewater with a B.S. degree in Criminology, I got a job as a police officer in Southern California, of all places. It was quite a culture shock for a small-town boy like me from Wisconsin, but I learned a lot about law enforcement, and I learned even more about human behavior, especially as it related to unlawful activities, unfortunately.

A few years later my long-time friend Tom Kaminski, a police detective in Chicago, told me that the Chicago Police Department was looking for a police officer. I jumped at the chance to work with him and to get back closer to Wisconsin, so I applied for and got the job. However, when the Pearl Lake sheriff retired a short time later and I was offered the job, I did not hesitate to accept it. Tom and I were both disappointed that we would not be working together in Chicago longer, but he knew how excited I was to be returning home and was genuinely happy for me. We both knew that we would still get together often, and time has shown that to be the case.

My friendship with Tom, a tall, strong, freckle-faced redhead, goes back a long way. We have been close friends as long as I can remember, probably since we were both about five or six years old. Tom's parents own a cottage on Pearl Lake, so he and his family frequently vacationed here, which is how we met. We were inseparable during most of the summer vacation months, and spent a lot of time on the water, either swimming, water skiing or fishing. We did our share of traipsing through the woods, too. Both of our fathers were avid sportsmen, and taught us how to handle guns, bows and arrows, and other weapons safely. These responsibilities were taught to us from an early age, and neither Tom nor I ever took them lightly. As it turned out, the lessons came in handy since we both ended up in the law enforcement field.

I was looking forward to seeing Tom and his wife, Amy, and their five year-old daughter, Elizabeth, again this weekend, even though we got together a month ago when they were here last. Similar to my parents, Tom's folks are now retired and live permanently in their Pearl Lake cottage.

∞

Our football team is scheduled to play a game in North Chicago on Saturday afternoon. I thought it would be fun for the kids to see the *Chicago Field Museum of Natural History* while we are in the area, so I arranged for the team to go to Chicago a day early.

Since it has a unique educational value, the school administrators gave the approval for the team to leave school early on Friday morning to drive to the museum and spend the day there. The only hitch was that each of the players would need to submit a written report of their museum experience to their history teacher when they returned to class. The players decided unanimously that it would be well worth it.

Most of the players and coaches have arranged to spend Friday night with various friends and family in the Chicago area to help keep travel costs down. Tom and Amy will put me up for the night, as they have many times before, and also have enough room for a few other players and their families.

Pearl Lake High School pays for buses for away games, which are usually one-day rides. When the team plans overnight trips like this weekend, the coaches and parents agree to pay for any additional costs over and above what the school would typically pay. The team conducts various fund-raisers throughout the year, such as candy sales and pizza sales, which help to pay for most of the added costs of our outings. Luckily, the parents overwhelmingly support our trips and do not mind pitching in a few dollars whenever they are scheduled.

Evidently, the parents and players must enjoy our team excursions because most of the requests I get are to schedule them more often, not less. They look at them as weekend getaways or mini-vacations that they wouldn't normally get to take during the school year. It enables the parents to support their kids in their sports activities, and the kids love it. Living in a small town in Wisconsin, it can be one of life's simplest pleasures.

« Chapter 2 »

THE PEARL LAKE COACHES and some friends usually gather at my place on the nights after our football games, and tonight was no exception. The temperature was still 69° outside on this early September night. The air was crisp and clear as we played poker on the screened-in porch overlooking Pearl Lake. The lake was calm as it glimmered under the light of the stars and nearly full moon. The big brick corner fireplace on the porch was stoked-up and emitting a comforting heat that took the chill out of the air and helped us to settle down from the excitement of our football game. The peaceful calls of the loons on the lake also had a calming effect on us all.

"Brandon had some pretty positive contact in the trenches today, Steve," Bob Colgate, our defensive coach said to Steve Dozier, Brandon's father, and coach of the linemen. Bob always seemed to speak in riddles, or talk around subjects so you always had to be thinking in order to figure out what the hell he was talking about. Instead of saying 'There wasn't a cloud in the sky', he would usually say something like 'There wasn't a cirrus or cumulus in sight in the lower atmosphere'.

"Did Brandon have happy feet, or athletes foot, or what?" Bob asked Steve. "Dealer takes one card," he added clearly with a smile on his face, as he threw in one card and dealt himself another in this five-card draw poker game.

Unlike the seven-card stud poker games that are currently popular around the country, five-card draw is a slightly faster-playing poker game. Each player is dealt five cards, and can then choose to discard and replace up to three cards, ending up with five cards in their hand. There are no shared cards that each player uses in their hands, as in seven-card stud. In five-card draw, each player plays with the final five cards in their hands. It tends to be a little less intense of a game, and is more conducive to our group of friends playing just for the fun of it, and not out for blood or money. That's not to say that we don't have our moments of spirited competition.

"Brandon played okay today," Steve answered Bob Colgate modestly. "He told me after the game how much fun he had. You're right though, Bob. Brandon was upset that he jumped before the snap and got called for an off-side penalty," he said, responding to Bob's 'happy feet' riddle. "Give me three cards," Steve added with a frown on his face. Apparently he was not too happy with the remaining two cards in his hand.

Eric Anders is a tall, Norwegian blond, with thick wire-rimmed glasses that cover his intelligent eyes that look like they are constantly computing, like a human calculator. Eric is the president of the Lakeshore Bank in Pearl Lake, and is one of my closest and most trusted friends. Having seen the football game, he said, "Brian gets so excited that it's hard for him to hold back sometimes. He just needs to settle down a little bit. He sure gives it his all on every play, though." Without expression, Eric added, "I'll take three cards."

Jim Johnson, Pearl Lake's big, scrappy varsity football coach, who we all called 'Bruiser', added, "I thought Brandon looked good today. He played with intensity, which I like to see." Jim was a tough, hard-hitting football player in high school. Everyone figured he must have left bruises on the opposing players every time he hit them, so they started calling him Bruiser. The nickname has stuck ever since. He looked down at the cards in his hand, frowning. "What the hell – I guess I'll take three cards, too!" he said as he discarded three cards.

"Brandon did have a good game today," I agreed. "He has really improved since the beginning of the season." I threw three cards away, kept a pair of fours, and requested three new cards.

"I would rather see him with fire in his gut, than have to light a fire under his butt to get him going," Bob said in an unusually direct manner. We all nodded our heads in agreement. "I'll bet three," he added with a cocky smile on his face as he threw the maximum number of chips allowed in our friendly poker game into the pot.

Bob Colgate used to help coach the Pearl Lake varsity football team a few years ago, when his son was on the team. After his son graduated and Bob's work schedule made it hard for him to get to practices regularly, Bruiser asked me if I could use another coach on the freshman team. Since our practices usually started a little later than the varsity practices, and we didn't practice as often, Bruiser thought that Bob could help me out with the freshman team. I didn't really know Bob that well at the time, but since we needed a defensive coach, with Bruiser's recommendation I brought him on board. I'd have to say it's worked out well for everyone.

Bob, who has sandy-colored hair and is about 5'8" tall, was born and raised in Chicago. He is the

President/Owner of Badger Finance Company, which he bought five years ago. The Badger Finance office is located in the city of Fond du Lac, which is about ten miles from Pearl Lake. Bob previously worked as a salesman for an industrial supply company, and obviously was very successful since he earned enough money to purchase Badger Finance at the relatively young age of thirty-eight. Ever since I have known him, Bob has been very well polished socially. He always seems to say the right things, dress appropriately in all settings, and tell the perfect jokes for every occasion. These are fine skills he has honed over many years of entertaining clients on the company's expense tab, and they have served him well, not only as the president of his company, but also as an assistant coach.

Steve Dozier, on the other hand, was born and raised on a farm here in Pearl Lake. Steve, who is a few inches taller and wider than me, has worked longer and harder than anyone I have ever known. His father proudly handed over the title to the family farm to him several years ago, along with all of the responsibilities that came with it. Steve's three sons, Bart and Andrew, both now in their early twenties, freshman football player, Brandon, and younger daughter, Sara, and his wife, Debbie, all help on the farm. As does his father, Louis, who at nearly seventy years old still seems to be as strong as an ox. His wife died of cancer several years ago, so Louis still lives on the farm with the family, and they are happy to have him.

I have a great deal of respect for Steve. He treats his wife and family very well. Whenever anyone in Pearl Lake needs anything, he and his family are always there to help. Many people in the area talk about how he often gives away corn, beans, melons or other crops from his fields to others who may be going through hard times or are struggling to feed their families. During the winter months, it is not unusual to see him in town with his pick-up truck pulling out vehicles stuck in the snow. The word gets around even though he tries to keep it quiet. It takes a lot of hard work and business savvy to make it in farming in Wisconsin these days. While many family farms go out of business each year in Wisconsin and around the country, Steve has continued to be successful.

"I sure can't get a decent poker hand tonight!" Steve groused good-naturedly, as he tossed in his cards and dropped out of the game.

"Aw, that's too bad," Eric answered Steve, unsympathetically. "I'll see your bet," Eric said to Bob. Still blank-faced, he threw in his chips and matched Bob's bet to stay in the game.

Bruiser laughed. "It looks like you guys are too serious about this hand. I'll let you fight it out. I drop."

I looked at the pair of fours that I was still holding, and picked up my three-card draw for the first time. One at a time, I added each card to my hand: a seven, a four, and another four! I had four fours! "Okay...I'll see your three, and I'll raise you three," I said, trying to stay calm as I pushed six chips into the pile on the middle of the table.

Bob was obviously no longer willing to put in more money on his bluff hand. He threw in his cards and dropped out of the game.

Eric looked at the growing pile of chips on the table. "Well, I can't let you take it that easily. I'll see your three, and raise you another three," he challenged, throwing his chips onto the pile, boldly adding to my earlier bet.

Eric remained stone-faced, but I didn't think he was bluffing. *He must have a very good hand*, I thought, but I've played poker many nights when not even *one* four-of-a-kind hand was dealt. Confident I had a winning hand, I slid my three chips into the pile and stayed in the game. "I'll call you," I said.

Eric coolly turned his cards over one at a time: Ace of clubs... Ace of hearts... Ace of diamonds... If Eric had another ace, my great hand would be beaten by an even *greater* hand. He next turned over a Queen of Spades...and then turned over a *Queen of Clubs*. A full house – Aces over Queens! It was definitely a strong hand, but not as good as four-of-a-kind!

I turned my hand over, revealing my four fours as everyone clapped and cheered, acknowledging my rare four-of-a-kind hand.

"Damn!" Eric yelled, laughing. "Great hand, Jason! Now you can buy the beer with your winnings for our next poker game."

"You've got a deal," I said as I hauled in the pile of chips. "Ahh...'Lucky in cards – unlucky in love,'" I stated, philosophically.

"Are you serious?" Eric asked incredulously. "The women are always swooning over you. You just don't notice it."

"What are you talking about?" I asked. Bob, Bruiser and Steve nodded their heads in agreement with Eric, and just smiled.

Steve Dozier patted me on the back, harder than he realized not knowing his own strength. "Oh, the right woman will find you yet, if you don't hide too much," he said. "Then maybe I'll be able to beat you at cards!"

« Chapter 3 »

KATIE'S PLACE RESTAURANT AND Bar in Pearl Lake is known for the wide variety of homemade items on its menu, which always seem to be prepared to perfection. Conveniently located on Main Street amongst a few friendly neighborhood bars, the General Store, a Piggly-Wiggly grocery store, and the Lakeshore Bank, the red brick building was built back in 1910 but still looked new. Katie bought the building, which used to be an old hotel and saloon, and totally refurbished it. She refinished the original wooden oak floors and restored the red brick on the inside and outside of the building to its original condition. She also updated the south, east, and west sides of the building with new, large, energy-efficient windows that have an old-fashioned appearance and blend perfectly with the style of the early 1900's building.

The tables and chairs inside are sturdy, comfortable antiques. Several bookshelves arranged throughout the restaurant are jam-packed with books, both old and new. Customers could regularly be seen leisurely browsing through the books while they were eating, or drinking coffee. 'That's what they're there for,' Katie always said.

A wide assortment of antique serving plates and dishes, and ceramic, brass, and wood-carved figures decorate the entire area. The walls are covered with interesting, colorful paintings. Katie had gathered quite an impressive collection of antiques over the years.

Along with the bookshelves and antiques, the restaurant is filled with live, plush green plants and miniature trees that are arranged to effectively break up the large space into several smaller, more private areas for dining and visiting. The bar area is a separate room on the right side of the restaurant as guests walk in. It is set up with several big-screen television sets to satisfy the many sports fans that frequent the place.

Katie's Place is impeccably clean, and everything always appears to be in its right place, just as Katie likes it. She always wears white clothes and white aprons, which remain clean and spotless. I could never understand how she can prepare so much food and always keep so clean, until I found out her secret. She constantly changes her aprons throughout the day – sometimes ten or more times a day. It is reassuring, though, along with the fact that she has a little meat on her bones.

∞

Katie, a friendly woman about fifty years old, met me immediately as I entered the front door. She had a serious expression on her face, which was unlike the typical friendly smile she usually greets me with when I come in.

"We might have a problem, Sheriff," she said quietly, so as not to upset her customers further.

Katie, along with most of the folks in Pearl Lake, usually kept it pretty informal and just called me Jason. So when she addressed me as *sheriff* I was immediately on alert. She nodded to LaRae Dawkins and her son, Devon, sitting at a table looking visibly upset, then turned her head towards the bar, directing my attention to LaRae's ex-husband, Darnell Dawkins. He was pulling out a bar stool to sit down, apparently having just left La Rae's table after seeing me come in.

I know LaRae and Devon, as I do most people in the small town of Pearl Lake. Devon is a wide-receiver on our freshman football team. He is a good, quiet kid who practices and plays hard, and stays out of trouble. Unfortunately, the same cannot be said about his father, Darnell. He has gotten into quite a bit of trouble in Milwaukee and Chicago over the years. LaRae told me a while ago that he has never paid her court-assigned alimony or child support. She made me promise that I would not arrest him for failing to pay them. She knew that Darnell could make her life a living hell if she gave him a hard time about it, and I was not foolish enough to believe that he wouldn't. She moved with Devon from Milwaukee to Pearl Lake a few years ago, largely to get away from Darnell. We have been friends ever since, and I was going to do everything I could to make sure she and Devon stayed safe.

"Are you okay?" I asked LaRae as I reached her table.

"We're fine, Sheriff," she answered as she wiped tears from her face. "It's tough trying to get through to him sometimes." She nodded coolly in Darnell's direction.

"What is he doing here?"

"I don't know. I'm afraid he's going to ask me for money, which I just don't have right now."

That's a good one, I thought. Darnell owes her alimony and child support payments, but LaRae is worried he is going to hit *her* up for money. I nodded in understanding, and walked over to the bar where Darnell was sitting.

"You know I will have to arrest you if you drink that beer, Darnell," I said to him quietly as the full glass of beer in his hand was inches from his mouth. I was fully aware of his recent release from custody, and also the terms of his parole, which specified that he not drink any alcohol for twelve months. "Let's go outside so we can talk," I suggested, smiling. I looked directly into his eyes so he knew I was serious. I hoped it looked like we were just having a friendly conversation to anyone that may have been watching us from the restaurant or bar.

"Well I can always count on you to keep me out of trouble here in Mayberry, can't I, Barney?" he replied with a crooked smile, looking longingly at the untouched cold beer as I led him to the door. His Andy Griffith-Barney Fife quip was so original – like I hadn't heard that one a million times before as a small town sheriff. Next would be the jab about the one bullet I'm allowed, à la Deputy Fife.

I opened the restaurant door for Darnell on the way out, and turned toward him so I could keep a close eye on him. I noticed him flinch involuntarily and raise his arms slightly in a reflex motion to protect his face. He grimaced after seeing that I'd noticed. Ever since his nose accidentally bumped into my elbow a few years ago during a tense situation very similar to this one, he seemed to shy away from getting too close to me. In that prior incident, Darnell had tried to hit me with a sucker-punch when he thought I wasn't looking. Luckily, I had seen the punch coming just in time to turn sideways to avoid it and swing around quickly to smash his nose solidly with my elbow, leaving his nose bloody and broken.

I had to shake my head. It had been over two years since LaRae divorced Darnell after he had been sent to jail after being charged with DUI in Milwaukee for the five-hundredth time or something like that. Darnell has been giving her a hard time ever since. LaRae had been granted full custody of Devon, but Darnell never cared about him.

"Can't a guy get a sandwich without getting harassed?" Darnell whined pathetically.

"Darnell, I am not going to continue having the same discussion with you that we had a few years ago. We both know that *you* are the one doing the harassing. You can make your life a lot easier by staying out of Arrowhead County."

"Is that a threat, Sheriff? You can't tell me where I can or can't..."

"Darnell," I stopped him quickly, "I'm not arguing with you, and I'm not threatening you," I explained calmly. "I'm just trying to help you out here. I could have let you take a drink of your beer, and hauled you in for violating the terms of your parole, but I didn't. I didn't arrest you for disturbing the peace with that stunt you just pulled in the restaurant. The next time you might not be so lucky. Just stay out of Pearl Lake."

Once again, Darnell knew he was not going to win the battle. "You're lucky you got your one bullet, Barney," he said, glancing at the gun in my holster as he turned to leave.

Well, surprise, surprise! I didn't answer Darnell. I just gave him a friendly, small-town sheriff smile as I let him go. Some people never learn.

∞

Katie gave me a little kiss on the cheek when I returned inside.

"That jerk came in and sat down uninvited at LaRae's table, and started swearing and banging his fists on the table. He was just beginning to get loud when you showed up. Thank you, Jason," she said gratefully. "You have a knack for showing up at just the right time."

"It's what I'm here for, Katie."

"Way to go, Jason," a man that I recognized from town said as I passed his table.

"That could have gotten out of control," a woman that I didn't know added as I walked by. "Nice job, Sheriff."

LaRae stood and gave me a quick hug as I returned to her table. "We were just sitting down to eat before we were interrupted, Sheriff. Devon and I would love it if you could join us for dinner."

"I'd like that," I answered, glad that she seemed to have recovered from the incident. Unfortunately, she was probably used to these types of antics from Darnell by now. "It's a pleasure to eat with one of Pearl Lake's best freshman wide receivers."

"We only have two," Devon pointed out, chuckling. The tension on his face was gone for the moment, too.

LaRae took in a deep breath of air and exhaled slowly as her shoulders began to relax. She had a beautiful smile, and it was good to see it reappear. As always, LaRae was dressed sharply. She was wearing black pants and a red and black patterned shirt that seemed to highlight her medium length jet-black hair as well as her tall, curvy figure.

"Did Devon mention that I can make it to the game in North Chicago this Saturday?" LaRae asked. "We're not scheduled to work overtime this weekend at the factory, so I will be able to go to the game."

LaRae worked in the office at Arrowhead Appliance Company, which produces small appliances such as toasters, crock-pots, and coffee makers. With over five hundred employees, Arrowhead Appliance is the largest employer in Pearl Lake.

"Devon told me. I'm glad you can make it," I answered. "How are things going for you at Arrowhead, LaRae?"

"I really like it there. The people I work with have been great. I always have a lot to do, so it keeps me busy, and the pay and benefits are good, too. I can't thank you enough for getting me this job, Jason."

"How long have you worked there now, LaRae?"

"I can hardly believe it, but it's been over two years already."

"You worked hard for everything you got, and have certainly proven yourself by now. You've earned it."

I could only imagine how tough it was for a divorced woman trying to make a decent life for herself and her son. I looked at LaRae across the table. Even though her ex-husband Darnell had given her a hard time a few minutes ago, she appeared calm and in control, and displayed a sense of confidence. She was a strong woman, and I admired her. LaRae and Devon seemed to be doing fine, despite Darnell.

"I never would have gotten the chance if it weren't for you," LaRae said as she looked directly into my eyes. "Being an African-American woman from Milwaukee, I was worried about moving to a smaller town where I didn't know anyone. You helped me get out of Milwaukee when I was desperate and had no place to go. Since I've been in Pearl Lake, you've helped me pick up the pieces and get my life together. You saved my life, Jason, and Devon's, too, and I will never forget it."

« Chapter 4 »

OUR FOOTBALL TEAM ARRIVED at the *Chicago Field Museum* on Friday morning as scheduled, and gathered in front of the wide sun-bleached white concrete steps leading up to the museum entrance so we could account for everyone in the group. The kids stared in awe at the panoramic Chicago skyline, with its towering, architecturally unique buildings becoming obscured as they reached up into the clouds and haze. The players were equally amazed when they turned around and gazed at the unending view of Lake Michigan as it blended with the azure blue sky over the horizon.

In stark contrast, the Pearl Lake town skyline that we were all accustomed to was set much lower on the horizon and was highlighted by a variety of trees, a church steeple, an occasional silo in the background, and Pearl Lake itself with its beautiful sandy beaches clearly visible on the opposite side of the lake.

As we walked through the front entrance of the huge museum, the entire team froze in astonishment as they stared directly into the face of 'Sue', the biggest, most well-preserved *Tyrannosaurus Rex*, or *T. Rex* for short, found to date. Sue was forty-two feet in length and weighed approximately seven tons when she roamed the earth 67 million years ago.

In 1990, Sue Hendrickson, a member of an archeological team from the *Black Hills Institute*, found dinosaur bone fragments near a dig site in the South Dakota badlands that she believed were part of a

T. Rex. After inspecting the bones more closely, the team confirmed her findings and decided to name the pre-historic discovery 'Sue', in her honor.

After a long-running dispute over the ownership of the dinosaur bones due to their discovery on the land of a Sioux Indian reservation, Sue was purchased at a public auction in 1997 by the *Chicago Field Museum*, where she has remained on display ever since.

Tiptoeing cautiously around the menacing *T. Rex*, which had been a ferocious meat-eater in its time, we slowly made our way around the museum. We passed through a section of ancient Egyptian relics and various African artifacts including a jungle display of the *Lions of Tsavo*, and stopped briefly at the North American Indian Exhibition.

The facts and history of various Native American Indian cultures piqued my interest since my great-great-great grandmother, born in 1856, was a Native American. I never learned much about my ancestors from that point in time, other than hearing a few stories from my grandparents before they died when I was in my late-teens.   Since the 1880's, none of the generations of my family were raised on Indian reservations or in a Native American environment. I still always had an appreciation of the Native American traditions and felt a strong sense of my heritage.

We moved on to the Special Exhibition Gallery, which was currently showcasing the largest display of pearls that the *Field Museum* had ever shown to date.

"Sue, look at this!" I heard Chris Garrett call out to Brandon Dozier.

Brandon noticed the inquiring expression on my face. "Chris thinks I'm big and vicious on the football field," he explained, "so he is calling me Sue, like the *T.*

Rex." Brandon and Chris were both smiling, so I knew they were having fun with it. It was Chris's way of paying Brandon a compliment.

"Maybe you could have used wings like a pterodactyl when you were being chased on your touchdown run in our last game," I said to Chris, joking.

Brandon answered for him. "You don't need wings when you are as strong and fast as a lion, right Tsavo?"

"I guess so, Sue," Chris replied as they proceeded, laughing, towards the pearl collection.

As I walked up next to Chris and Brandon, I noticed them staring at the *La Peregrina* necklace, which was prominently displayed as the Special Exhibition's main attraction. The necklace was adorned with a huge 1-½ inch pear-shaped pearl.

Steve Dozier read the sign in front of the display out loud to us: "Various English, French, and Spanish royalties have owned the *La Peregrina* necklace for the past several centuries. Richard Burton bought the necklace for Elizabeth Taylor in 1969. The *Chicago Field Museum* expresses our appreciation to the Elizabeth Taylor estate for allowing us to display this precious necklace as a part of our Special Exhibition."

"Wow!" LaRae Dawkins whispered as she admired a stunning string of pearls that Marilyn Monroe had received from Joe DiMaggio on their honeymoon. Devon walked up beside her to see what she was looking at.

"Mom, you have a necklace at home that almost looks like that."

La Rae laughed.

"There's just one little difference," she answered. "My necklace is made of *faux* pearls."

"What's that?"

"Faux is a French word for fake. Mine are imitation pearls."

"Really? They look real to me," Devon answered innocently.

"Thank you, Devon. That's nice of you to say," LaRae said, smiling.

We continued on through the pearl exhibition, which had nearly half a million pearls on display. There were royal broaches and pearl necklaces once owned by Empress Josephine, the kings of Kuwait and Poland, Queen Mary of Scots, Queen Victoria, and other priceless items from China, India, Japan and the Middle East. It looked like the adults in our group appreciated seeing the rare display of pearls the most, but the boys seemed to be enjoying the experience, too.

We discovered that the museum's physical geology collection displayed on the second level was just as impressive. The most eye-opening gem on display was a very clear, light yellow 62,000-carat crystal of topaz. Everyone in our group seemed to be completely mesmerized as they gazed at the topaz crystal.

"Just think," Chris said. "If you shaped the crystal to make it round, it would make a great crystal ball!"

Brandon did his best fortune-teller impression, moving his hands in a circular motion around an imaginary crystal ball. He said slowly, "l o o k, l o o k d e e p into my crystal ball. I see Chris running for another touchdown tomorrow during our football game against North Chicago."

Everyone laughed as Brandon's joke broke the hypnotic state that they seemed to be under from gazing at the soft yellow topaz crystal.

"Okay, everyone," Steve Dozier prodded, still chuckling. "We've got a lot more to see yet, so we had better keep moving."

We wound our way through the rest of the museum, stopping periodically to look at the other various displays that caught our attention. At least a few of the players on the team would remember this trip to the *Chicago Field Museum*, I figured. They certainly would remember it more than they would have had it been another typical day in school.

One by one the players called out their enthusiastic farewell wishes:

"Don't eat anyone, Sue!"

"Don't forget to brush your teeth, Sue!"

"Good bye, Sue!"

They each waved affectionately at the *T. Rex.* on their way out of the museum. Yes, they definitely would remember this visit to the *Field Museum*.

∞

After eating *Chicago-style* deep-dish pizza together at a local pizzeria, the team and their families all headed to the various locations around town where they were staying for the night.

Steve and Debbie Dozier, Brandon, and their daughter Sara had set up camp-style in the Kaminski living room for their overnight stay. There were two clotheslines strung across the room with blankets draped over each one, forming separate tents for Brandon and Sara. They each had their sleeping bags and pillows laid out under them on the carpeted floor.

Steve and Debbie were sitting on the sofa, which they would soon turn into a pullout sofa-bed to sleep on for the night. Steve's father, Louis, and older sons Bart and Andrew were staying behind in Pearl Lake to handle the farm chores.

Chris Garrett and his grandparents were staying down the hall in Elizabeth Kaminski's bedroom, while Elizabeth planned on sleeping on an air mattress in Tom and Amy's bedroom. I was content to be sleeping on the couch in their office/den.

We were all sitting in the living room, relaxing after our day of adventure at the museum. Taking in all that history can be quite exhausting.

"How did you like the *Field Museum*?" Amy Kaminski asked everyone.

"It was awesome!" Brandon exclaimed.

"There was a lot of cool stuff there," Chris added. "Did you know that those two ferocious *Lions of Tsavo* from East Africa killed over one hundred and forty people in less than a year?" Brandon and Chris whispered to each other and chuckled again. I heard Brandon calling Chris *Tsavo* under his breath.

"Yes, it's amazing," Debbie Dozier answered Chris. "One of the lions was measured at over nine feet long. My favorite part of the museum is still the gem collection, though."

"Of course, you would be most interested in the jewelry section," Steve teased Debbie good-naturedly.

"Oh, I'm quite content with the jewelry I have," Debbie said, smiling. "Amy, have you seen the Special Exhibition of Pearls?" she asked.

"No, I haven't had a chance to see it yet, but I have seen their geology and gem collection. The diamonds, emeralds, pearls, rubies and sapphires take my breath away every time I see them."

"Yes, the gems were all so beautiful!" Debbie agreed.

"Enough already!" Tom laughed. "I'm exhausted just hearing you talk about all of the precious gems."

Amy smiled. "Oh, I know. I do get carried away talking about them. I'm so glad you all enjoyed the museum."

"Well, I think it's time for bed," I announced. "We have a few football players that need their sleep so they are rested for the football game tomorrow. Isn't that right, Chris? Brandon?"

"I guess so," Brandon, not yet ready for bed, answered without enthusiasm. Neither Brandon nor Chris would probably admit it, but with all of the activity they had gotten today, I was sure they both would sleep pretty well tonight.

"Thanks for letting us camp out here tonight," I said to Tom and Amy as I rose to find my sleeping spot for the night.

"It's always our pleasure," Tom said sincerely. "You know where everything is," he said to everyone, "so please make yourselves at home."

Amy nodded in agreement. "Good night," she said, yawning, as the group turned in for the night. "Sleep well."

« Chapter 5 »

WE DIDN'T SLEEP WELL. At least Tom Kaminski and I didn't. I was used to being awakened by telephone calls at all hours of the night, and heard Tom's phone when it started ringing. I checked my watch. It read 12:44 a.m.

I sat upright, figuring that the call would probably *not* be of a social nature. Confirming my suspicion, Tom walked into the den in his pajamas while he was talking on his cordless telephone, so as not to disturb Amy and Elizabeth in the bedroom, I thought. He nodded at me with understanding, from one cop to another, not surprised to see me awake and aware that something was going on.

"Was anyone hurt?" he queried into the phone, and listened to the apparently detailed answer.

"Have Carole bring her Crime Scene Investigation team in right away. If they left anything, Carole will find it." Tom listened to the caller again. "How old did you say he is?" he asked. "Yeah. That's quite a physical trauma for a sixty-two year old to go through."

"Now Perry..." Tom said deliberately. He must have been talking to Perry Williams, I figured. Perry was one of Tom's fellow detectives in the Chicago Police Department. Tom had introduced me to him a few years ago. "You know this is going to get a lot of attention," Tom continued. "When the media hears about it they will go into a feeding frenzy! Mount Rushmore won't have as high of a profile as this case once the word gets out. As always, we need to be procedurally clean on everything we do. Every move we make will be closely scrutinized. Thanks, Perry. I'll be there in a few minutes." He hung up the phone.

"Holy shit!" Tom exclaimed. "Now that you're awake, Jason, would you like to join me for some excitement tonight, or this morning, I should say? I'll fill you in on the way there if you are up for it. This is big."

I would not involve myself in one of Tom's cases unless he asked, and I was glad he did.   This was his turf now, and the Chicago PD did not take kindly to outsiders sticking their noses into their business. But I knew I wouldn't be an outsider if I were with Tom, and that he wouldn't have suggested I join him if he didn't think I could help.

"Hell yes," I answered, nodding my head in the affirmative as he fully expected. I already had my jeans on, and reached for the rest of my clothes and shoes.

"Good. I thought you would say that."

"I'll fire up the coffee while you get some clothes on," I told him. "Don't worry, I know how you like it – black and thick as tar."

"Damn right," Tom replied, with his mind still preoccupied by the details of the phone call.   He hurried back to his bedroom to get dressed, and to confirm with Amy what she probably already knew through experience – that he needed to leave on urgent police business.

∞

"Someone broke into the *Chicago Field Museum*," Tom explained as we drove there in his unmarked police vehicle. "The jewelry from the Special Exhibit Gallery has been stolen, including the *La*

Peregrina necklace. Some of the museum's gem collection has been taken, too. Even the yellow topaz crystal is gone."

"That's unbelievable," I said.

"You can say that again. Nothing like this has ever happened at the museum before," Tom replied. "You know this is all strictly confidential, right?" Tom asked unnecessarily.

"Everything will always remain totally confidential with me, Tom."

He nodded in acknowledgement. "I know. Just making sure."

"Did someone get hurt?" I asked, recalling that he had inquired about someone's health earlier in his telephone conversation.

"Yeah. The museum guards were shot with tranquilizer darts. They have all regained consciousness, except for a sixty-two year-old guard. He was hit in the neck with a dart, which may have triggered a heart attack or a stroke. He's being taken to *Chicago General Hospital* right now."

"It's better than getting shot with .38's or AK-47's or something," I said. "It's much cleaner anyway. It says something about the guys that did it, though."

"It does," Tom agreed. "They could have used real bullets just as easily as tranquilizer darts. They wouldn't have had to worry about anyone identifying them or testifying against them if they had killed them all. Luckily for the guards they didn't use real bullets."

"They went out of their way to *not* kill anyone in the robbery," I commented.

"It looks that way, Jason."

"It could make a big difference if they're caught and convicted," I said. "It would potentially reduce the sentence from a maximum of life in jail down to maybe ten to twenty years, or even less with parole, depending on priors."

"I see what you mean," Tom said. "Maybe the robbery was committed by some high-class jewelry thieves or museum burglars, as opposed to a bunch of petty thieves or organized crime members."

"That could make this crime even more difficult to solve."

"Yes, it could," Tom agreed.

Most of the bad guys have records that typically paint quite accurate pictures of the crimes they have committed. Even though criminals unfortunately sometimes get better with practice, they also tend to follow the same patterns and use the same methods that they've used in the past. Fortunately, their *modus operandi* often help to steer law enforcement officials directly to them.

However, jewelry thieves and museum burglars are often a different breed of criminal. They don't always have long records, and sometimes may only plan and commit one or two major crimes in their lifetimes. If they are successful, they may rake in a few big hauls and then retire from the life of crime forever.

Tom had better fasten his seatbelt, I thought, because this case could be sending him on a bumpy ride.

Little did I know that it would be taking me on a dangerously wild ride of my own.

« Chapter 6 »

PERRY WILLIAMS MET US when we arrived at the museum. There were enough Chicago police officers on the premises to fill an entire town the size of Pearl Lake. Some officers were sealing off a small area around the museum front entrance door with yellow police tape.

Tom stopped before we entered the building, and visually scanned the scene.

"Officers," he said to the policemen with the yellow tape, "would you please seal off the entire perimeter of the museum grounds? I need the property cordoned off around the whole building – all the way to the water." He pointed to the Lake Michigan lakeshore, which was about forty yards from the museum. The area was brightly illuminated by the headlights of all of the police vehicles scattered around the property.

"Yes, detective," the officer's acknowledged.

"Perry, do you remember Sheriff Avalon?"

"I sure do." Perry smiled in greeting as he reached out his hand. "It's good to see you again, Sheriff. What's the matter? There isn't enough going on in Pearl Lake, so you gotta come to Chicago to get some action?"

"This kind of action I don't need, Perry," I answered as I shook his hand. "It's good to see you again, too. Please call me Jason."

"We don't need this stuff either, Jason. It just always seems to find us," he answered with a soft, deep laugh that resonated from the bottom of his stomach as he led us into the building. I stayed a step behind Tom and Perry in order to be as unobtrusive as possible, yet remained within earshot.

"What have you got so far, Perry?" Tom asked.

"There were three museum guards on duty during the robbery. One of them is at the hospital already. The other two are still here. They seem to be doing okay now that the effects of the tranquilizers are beginning to wear off. I thought you'd want to talk with them, if possible, before they are taken to the hospital."

"I would. Thanks, Perry," Tom said.

The guards and a policeman were up ahead of us on the main floor next to the museum's information/security desk. An ambulance crew had hooked the guards up to IV's, and was placing them onto gurneys. The guards both had dazed expressions on their faces, but otherwise looked to be okay. They were probably used to a routine of giving directions, pointing out the restrooms, and watching the security monitors until their eyes glazed over. Right now, they were probably telling themselves this was *not* the duty they signed up for. They were lucky to be alive.

Tom showed his badge when we reached them.

"I'm Detective Kaminski of the Chicago PD," he said, "and these are my colleagues Detective Williams and Sheriff Avalon." Perry and I dutifully flashed our respective badges. They didn't need to know that I was just a small town sheriff from Wisconsin, nor did they notice from glancing at my badge.

"I know you have all been through one hell of a night," Tom said to the guards, "but can you help us out by answering a few questions before you leave? Do you feel up to it?"

He directed his questions as much to the ambulance paramedics as to the injured guards. Tom knew that the paramedics were responsible for the guard's medical care. Accordingly, the paramedics were the ones that would determine whether they felt the guards were fit to talk to us now, or not.

One of the guards, a thin white man that looked to be about thirty years old answered. "Hell, I've been knocked out harder than this by my old man when I was a kid. I'm all right. How are you doing, Kenny?" He looked at his fellow guard, a well-built black man, maybe in his late thirties. Kenny appeared to be a little more subdued.

"I'm okay. Needed a little nap anyway, I guess," Kenny answered with a smirk.

Tom and I looked at the paramedics.

One of them held out two fingers. "You've got two minutes," he stated firmly.

"Thank you," Tom replied. He immediately turned to Kenny.

"Kenny, what was the first sign that you noticed something was going on?"

Kenny took a deep breath and slowly exhaled in a futile attempt to quickly rid his body of the effects of the tranquilizer. "I was right here at the security station when I noticed someone open the north door and walk right into the building. The doors were all supposed to be locked." He looked toward the steel doors at the back of the museum, which were approximately fifty yards from where we were standing – about half the length of a football field.

"I couldn't believe it," Kenny continued. "I checked my security monitors that show those doors from four separate camera angles, both inside and out.

They were clear. No one showed up on any of the cameras. I knew something was wrong, and turned to sound the alarm." He pointed to a square red button on the left side of the security instrument panel. "I felt the dart hit me in the back, right between the shoulder blades."

Kenny reached behind his back, straining to touch the spot where the dart hit him. He shook his arms and rotated his neck trying to loosen up the muscles that were already beginning to stiffen from the impact of the tranquilizer dart.

"What happened next?" Tom prompted him to go on.

"I thought, 'Lord, I've been shot'!" Kenny continued. "I thought it was a regular bullet and that I was as good as dead. I tried to reach the alarm button a few feet away anyway. Seems I didn't make it." He shook his head in dismay. "That's the last thing I remember until I came to with Officer Davis here holding a wet handkerchief on my forehead."

Kenny pointed gratefully to the short, stocky policeman that first appeared on the scene, standing off to the side. Officer Davis nodded in response, still keeping close watch on the two guards. It was obvious he was going to make sure they were okay right up until the time the paramedics got them to the hospital.

"Kenny, do you have any idea what time it was when this happened?" Tom asked.

"Yeah. I saw the clock above the monitors. It was exactly 12:13 a.m."

Perry Williams jumped in. "You said that you checked your security cameras at the same time you saw someone walking through the north doors, but the cameras didn't show that anyone was there? How could that be?"

"Damned if I know," *Kenny the Guard* shook his head. "Never saw nothing like it before. The monitors showed the north doors as though no one was anywhere around. When the museum is closed, we have motion sensors and door alarms that sound when the doors are opened. But I swear that the monitors were clear and no alarms went off!"

"Did you get a good look at the person coming through the door?" Tom asked.

"Not really. All I can tell you is he just seemed average – not too tall, too fat, or too skinny. He was wearing all black, including a black ski mask pulled down over his face. It all happened so fast, that's all I noticed. How is Clifford doing?" he asked, obviously concerned. "He's the guard who has already been taken to the hospital."

Tom, Perry, and I looked at each other, not knowing the answer. One of the paramedics did. "He was alive," he said to Kenny, "but was still unconscious when he arrived at *Chicago General*. I'm sorry, but that's all I know."

"Thanks," Kenny nodded, appreciating getting the updated health status of his fellow guard.

Perry directed his attention to the other guard.

"How are you doing? Can you answer a few questions?"

The guard nodded, still appearing a bit befuddled by the circumstances.

"Sure," he said weakly.

"What do you remember?"

"Not too much," the guard answered. "I was stationed inside the main entrance doors on the south side of the building, right next to the *Field Museum* Gift Shop over there." He pointed to the front entrance doors that he had guarded along with Sue, the museum's in-house guard *T-Rex*. They must have done a good job because it looked like the intruders did not gain entrance from those doors.

"I stay at my desk station most of the time," the guard continued. "It has one monitor that shows a wide view outside the main entrance. Once in a while I get up and walk past the front doors and through the front area of the museum, just to move around a little bit and to look at something other than the monitor. I was walking back to my desk when I got hit with a dart, right here in my left arm." He turned to show us the spot directly above his elbow. It had a big, swollen red welt about four inches in diameter. A needle mark from where the tranquilizer dart hit was still clearly visible in the middle of the red spot.

"Did you see who shot you, or see anything else?" Perry asked.

"No, I didn't. I'm sorry, but that's all I can remember."

The paramedics stood up to load the guards into the waiting ambulances. It was our cue that question-time was over.

"Thank you for your help," Tom said to the guards. "Good luck, and recover quickly."

"Officer Davis," Tom turned to the police officer, still waiting patiently and taking it all in. "Would you mind telling us what happened since you arrived on the scene?"

"Sure. Whatever I can do to help."

"Thank you, officer. Go ahead," Tom said.

"I was patrolling in the general vicinity of the museum area, as I do occasionally when I am on the night shift. I received a report that came in from the owner of one of the yachts that was docked on the pier located just adjacent to the museum. He said he noticed some people walking around the outside of the museum and thought it was a little unusual at this time of night, so he called it in to the police department. I..."

"What time did you receive the call?" Tom interrupted.

"It was about twelve-thirty," he answered. In detail, Officer Davis took us through his actions from the time he entered the open, unlocked back doors on the north end of the building, until he saw *Kenny the Guard* unconscious at his workstation.

"As soon as I saw the guard sprawled on the floor I immediately called for back-up and went to check on him." The expression on his face registered the same concern that he must have had at the time he made the call. "I didn't know whether the burglars were still in the building, or not. Kenny was starting to come to, and thank God, it appeared as though he was going to be okay. I looked around the museum and noticed the other guard lying on the floor by the front doors. I went over to him to make sure he was all right, and found that he was beginning to regain consciousness, too."

Officer Davis is an unsung hero, I thought as I listened to him describe what had happened. He didn't know whether he was in imminent danger at the time, or not. If he had followed procedure, he would have stayed behind and waited for back-up to arrive. Instead, he rushed into the building to see if anyone needed help.

"By then," he continued, "the back-ups had arrived and confirmed that the burglars were no longer in the building. That's when they found the other guard on the second floor, still unconscious."

Tom and the entire Chicago Police Department would be under tremendous pressure to solve this *Chicago Field Museum* robbery. If anyone could do it, I knew Tom could. In a way, I envied Tom for the unique challenges that he would face with this case. But a part of me was glad that I didn't have to deal with anything on this large of a scale in Pearl Lake.

That was soon about to change.

« Chapter 7 »

THE COACHES WERE HAPPILY packing up the team equipment after our football game against North Chicago, a satisfying 28–6 victory.

I overheard Bob Colgate quietly boasting to Steve Dozier while I was loading a case of team supplies into the car. "It was like the goose that laid the golden egg," Bob said.

Steve nodded unenthusiastically as he stuffed our team footballs into a travel bag.

"I made over ten in less than a month," Bob continued, putting the finishing touch on what I figured was the financial equivalent of a 'big fish' story.

"Ten dollars?" Steve asked before he could catch himself. He immediately winced in regret, realizing he had taken the bait.

Bob smiled slyly. "Oh, no," he said, reeling Steve in. "Ten *thousand* dollars!"

Steve rolled his eyes. Bob often seemed to find subtle ways of bringing up examples of his exceptional ability to make money in his Badger Finance business. Ironically, I just heard from a reliable source that Bob recently lost a large sum of money, which ran into six figures, on investments that didn't quite pan out. Funny he didn't seem to mention instances like that to us. Steve knew it, too, which is probably why he was rolling his eyes as he listened to Bob. I figured that Bob's comments were meant for both Steve and me to hear – for maximum exposure.

"Congratulations on another good game, Jason," Steve Dozier complimented me, attempting to change the subject.

"Good game to you, too, Steve and Bob!" I returned the compliment, gladly obliging Steve in changing the topic of discussion. "The kids played pretty good today, didn't they?"

"That's three big *W*'s and no *L*'s," Bob said, happily touting the team's 3-0 record to start the season in his unique riddle-speak way.

"Chris Garrett is turning out to be a very good ball player, Jason," Steve noted. "He scored two touchdowns today!"

I smiled hearing Steve's comments. Even though I get along well with most of our players, he knows that Chris and I are especially close. I have to admit that I do feel a sense of pride with him.

Chris was still surrounded by a bunch of players gathered together on the sidelines, talking about the game. The players seemed to be drawn to Chris like a magnet, and he accepted their compliments quietly.

"Did you see the move Chris put on the defensive back on his first touchdown run?" Brandon Dozier asked one of the other players. "Chris got around him, and he was so quick that the player never even got a hand on him!"

"I never would have gotten that far if Brandon hadn't leveled the linebacker like he did," Chris responded. "Did you see the block he made? Brandon knocked him on his butt!"

They all laughed. It was great to hear Chris give credit to his teammates, and to see the players rally around each other.

I noticed Chris look around until he located Devon Dawkins. Devon was sitting off to the side by himself, taking off his shoulder pads. He had scored a touchdown in the game, too, on a spectacular long pass reception. Chris whispered something to the players around him, and they all immediately stood up and ran over to Devon – screaming and cheering.

"Good game, Devon!"

"That was a nice catch!"

"Great touchdown, Devon!"

In fun, they dragged Devon to the ground and piled onto him mercilessly. Steve, Bob, and I watched them closely to make sure they didn't smother the poor kid. The players eventually got back to their feet, pulling Devon up with them. He sat up with a wide smile covering his entire face and joined in the laughter with the rest of the team.

Chris had a fantastic game today, I thought, *but the move he just made was his best move of the day.*

∞

"I heard that you got a special tour of the museum early this morning with Tom Kaminski," Bob Colgate said to me. "Didn't you see enough when we were there with the team yesterday?" Apparently he had seen the news regarding the robbery, and heard that I had gone back to the crime scene with Tom.

"It's hard to believe, isn't it?" I answered. "Tom is going to have his hands full trying to solve this one."

"What did they get away with?" Bob asked.

"I don't know exactly what was taken. I left when the curator of the museum and the insurance officials started arriving. They were going to do a complete assessment of everything that was missing."

"All they said on the radio was that there were several items stolen," Steve Dozier said.

"I thought I heard this morning that the *La Peregrina* necklace is missing," Bob added, "and they said that one of the guards has not recovered yet from getting hit by a tranquilizer dart. Have you heard how he is doing, Jason?"

"No, I haven't heard anything recently. It's amazing how fast the news reporter's cover stories like this," I replied, not wanting to go into any details about the crime. Tom had warned me there would be a lot of rumors being spread about this case. I didn't want any of them inadvertently coming from me.

"Tom's job sure won't be any easier with all of the reporters on his tail. I wouldn't want to switch jobs with him right now," Steve said.

I thought of some of the jobs that Steve did regularly on the farm, such as birthing calves and shoveling manure. We all knew that Tom, the big-city Chicago boy, was not much for getting his hands dirty from farm work. He would much rather get them dirty by grabbing a criminal by the scruff of his neck.

"Somehow, even with all the attention on this *Chicago Field Museum* robbery," I answered Steve, "I don't think that Tom would want to switch jobs with you either." We all laughed as we pictured Tom shoveling manure and doing other farm chores, and conversely, Steve as a Chicago cop. We cheerfully got into our vehicles for the ride home to the peace and quiet of Pearl Lake.

« Chapter 8 »

ON SUNDAY EVENING THE water on Pearl Lake glimmered as the sun began to set. The sun cast out deep shades of red, yellow and orange which transformed into gold, silver and diamonds as it reflected on the clear blue water. I relished breathing the fresh air, filtered clean through the abundant leaves on the trees in the Wisconsin woodlands. I could feel the soothing effects of the wind rustling through the trees and the waves lapping rhythmically onto the lakeshore as I sat on the porch. It had been a good summer.

The ringing telephone shattered the serenity. I checked the caller ID display on the handset before I picked it up. It read 'Pearl Lake Pub'. All emergency calls go directly to the Sheriff's Office in town, which is a room inside the Pearl Lake City Hall building. I use the office to access the police computers, and for a place to meet when people need to see and talk to me. Whenever I am not in the Sheriff's Office, which is most of the time, the calls are forwarded to me either on my home telephone or cell phone. In this case, the display on the telephone showed that the call originated from the *Pearl Lake Pub*.

"Sheriff Avalon," I answered.

"Hi Sheriff. This is Candy over at the *Pub*. It's not an emergency or anything, but someone just punched Harry Wilson and knocked him clear off his barstool. He's okay, but I was hoping you would come over to check it out." Seventy-three year old Harry Wilson had settled down in Pearl Lake after retiring as an electrician about ten years ago.

"Candy, are you sure that Harry is okay? If he needs medical attention you need to call 9-1-1 right away."

"I'm sure, Sheriff," she answered nonchalantly. "He said he's not hurt, and he seems okay and everything."

"Is everyone else there alright, too?"

"Yeah, everyone's okay."

"Is the guy who hit Harry there yet?" I asked.

"No, he's not here anymore. He left right after he punched Harry."

"Do you know who it was?"

"No, I didn't recognize him. No one else did either. But I'd say he was maybe in his late-thirties. He has black hair, and he is a little bigger than average, like he has muscles. I saw him drive away in a green Ford pick-up truck."

"Did you get his license plate number?"

"No, I didn't."

"Okay, I'll be there right away. Please do your best to keep everyone there, would you Candy?"

"I always do, sheriff," she said before hanging up the phone.

∞

On the way to the *Pub* I called the incident in to the Arrowhead County Sheriff's Department that was staffed around the clock seven days a week. I requested that all of the personnel on the road keep a lookout for the person matching the description that Candy gave me.

There was rarely any trouble in Pearl Lake, but it seemed that when there was, it usually happened at the *Pearl Lake Pub*. Over the course of a year, the Sheriff's Office probably got five or six calls from the *Pub* requesting assistance. That might not sound like a lot, but it is for our small, quiet town. When you mix alcohol with a large group of people watching sports on television and rooting for different teams, or with a bunch of hunters returning from the woods without having any luck, there are bound to be a few unhappy drinkers occasionally. Sometimes situations can get out of control if they are not handled properly.

Katie's Place, on the other hand, very rarely has problems that get out of hand. Katie and her staff always seem to have a knack for noticing potential problems before they turn into full-blown incidents, and one way or another they prevent them from escalating. Unfortunately, the people who run the *Pub* do not have the same ability.

Everything was quiet when I got to the *Pub*. Candy was behind the bar talking to a few patrons, and was acting as though nothing had happened. There were only a few small groups of people in the bar at the time, about a dozen total. I knew about half of them, and exchanged 'hello's' with them as I walked over to Candy.

"Hi Sheriff Avalon. Thanks for coming," she welcomed me with a warm smile. Candy is a cute, big-featured woman around twenty-five years old. She has a full, curvy figure, accompanied by a pair of big, brown eyes, and a big smile, too.

"Hi Candy. Is everything still okay?"

"Sure, everything's fine now," she answered. She turned around to look at Harry Wilson, who was watching TV with a few others at the opposite end of the bar. "Hey, *Harry*," she called out loudly, nodding in my direction after she got his attention.

"How are you doing, Sheriff?" Harry called across the bar, with a slightly pained expression on his face as I walked towards him.

"I'm doing just fine, Harry, but I didn't get knocked off of a barstool. How's the noggin'?" I asked, looking at his head.

"Oh, I'm alright. I just have a little egg on the side of my head that's a little sore." He had some ice wrapped in a small towel, and was pressing it gingerly against his head. He removed it to show me a good-sized lump just above his right ear. Fortunately he still had one free hand that enabled him to lift a bottle of beer to his mouth, apparently to help alleviate the pain.

"What happened?" I asked.

"Damned if I know, Sheriff." He took another swig of beer and set the bottle down. "A few of us were watching the football game, minding our own business," he explained, pointing to a television mounted above the bar. "We were all cheering because the Chicago Bears just got beat by the Detroit Lions from a last-minute field goal. The next thing I know, I found myself sitting on the floor. It felt like a brick wall fell down on me. I was a little dazed for a while. It wasn't that I had too much to drink," Harry quickly pointed out.

"That's right, Sheriff," Candy vouched for him. "He's only had a few beers. After we checked on Harry and got him back to his seat, I noticed a big, muscular guy walking out of the bar. He was in the bar when I got here at three o'clock this afternoon. I served him four, maybe five drinks. He was drinking screwdrivers, not beer like most of our regular customers. I really wasn't paying too much attention to him. When I looked out the window I noticed him get into his truck and drive away. I thought he might have been that Hector guy who works for Mr. Dozier on the farm, but I'm not sure. I know Hector drives an old green pick-up truck like the one I saw, but he never comes into the *Pub* so I don't know him very well. I see him around town once in a while, but that's it."

"You weren't able to get the license plate number?" I asked again to confirm what she had said earlier.

"No. He pulled out so fast I didn't get a chance to see it."

Jack Trader was sitting at the other end of the bar. "Nothin' ever freakin' happens in this town," he said boisterously to someone next to him, "and when it does, it's someone getting knocked off their barstool. Pearl Lake is so boring. Hell, back in Chicago there is *always* something interesting going on."

Jack Trader was born and raised in Chicago. He moved to Pearl Lake with his parents about thirty years ago when he was around sixteen years old. He must not have forgiven his parents for taking him away from what in his mind was the perfect city. His father retired from a good production job at the Arrowhead Appliance Company, and Jack has been working there for over twenty years himself now.

Someone piped up in answer to Jack. "Then why don't you do us all a favor and go back to Chicago?" Everyone else in the bar cheered in unison.

Thankfully, without comment Jack resumed staring aimlessly at the half-full glass of beer sitting in front of him on the bar; or in Jack's case, the half-*empty* glass of beer.

I turned back to Harry and the group surrounding him. "I'll check it out," I assured them. "Harry, do you want to press charges when I find the guy?"

"Hell no, Sheriff. What good would that do? I'll be okay. I'd just like to know what his problem was," he said, shaking his head. He winced in pain as the movement aggravated the sore spot over his ear.

Harry promptly put the ice pack back on the still-visible lump, and took another drink of his liquid painkiller.

« Chapter 9 »

I DROVE TO THE Dozier farm to see if I could find Hector Velasquez. I hadn't said anything to Harry or Candy at the *Pub*, but this did not seem like something that Hector would do. Hector had been working on the Dozier farm for over thirty years. Hell, since he was a kid. He came to Wisconsin from Mexico with his folks during the summer months to do farm work in order to make a better living for their family. Hector was only twelve years old at the time. When his parents could no longer take the rigors of the manual labor after working in the fields for over twenty years, they returned to Mexico. But by then, Hector had met and fallen in love with a beautiful woman named Marie. Even though the rest of his family had returned to Mexico, Hector and Marie decided to stay. Both of them had been in Wisconsin longer than they had been in Mexico and considered Pearl Lake to be their home. After they received their U.S. Citizenship about five years ago, they were married in Pearl Lake.

Hector and Marie had also grown very close to the Dozier family. Steve had praised Hector many times over the years for being such a hard worker on the farm. Their family had also known and liked Marie since she worked on another nearby farm in Arrowhead County with her family. Steve was so close to Hector and Marie that he knew they were seeing each other long before either of their parents did.

When Hector and Marie announced that they were planning on staying in Pearl Lake, the Dozier's were elated. Steve, Debbie, and Louis Dozier discussed the matter amongst themselves and decided to give the Velasquez couple a ten-acre parcel of land on the edge of their property. Ten acres might not sound like a lot, but it was enough for Hector and Marie to build the house that they had dreamed of together, and to plant some crops on a plot of land that was their very own. They cried for joy when they heard the Dozier's offer and said that it was the best gift they had ever received. Maybe it was, until their beautiful baby girl, Theresa, arrived a year later. Their baby boy, Antonio, was born the following year. Hector had never been in any kind of trouble for the thirty years I had known him. None. And I didn't believe he would get into any trouble now.

∞

Steve's boys were returning to the house from the barn as I drove into the Dozier driveway. They must have just finished milking the cows or completed some other chores. Steve was still working over by the barn.

"Most people rest on Sundays," I said to Steve as I approached him.

"A farmer's work is never done, Jason," he answered, smiling. "You're one to talk. You're *always* working." He watched me closely as I walked towards him. "Be careful where you step, Jason," he cautioned. He was moving kernels of corn that were piled high on the ground into a silo that was adjacent to the barn. The corn stored in the silo would be used to feed his cattle over the winter months. The corn was piled on top of an underground grain auger, which was like a giant fan with sharp, powerful blades that helped to vacuum the corn into the silo. The corn covered up the auger so it couldn't be seen, but I knew it was there. I had been around farms long enough to know that augers could be dangerous and to stay away from them. Farmers have lost their legs, if not their lives, by getting caught in operating grain augers.

"I see it. Thanks, Steve." I appreciated the fact that Steve was looking out for me and was making sure that I stayed safe on his farm.

"Can't be too careful."

"You're right about that. You're right about the work part, too, Steve. I was just at the *Pearl Lake Pub*. Someone took a punch at Harry Wilson over there, apparently unprovoked, and knocked him clear out of his barstool. Candy at the *Pub* got a brief look at the guy who may have hit him as he was leaving the bar. The guy drove away in an old green pick-up truck just like the one Hector drives. She didn't really get a good look at him, but said it was possible that it could have been Hector."

"Jason, we both know Hector would never do anything like that," Steve said matter-of-factly.

"I know he wouldn't," I agreed.

"Besides, Hector has been here all afternoon helping me with the chores. He just walked home a few minutes ago. When did it happen?" Steve asked.

"About an hour ago. Obviously Hector can't be in two places at one time, so that rules him out. Not that he needs an alibi as far as I'm concerned."

The wireless police department radio that hung on my belt began to squawk.

"Four-four-one. Four-four-one". It was Cheryl, our county dispatch officer calling me using my sheriff's department call number.

"Four-four-one. Hello, Cheryl," I answered.

"Hi Jason. I have an update for you on the disorderly conduct incident at the *Pearl Lake Pub*. A Waushara County Officer picked up a suspect that fit your description: A male, thirty-nine years old, driving a green 2007 Ford pick-up. His name is Richard Thomas Bonline. He was tested with a Blood Alcohol Content of .16. He was arrested and is being held in the Wautoma jail."

The city of Wautoma is about twenty minutes away from Pearl Lake. He must have driven straight there from the *Pub* in Pearl Lake. Well, obviously not too straight.

"When he was brought in and questioned," Cheryl continued, "Mr. Bonline admitted punching someone at the *Pearl Lake Pub*. Apparently Mr. Bonline, a Chicago resident, is a Bear fan. He became upset when he saw the results of the football game on TV and heard the guys in the bar gloating over the Bear's defeat."

"So he decided to take out his frustrations on a harmless, seventy-three year old man who was minding his own business," I concluded. "I'm glad they got him before he could hurt anyone else. Thank you, Cheryl. Have a good night."

"You're welcome, Jason. 'Bye now."

"I guess that wraps that up," I said to Steve. I looked behind him, past his barn and down the driveway that led to the Velasquez house about a city block away. I could see Hector playing with his kids in the back yard.

Steve turned around, and saw Hector, too. "Yeah, there he is."

"I'd like to go say hello to him as long as I'm here," I said. "I haven't seen him for a few weeks."

"You're not going to say anything to him about the *Pub*, are you?"

"No. There's no need to bring it up to him."

"You're right," Steve nodded. He seemed glad that I was not going to burden Hector with what happened at the *Pearl Lake Pub*. "Well, I've got to finish up here so I can get in to supper. I'll see you tomorrow at football practice."

"See you then. Have a good night, Steve."

∞

I left my car and walked down the long driveway to the Velasquez place. Hector was on the ground wrestling with his kids when I got there. It looked like four year-old Theresa and three year-old Antonio were winning the match.

"Do you need any help here, Hector?" I asked. His arms were both pinned firmly to the ground, with Theresa laying on one, and Antonio laying on the other.

"No, thank you, Sheriff. I'll be okay," Hector answered. He effortlessly lifted his son and daughter to their feet, and got up himself.

"We were just playing, Sheriff Jay," Theresa explained innocently. "Papa doesn't need any help. Do you Papa?" she added as Hector shook his head and laughed.

"Hi, Mr. Sheriff Jay," Antonio greeted me politely.

"Well, hello there, Antonio!" I answered, amazed at how well he was talking for a three year-old.

"What great kids you have, Hector," I complimented.

"They are the best!" he agreed. Theresa and Antonio beamed with pride hearing the loving words from their big, strong father.

"Now, go on in and clean up for supper," Hector said as he steered them towards the back door. They obeyed without hesitation and walked back to the house, hand-in-hand.

"I'm just putting some hamburgers on the grill, Sheriff. We have plenty. Would you like to join us?"

"No, thank you, Hector. I appreciate the offer but I've got to run. I was just over at Steve's and thought since I hadn't seen you for a while that I'd stop over and say hi."

Just then Marie opened the back door. Marie was a fairly short woman with a glowing bronze complexion and a shapely body, and fiery green eyes that did little to hide the passion within. Hector knew that she was a knockout and always told the men in town that it was okay for them to look once in a while, but not to touch. He didn't have to worry, though. Marie was madly in love with Hector and never gave him reason to doubt it.

"Hello, Sheriff Jason!" she greeted me with a warm smile. "We'd love it if you would join us for supper."

"Hi, Marie. Hector just asked me, too, but I can't stay tonight. Thank you for the offer."

"You are going to hurt my feelings if you don't join us for dinner one of these days, Jason," she said as the fire in her eyes flared briefly. *Hector is a very lucky man*, I thought. Marie was lucky to have him, too. He was a hard worker, and from everything I had seen and heard, was a good husband and father.

"Aye!" Hector whispered to me under his breath. "I have seen that look before, amigo. If you know what is good for you, Jason, you'd better accept her next dinner invitation."

"Okay, Marie," I answered her, nodding to Hector in appreciation for his friendly warning. "I sure don't want to hurt your feelings. I'll definitely take you up on your offer soon."

"You do that, Sheriff," Marie said, holding me to it. She smiled and waved good-bye as she stepped back into the house.

"Whew," Hector sighed. "That was close."

We both laughed.

"Hector," I said, "I don't need to tell you that it will be my pleasure to come back and have dinner with you and your family. You and Marie are both great cooks, and I couldn't find any better company."

"Come back anytime, Sheriff Jason," Hector said. "Our door is always open to you."

« Chapter 10 »

WORKING OUT WAS THE last thing I felt like doing when I woke up Monday morning, but I headed to the local fitness center across the street from the Sheriff's Office anyway.

I tended to agree with Neil Armstrong, the first man to walk on the moon, when he said '*I believe that the good Lord gave us a finite number of heartbeats, and I'll be damned if I'm going to use up mine running up and down a street*'. Despite that, I ran a few miles on the treadmill, letting my mind wander aimlessly. Then I moved on to one of the fitness center's latest and greatest fitness stations and did some strength exercises. By the time I was done with the workout and was all showered and dressed, the activity in Pearl Lake was beginning to pick up. As I often do, I decided to do my beat-cop routine and walked around downtown Pearl Lake – all two blocks of it.

I walked next door to the Drake Realty and Antique Shop, which are both housed in the same building. John Drake runs the realty office and his wife, Barbara, handles the antique shop. Both in their late-fifty's, Barb and John have lived in Pearl Lake for over five years now. I accepted their offers for a cup of coffee, and visited with them for a while before continuing to make my way around town.

Next to the Drake Building was the Pearl Lake Factory Direct Store. I could see the owner, Dan Abrahms, through the front window as he was stocking the shelves. I entered the front door, which was unlocked even though it was still an hour before opening time.

"Good morning, Mr. Abrahms. Working hard already?" I asked as the bells on top of the door jangled when I entered.

"Good morning, Jason. Oh, you know how much I enjoy doing this. It's not work to me."

That was obvious. Dan Abrahms is in his early seventies now, and is apparently no closer to retiring than when he first opened his store over forty years ago. His son and daughter, Rod and Cindy, both in their late-forties, help him with much of the work in the store now. Even their kids, Dan's grandchildren, have been getting more involved in the store lately.

"Jason, how many times do I need to ask you to call me Dan?" he asked. "I've known you all of your life, and you've been the sheriff for, what, five years now?"

"It's been a little longer than that, Mr. Abrahms." Actually, it had been over eight years already. "Time flies when you're having fun."

"Believe me," he said, smiling, "I do understand."

I was raised to respect my elders, and felt it was a sign of respect to call Dan 'Mr. Abrahms'. He has been a successful businessman as long as I have known him. I don't know how much money he makes running the Factory Direct Store, but obviously the store has been profitable enough over the years to provide a good living for himself and his family. Especially now, since it must generate enough income to help support some of his grandchildren, too.

Like Steve Dozier, Dan Abrahms has done a lot for the people in Pearl Lake. He may do it in different ways than Steve, such as through his involvement in St. Paul's Catholic Church charitable activities, or the local

Rotary Club. Nevertheless, he helps behind the scenes and without fanfare.

"That sure is a nice computer we have in the Pearl Lake Library," I said. "Emily tells me it brings us into the twenty-first century."

Emily, our town librarian, mentioned to me a few days ago, against Dan's wishes, of course, that Dan had bought a new computer system for the Pearl Lake Library. It had state-of-the-art capabilities designed specifically for libraries. Previously, the library had still been using an archaic computer system for searching and checking out books and other publications and reference materials.

Dan glanced at me briefly, barely breaking his rhythm of restocking the store shelves.

"It is nice, isn't it?" he confirmed. I detected from the quick look he gave me that he knew I was aware of the fact that *he* was the reason our library had a new computer.

"Well, I have to get going," I said. "By the way, Mr. Abrahms, have I told you how much I admire you? We are so lucky to have you here in Pearl Lake."

He smiled sincerely. "Seems to me I recall you mentioning it to me before. I appreciate it," he replied as I walked to the door. "Hey, Jason," he called out. I stopped, turned, and looked back at him. "The feeling is mutual."

I continued my excursion through downtown Pearl Lake, stopping in at the Piggly-Wiggly grocery store, and the Gas Station and *Pearl Lake Pub* across the street on Highway 21. Then I crossed back over the highway and stopped at the Lakeshore Bank, the Pearl Lake Antique Shop, and the General Store. I ended up at *Katie's Place*, where I chatted briefly with Katie over an orange juice and breakfast muffin.

As usual, the spirit and enthusiasm of the folks in Pearl Lake lifted me up. By the time I reached my office in the Town Hall Building, my earlier Monday morning *blahs* were long gone.

Tom Kaminski telephoned not long after I had begun working on some paperwork.

"Good morning, Jason," Tom greeted me. "How is life up in the northwoods?"

"Hi, Tom. It's beautiful, as always," I answered truthfully. "How are things in the big city?"

"Actually, I have some news about the *Chicago Field Museum* robbery. Do you have a few minutes?"

"I sure do," I assured him. Tom and I often talked to each other about the various aspects of the cases each of us were working on at the time. Sometimes it was merely as a sounding board, and other times it was in an effort to help each other fill in the blanks that occasionally we were unable to do on our own.

"Okay," Tom began. "The burglars had detailed knowledge of the museum's security system. We learned that the museum updated their security system a few years ago, but in order to keep the costs down they only updated part of the system. They chose to leave the existing wiring for the portion of the alarm system belonging to the north side entrance doors on the old circuit panel on the second floor of the building."

"So the north side entrance doors were still hooked up to the *old* alarm system?" I asked.

"That's right," Tom confirmed. "The north side of the building incurred water damage around ten years ago. They updated the security system at the same time they made the repairs for the water damage. The security system on the rest of the building wasn't updated until the museum had enough money in their budget to do it, which was a few years ago.

"Sometime shortly before the robbery," Tom continued, "the burglars installed a timing device on the old circuit panel. The timing device was set to turn off the alarms on the north side entrance doors minutes before they entered the building. That is why the guard named Kenny was surprised when he saw the man walk right through the doors without any warning lights showing up on the monitors, or without setting off any alarms. He was so stunned to see a man inside the building that he hesitated for a moment before he double-checked the monitors to verify what he was seeing. That hesitation allowed the intruders enough time to take a few steps into the building and shoot him with a tranquilizer dart. Before the other guard knew what was going on, he was shot with another dart at point blank range by one of the other robbers."

I could hear Tom on the telephone shuffling through the pages of notes that he had accumulated on the case.

"Here it is," he said after he found the note he was looking for. "The type of tranquilizer used in the robbery is a generic brand used by thousands of veterinarians around the country. It obviously works as well on humans as it does on animals. It is a fast-acting tranquilizer that the experts say takes effect in a matter of seconds on an average-sized person. Its usage is so widespread that there is no way to trace where it was obtained."

"It sure sounds like this was an inside job, Tom."

"It does," he agreed. "We've already talked to everyone who currently works at the museum, including the guards, staff, and museum curator. It's early in the game, but at this point they all check out clean."

"Whoever it was knew about the wiring of the security system," I said, stating the obvious. "If it wasn't someone currently employed by the museum, could it have been someone from the security company or another outside contractor?"

"We're checking out all of those possibilities now," Tom answered.

"Has it been determined exactly what has been stolen?" I asked.

"It sure has," Tom replied, "and you won't believe it. Many of the items that were displayed in the Special Exhibition were stolen, including the *La Peregrina* necklace, Marilyn Monroe's pearl necklace, the collection of royal jewels and broaches from around the world, as well as the centerpiece of the *Chicago Field Museum's* collection, the yellow topaz crystal. Oh, they also managed to smash a few displays in the Native American Indian exhibition and grab several Indian headdresses on the way out."

"Indian headdresses?" I asked. I pondered the circumstances of the robbery. "Well, why not? What one person considers worthless, another may believe to be priceless."

"That's deep," Tom said, "but I suppose it's true."

"Did they put a dollar value on what was taken?" I inquired.

"Yeah, I've got a copy of the insurance paperwork right here. The total value amounts to over $200 million."

"Two hundred million dollars!" I repeated incredulously. "That's not bad for a half-hour jaunt through the museum," I said, realizing full well that the burglars must have taken several weeks to prepare for a crime of this magnitude.

"Oh, and Jason," Tom added quietly, "now for the bad news. Clifford, the museum guard that didn't regain consciousness after getting hit by the tranquilizer dart? I'm sorry to say that he died in the hospital this morning."

« Chapter 11 »

"NO," I SAID TO TOM, shaking my head sympathetically. "I thought he would make it."

"I certainly hoped so, too."

"Even though it seemed like the robbers were trying to avoid killing anyone, a guard ended up dead anyway. That's a tough break."

"Especially for the guard," Tom said.

"That's what I meant. Have you released the news to the media?"

"Not yet. We'll make the announcement sometime this afternoon. We had previously informed the media immediately after the robbery that there was a shooting involved, but we didn't release any other specific information. We mentioned the *La Peregrina* necklace and a few other pieces of jewelry that were taken, but we didn't release the complete list of what was stolen. I'd like to keep our cards close to the vest for a little while longer."

"How is the top brass handling all of this?" I asked, knowing the politics involved in such a critical case as this in a major metropolitan city like Chicago.

"Actually, the police chief, the mayor, and the DA have all been pretty good so far. Obviously, they want this thing solved. They have been deflecting most of the heat, keeping it off of me and letting me do my job. But I don't know how long their patience will last, especially once the news of the guard's death gets out."

"They have confidence in you, Tom, and they're all smart enough to let you do your job."

"Time will tell," he said.

"Yes, it will. You'll show them."

"Thanks, Jason. By the way, I received some information that you might find interesting."

"What's that?"

"You won't believe it, but you know that guy Darnell Dawkins that you are always talking about running into up there? We believe he was in the vicinity of the museum on the night of the robbery."

I paused to let the information sink in. "No," I shook my head. "Darnell isn't smart enough to plan something like this. He doesn't even know right from left, much less right from wrong."

Tom chuckled.

"I know," he said, "but if he was seen in Chicago at the time, it's possible that he could have been one of the robbers, if not the lead man. It's just too much of a coincidence to not investigate it further. We've got a team staking out his place in Milwaukee. I was hoping that when he shows up, you would help me out and join me while I go talk to him. With you knowing him personally, and both of us knowing the details of the crime, I thought between the two of us we could get a good take on whether he was involved or not."

"You can count on me, Tom." Unless, of course, a major emergency would happen to take place in Pearl Lake in the meantime, which was highly unlikely.

Little did I know that a major crime would soon take place in Pearl Lake, and I would become immersed in the *Chicago Field Museum* case to a greater degree than I could ever have imagined.

"I can always count on you, Jason," he answered. "I wouldn't have asked if I didn't know it."

∞

I was back in the sheriff's office when Chris Garrett came in shortly after three o'clock that afternoon. School must have just gotten out for the day. Chris must have had something on his mind. Whenever he needs to talk to someone, he will often came to my office when he knows I will be alone and we will be able to talk privately.

"Hi, Coach Jason," Chris greeted me with a smile.

"Hello, Chris. How was school today?"

"It was enlightening," he replied with a slight smirk on his face.

"Enlightening? How so?"

"Well," he pondered briefly, "Algebra class was good today."

"Really? Algebra?" I asked, somehow doubting his sincerity.

"Sure," he said trying, unsuccessfully, to look serious. "Here is a question for you: If there is a body buried under each headstone in the St. Paul Cemetery, and there are one hundred rows of headstones, without knowing how many columns of headstones there are – how many people do you think are dead in that cemetery?"

I thought about his question for a few seconds, and then chuckled.

"Hmm," I answered. "I suppose *all* of them." *Very funny*, I thought.

He smiled and nodded, not surprised that I did not fall for his trick algebraic riddle. I had plenty of practice from talking with Bob Colgate – the riddle-speak king.

"Coach Jason, can I talk to you about something?" he asked seriously.

"Of course you can. Here, have a seat." I pointed to the chair next to my desk. "You know you can always talk to me, no matter what – good or bad – don't you, Chris?"

He nodded. "I know."

Chris settled into the chair with his eyebrows wrinkled together, deep in thought. I let him organize his thoughts and waited patiently until he was ready to talk.

"I was thinking about Devon Dawkins," he said after a few moments. "He has been really quiet. I wonder if something is wrong. Devon seems like a cool kid. I think everybody on the football team likes him, but he doesn't really ever open up or say much. Plus, whenever the guys on the football team do something, he never comes with us. I know he is one of the few African-American kids in town. Maybe it seems weird to him, but I don't ever hear anybody on the team say anything about it. I don't think anybody cares about that. I mean, I don't think anyone is prejudiced or anything. Do you think *he* is? Do you think maybe he doesn't like us?"

Once Chris got started, the words poured out freely as he let out what had probably been bottled up inside for a while. *He is quite a kid*, I thought. He was fourteen years old, yet wise enough to notice that one of his teammates might be struggling with something personally, and conscientious enough to care.

"Has Devon ever said anything to you about being unhappy?" I asked. "Could it just be that he is a quiet kid?"

"No, I don't think so. He laughs right along with us whenever we joke around. I haven't ever heard him talk about being unhappy, or about being mad or anything like that."

"Do you think it's a race issue?" I asked.

"No, he's faster than anyone else on the team," Chris said with a straight face.

"Very funny," I moaned, attempting to hide my smile. "You know what I mean."

Chris continued, answering my question seriously. "No, I don't think it is a race or prejudice thing at all. I have never heard anyone say anything like that. Everybody I know likes him personally, and everyone on the team likes him because he is a good football player."

"When you guys go to the mall or go to see a ball game or something like that, what does Devon say when you ask him to join you?"

Chris thought about it. "I guess we all talk about it, and whoever wants to go just gets together and goes. We don't really ask anybody," he explained.

"Remember," I pointed out, "the rest of your friends and most of the guys on the team have known each other your whole lives. Devon has only been here for about two years. What the rest of you do might be automatic to you, but maybe it isn't to him. Do you think you could make a point to include him in the plans when you do something the next time? You don't need to make a big deal out of it. Just make sure he knows he is welcome to join you all, or better yet, that you would all really like it if he did."

"That's a good idea," Chris nodded. "He probably would like it if we let him know we want him to do stuff with us."

After we talked for a while longer, I could tell that Chris felt a lot better after unloading some of the things that had been bothering him.

"Can I ask you about something now, Chris?"

"Sure."

"I'm planning to ask the rest of the team later today," I said, "but in the meantime I'm curious to hear what you think about it. On the way to our football game this coming Friday at Janesville, I was thinking about stopping at the Marshall Farm to see a buffalo named 'Miracle'. How does that sound to you?"

The Marshall Farm is located just north of the city of Milton, and would be right on the way to the game if we chose to stop there.

"Do you mean Miracle, the white buffalo?"

"That's right." I was glad to hear that he had heard of the sacred buffalo.

Chris thought for a moment, and said carefully, "I don't think the team would think it is a totally lame idea."

"By 'not a totally lame idea', do you mean the rest of the team might possibly think it would be fun?"

Chris nodded coolly.

"Okay, let's see what the rest of the team thinks," I said. "If they like the idea, we'll do it."

Chris nodded and stood up to leave.

"Chris," I said as he reached the doorway. He paused and turned to look back at me. "It's good that you noticed those things about Devon, and care enough to want to help him. You're a good kid."

"I know," he said, smiling. "Just don't tell anyone," he quickly wiped the smile off his face, and added sternly, "I don't want to ruin my reputation."

∞

I asked the football team after practice a few hours later if they would be interested in seeing 'Miracle'. Most of the players looked back at me with blank expressions on their faces.

"How many of you have heard of Miracle?" I asked.

Only Chris and a few other players raised their hands. The remaining players either hadn't heard about Miracle, or didn't care.

"Would you like to hear the story of the white buffalo?" I asked.

The team did not exactly answer with a resounding '*yes*', but when they all sat down quietly with curiosity showing on their faces, I could tell that they were interested. I sat down with them surrounding me, and told the story.

"In order to tell you about Miracle, I must first share a legend with you. This legend is one that has been passed on from generation to generation of many Native Americans over several centuries. Imagine America as it was hundreds of years ago, before the colonists reached the shores of our country, and before millions of immigrants came in search of freedom and better lives for their families. It was a time when many Native American tribes roamed the land in what was an immense undeveloped territory between the Atlantic and Pacific Oceans. They lived as one with the land among the deer, elk and buffalo. They fished and hunted only what it took for them to survive, and they were generally content."

I glanced around the room. The entire team was looking back at me with interest showing on their faces, waiting for the story to continue.

"It was during this time that an astoundingly beautiful woman..."

"Ooh..." the team burst out in a chorus of gasps. Not surprisingly, the young teenagers that had reached the age where most were thinking more and more of teenage girls and beautiful women, became increasingly interested in the story.

"That's right," I said, nodding. "A beautiful woman," I repeated, "dressed in white buckskin and holding a wooden pipe, appeared to the Lakota tribe. On the first day she was with them, she presented the wooden pipe to the tribe and proclaimed that if they lived good lives, it would bring peace to all on earth. The beautiful woman then rolled on the ground and arose as a giant black buffalo. On the second day, the buffalo rolled on the ground and turned red. On the third day it rolled again and turned yellow. Finally, on the fourth day the buffalo rolled on the ground one last time and arose as a great, white buffalo. The white buffalo then ran off and disappeared into the sunset in a cloud of dust.

"Ever since, the sacred wooden pipe has been handed down from generation to generation of the Lakota people. In addition to the sacred pipe, the prophecy itself has been passed on that the great white buffalo will return again, and will bring peace to all people around the world."

As I paused and looked around the room, the boys were looking back at me, anxious for me to continue the story.

"Now," I continued, "a very rare and mystical buffalo was born this spring on a farm outside of Milton. She is a pure white buffalo named 'Miracle'."

The players started talking to one another.

"Miracle must be the buffalo from the legend."

"But we still have wars going on now, it's not a time of peace."

"Wow, we're going to see Miracle!"

"Coach Jason, do you think that Miracle could be the white buffalo from the story?" Chris Garrett asked. "Is she returning now like the legend says?"

"Whether you believe in the legend or not, Miracle is truly a rare white buffalo," I answered. "The leaders of many Native American tribes have come to honor her with spiritual ceremonies. Miracle has also been visited by the governors of several states, various church leaders, and even the Dalai Lama. Over one million people have come to Milton from around the world to see Miracle since she was born."

"We want to go see Miracle!" Brandon Dozier spoke up after talking to some other players. The rest of the team shouted in agreement.

"All right! All right!" I acknowledged, laughing. "We will plan on visiting Miracle on the way to our game on Friday. The team has spoken."

« Chapter 12 »

Sᴏᴍᴇ ᴍᴇɴᴛᴀʟ ʜᴇᴀʟᴛʜ ᴘʀᴏғᴇssɪᴏɴᴀʟs and sleep experts believe that humans function at various levels of consciousness. The most basic level of consciousness, the subconscious level, is an accumulation of all of our life experiences. They include experiences that we often remember in our conscious level of awareness as well as ones that we may not remember. Sigmund Freud believed that a tremendous amount of information about ourselves resided in the subconscious level. Our dreams are a part of this subconscious level of awareness, and may simply be recollections of the past, or may be random thoughts, images, or emotions. Dreams that hold deeper meanings are considered by many to be a form of spirituality.

Some individuals are able to gather their life experiences, memories, and dreams from the subconscious level and integrate them with the reasoning and intellectual abilities in their conscious level, to reach a *superconscious* level of awareness. This superconscious level of awareness is often believed to be a state of enlightenment. People that function in a superconscious level of awareness are often considered to be psychic, or shamen, or even prophets.

There have been confirmed cases of surgery patients who saw and heard things that actually happened in the operating rooms during their surgeries while they were under anesthesia. Medical documents have detailed how individuals described passing through tunnels, beckoned by white lights and feelings of contentment after doctors had declared that they had passed away, before they were resuscitated and regained consciousness. These incidents may be unexplainable, but nonetheless have been proven to be true. They have been described as instances of premonition, or intuition, or déjà vu. Regardless of how the incidents are described, certain individuals can function with a heightened level of awareness of what is going on in the world around them if they have the ability and desire to do so.

∞

That night I had a dream about the buffalo from the Lakota legend. I was standing with the gigantic, black-haired buffalo in a large prairie surrounded by rolling hills as far as the eye could see. The tall prairie grass was swaying in the wind, turning dark green as the wind pressed it down to the ground, and returning to its light yellow-green color as it sprang back upright when the wind passed and it was illuminated by the sun's rays once again. The pungent smell of the mixture of dry soil and prairie grass permeated my nostrils.

As I looked over the rolling plains the scene changed before my eyes. The golden prairie transformed into a green wooded area with rolling hills and a wide river running through it. There were hundreds of Native American Indians riding their horses along the riverbank. Their faces and bodies were painted with streaks of white and yellow. A warrior that had a black hawk circling high over his head was leading them. They were whooping and hollering, celebrating what my instincts told me was a decisive victory in battle.

I turned toward the buffalo as it changed color from black to red. The Native American leader also took on more color as I looked at him more closely. His head was shaved except for a tuft of long red hair that ran over the top and back of his head, matching the now red color of the buffalo standing next to me. Attached to the leader's red hair was a headdress of a type I had never seen before. The headdress was wrapped around his red hair. It had three large feathers in front: a black feather in the middle, flanked by white feathers on each side. Two thick strings were attached to the sides of the headdress, one falling onto his right shoulder and the other onto his left. Each string had stunning circular attachments hanging from them, covered with multi-colored beads and feathers, and jade, silver, and gold adornments. The black hawk was still flying high above him, casting fleeting shadows on the ground as it passed.

As the color of the buffalo turned from red to light yellow, the wooded area of rolling hills once comprised of various shades of green was now covered with a deep blanket of white snow. There were only about one hundred Native Americans remaining in the group, which was now made up of men, women and children. They were no longer celebrating wildly, but were slowly trudging along through the snow, looking utterly exhausted.

Off in the distance, a group of soldiers that out-numbered them by five-fold were following them doggedly. They were each bundled up in thick cotton, wool, or leather coats and hats. With only a few men in the group wearing uniforms, they looked more like a bunch of farmers than trained soldiers.

The red-haired Native American leader, with the ever-present black hawk still circling overhead, gathered together all of his men that were still able to fight.   The remaining women and children were ushered silently into the cold, icy river in an attempt to swim to safety on the other side. He and his men then turned to face the approaching enemy to make what would be their last stand.

As I gazed once again at the buffalo standing beside me, its hair turned from light yellow to white, as white as the freshly fallen snow.   Understanding the tragedy that was unfolding before our eyes, an intense feeling of sadness that I knew I shared with the white buffalo came over me.

Suddenly, the buffalo rolled on the ground, stirring up a cloud of fine, white dust. As the dust cloud slowly thinned, I watched the buffalo's white hair grow long and its gigantic shape transform into that of a sleek woman.   The woman was kneeling, hunched forward with her head down and her hands on the ground. She slowly straightened up into an upright position, with her shoulders arched back and her head held high. I could see her clearly as she rose gracefully to her feet.   The dust had completely settled, and it appeared as though her entire body was surrounded by a bright yellow-white aura. She was the most beautiful woman I had ever seen.

She looked at me with sparkling eyes that were as blue and warm and inviting as the Caribbean Sea.   She was nearly as tall as me. Her body was long and lithe, and her smooth, slightly tanned skin had a shiny, healthy-looking glow. She had luscious lips and long, light blond hair that flowed over her shoulders and down to her full, bare breasts.

I woke up from the dream with a jolt. My heart was pounding wildly. My eyes were wide open, and the image of the stunning woman was still etched pleasurably on my brain.

"*Damn!*" I swore to myself. "*Why did I have to wake up now?*"

« Chapter 13 »

ALTHOUGH I DIDN'T REALIZE it, I still must have been smiling thinking about the dream when Tom Kaminski telephoned early that morning. It almost sounded like I was laughing when I said 'hello'.

"What's so funny?" he asked.

"Nothing," I answered.

He hesitated. "Are you up?"

"I sure am," I said, chuckling to myself.

Tom hesitated briefly. "Are you alone?"

"Of course, I'm alone," I said, wishing that I wasn't. I longed to gaze into the buffalo-woman's eyes once again. I was still mesmerized by the vision. The dream was so real that it seemed like it had actually happened in real life.

"It sounded like there might be someone there," he said. "Is this a good time to talk?"

"Sure," I answered. "There's no better time than now."

"Okay. Good."

I turned my focus on Tom's telephone call and began again. "Good morning, by the way."

"Oh, sorry. Good morning, Jason. Hey, I'm calling to let you know that Darnell Dawkins returned to his apartment in Milwaukee. He was arrested without incident by the local authorities. I'm planning on heading there now to talk to him about the museum robbery. Can you meet me there?"

"What time?"

"One o'clock this afternoon. I'm sorry for the short notice. This all just happened this morning. I'd really appreciate it if you could make it."

"No problem, Tom. I'll be there."

As soon as I hung up the phone I took a quick, cold shower to help me wake up and snap out of the enchanting effects of the dream.

∞

"We've nearly completed the background checks on the current guards and employees at the *Chicago Field Museum*," Tom filled me in when we met at the Milwaukee Police Station where Darnell Dawkins was being held.

"Did you find anything so far?"

"No, nothing suspicious," he replied. "We still need to check out the past museum employees and outside service contractors, including the ones that upgraded the security system."

"Well, you're making progress."

"We are," he acknowledged. "All of the detectives – hell, the entire Chicago PD has been working their asses off twenty-four hours a day on this. We *need* to make progress."

"Tom, you and your fellow detectives and Chicago police officers are too smart, and too savvy to let anyone get away with this. You'll solve it," I said confidently as we waited for Darnell to be brought to the interrogation room.

∞

"Mr. Dawkins," Tom greeted Darnell as he was led into the room a minute later, "I'm Detective Tom

Kaminski of the Chicago Police Department. I believe you know my associate Sheriff Avalon of the Arrowhead County Sheriff Department here in Wisconsin."

"You have got to be kidding me," Darnell said sarcastically. "What the hell is going on? What am I doing here?" He looked back and forth at Tom and me, like a dog watching a Ping-Pong match. He was obviously anxious about what we wanted with him.

"We're here to talk to you about the *Chicago Field Museum* robbery," Tom said. "Where were you Friday night and Saturday morning?"

Darnell's jaw dropped, and a flicker of fear showed on his face. Tom's question clearly took him by surprise.

"The big Chicago museum robbery that's been plastered all over the news? Do you actually think I got anything to do with that?" Darnell asked, dumbfounded.

"Just answer the question," Tom said. "Where were you Friday night and Saturday morning?"

"What the hell," Darnell said to himself. "I go to Chicago for a few days to chill and stay out of trouble, and end up getting something like that pinned on me?" he whined. "I went to visit my cousin in Chicago for the weekend," he answered, finally. "I got to his place around seven o'clock Friday night. Then, we went out for a big, fancy dinner. We ate at the McDonald's that was right down the road from his apartment, okay? After that we went to Shady's Bar for the rest of the night. Don't worry," he turned to me and quickly added, "I drank soda the whole time. We were there until two o'clock in the morning."

"Where did you go from there?" Tom asked.

"We went straight back to my cousin's apartment and crashed. I swear," he added, "I didn't have nothing to do with that robbery."

"I hope not," Tom said. "What time did you go to McDonald's?"

"I guess we were there sometime between nine o'clock and ten o'clock."

"How did you get around that night?" Tom continued. "Did you take your car?"

"No. Everything was within a couple blocks of my cousin's place, so we just walked. The McDonald's was a block away, and Shady's was right across the street from there. I left my car in the apartment parking lot the whole time."

"Darnell, did you go anywhere else that night?" Tom asked. "It's important that you tell us everything."

"No, we didn't go nowhere else." Darnell thought for a few seconds. "Well," he added, "after we ate we did stop at the bank across the street on our way to Shady's. My cousin needed to use the ATM to get some cash. I think he took out forty bucks. That's all we did."

Tom asked Darnell a few more basic questions to confirm his cousin's name, address and other pertinent information, then pored over his notes to make sure he didn't miss anything. He was very thorough. When he was done, he gave me a slight, almost imperceptible nod.

That was my cue. It was my turn.

"Darnell," I asked, "did you talk to anyone about the *Chicago Field Museum* robbery?"

"No. I didn't talk to no one about it," he answered without hesitation.

I have talked to several very good liars who could look me in the eye and lie convincingly. Some would lament about the unfairness of having the blame for something put on them falsely. Others would swear on a stack of bibles, or swear on their mother's graves, that they did not do what they were accused of doing – all the while being totally guilty. Whatever Darnell was, he was not a very good liar. I tended to believe him when he claimed that he was not involved in the robbery.

"Have you ever been to the *Chicago Field Museum*?" I asked.

"Hell, no. Never been there."

"Have you ever worked there, either directly or through an outside contractor?"

"No. Like I said, I ain't ever been there, period. Not as a visitor, or working there for nobody."

"Do you know anything about the jewelry or gems at the museum, such as the yellow topaz crystal or the *La Peregrina* necklace?"

"No, I don't know nothing about any jewels, or a peregrine falcon, or whatever you said," he answered with a blank stare. He didn't know what the highly valuable gems or the *La Peregrina* necklace even were. This was all way over his head.

"What did you think of the big elephant when you walked into the museum?" I asked.

Darnell was puzzled by the question. His eyes blinked rapidly several times as he tried to imagine an elephant in a museum.

"What?" he asked uncomprehendingly. "A big elephant? Made of jewels or something?"

I could see him trying to picture a big, diamond elephant in his mind. He couldn't really do it. He couldn't imagine an elephant in a museum, made of jewels or otherwise. Nor did he correct me and say,

'That was a *dinosaur* in the museum, not an elephant'. He didn't know anything about the *Chicago Field Museum* robbery.

"Honestly guys, I ain't ever set foot in the place, and I really ain't ever talked to nobody who has, so I don't know what's in there or not. But you know what? It sounds like there's some pretty interesting stuff in there. Maybe after you let me out of this dump I'll go visit that museum sometime."

Darnell thought about it again, and realized the scope of the crime that he was being associated with. "The hell with that," he changed his mind. "I ain't going nowhere near that place."

« Chapter 14 »

THE CLOUDS BEGAN ROLLING in – thicker, darker, and looking ominous as we boarded the team bus to travel to our football game in Janesville, with the brief visit to the Marshall Farm and Miracle along the way. Steve Dozier was riding on the bus with the team. Bob Colgate and I were each driving our own cars. Bob had some Badger Finance business to conduct in Janesville over the weekend, or in his words, he 'needed to perform some value-added money-making magic' while he was in town. I had plans to visit some friends in the area after the game.

I followed the team bus as it pulled into the Marshall Farm. Everyone piled out of the vehicles and stretched their cramped legs to get their blood circulating again. We walked together along the farm's driveway, passing a large white buffalo banner that adorned the front yard and continuing on to admire a large stone buffalo decoration when we reached the back yard.

I was surprised to see so many people gathered at the farm. There had to be at least one hundred people there. We reached a tall, wooden fence that separated the onlookers from the goats, horses, llamas...and buffalo grazing out in the pasture. Several teepees and a few tents were set up in a large circle in the back yard. Next to the tents there was a small, open-walled gift shop that was filled with shoppers. Two people on the other side of the fence, dressed in sweatshirts and blue jeans, and carrying wooden buckets were talking to another group of people. They must be the owners of the farm, Chad Marshall, and his wife, Gloria, I figured.

We stopped at a section of the fence that was directly across from the barn, which was about seventy-five feet away from where we were standing. A few beams of bright sunlight were shining through the now mostly cloudy sky. Four large, brown buffalo were in front of the barn eating out of an open trough. Standing next to one of the buffalo and eating alongside it was a small, snow-white buffalo. It was Miracle!

The players on the team were excited to see the rare white buffalo, and talked to each other in hushed voices. Miracle was illuminated by a golden ray of light created from a thin sliver of sunshine making its way through the clouds. A dazzling rainbow painted a semicircular frame around what appeared to be a magical picture of the white buffalo.

"Wow," Brandon Dozier said softly.

"Look at how white and fluffy she is!" Jacob Kampo exclaimed.

"You weren't exaggerating, Jason," Steve Dozier said to me. "Miracle is an impressive creature."

I tried to get a good view of Miracle as I stood alongside the fence with the rest of the team. I leaned against the fence, grabbing it with my right hand at waist height, completely awestruck by the white buffalo.

When the small herd of buffalo were done eating, Miracle and the large buffalo near her, probably her mother, began working their way towards the section of the fence where we were standing. I wondered if they thought we had food or treats for them. The snow-white buffalo slowly continued to move towards me, returning my steady gaze. When she reached the other side of the fence directly in front of me, she reached up and gently rubbed her warm nose on my hand that was still grasping the fence. Even though the young buffalo still probably weighed less than one hundred pounds, I probably should have been more cautious. Buffalo weren't exactly tame creatures, but I wasn't worried. It looked like Miracle was smiling.

"Hi girl," I whispered softly as she nudged my hand affectionately. Miracle certainly was an awe-inspiring buffalo.

I continued to take in the presence of the sacred buffalo, and suddenly recalled my dream from the prior night. Once again, I felt a close connection with the buffalo, as I did in the dream.

Out of the corner of my eye I noticed someone moving cautiously toward us on the other side of the fence.

"What are you doing there?" Chad Marshall called out. "No one is allowed to feed the animals!" He looked at the two buffalo near me as they backed up slowly, unfazed by his outburst. He noticed that they were not chewing or eating anything, and that none of us had any food in our hands.

"You weren't feeding her, were you?" Chad said, more as a statement of fact, then as a question.

"No, I wasn't," I answered. "I'm sorry if I got too close. Are you Chad Marshall?"

"I am," he replied with a surprised expression on his face, "and this is my wife, Gloria," he said as she came over to stand beside him to look at me, the source of all of the commotion.

"Hi Mr. and Mrs. Marshall. My name is Jason Avalon, and this is the Pearl Lake freshman football team." I directed his gaze to all of the players around me, dressed in their black and red uniforms. "We stopped here to see Miracle on the way to our football game against Janesville tonight."

Chad Marshall looked around and greeted our entire team.

"Thank you all for stopping," he said, smiling, before turning back to me. "It's good to meet you, Jason."

"That was absolutely incredible!" Gloria Marshall exclaimed.

"I'm sorry," I apologized again to her. "I didn't realize it was dangerous to let Miracle touch me."

"Oh, no, that's not what I meant," Gloria explained. "Miracle is typically quite shy. She very rarely comes near the fence. It was highly unusual for her to walk up to you and touch you like she did. That's what was incredible!"

"It was a surprise," Chad said. "Miracle is a gentle, friendly animal, but she usually sticks very close to her mother by the barn. The only other time I can remember her coming up to the fence was when Denby Sage was here a few months ago."

Chad Marshall waved to a man who was walking toward us on our side of the fence. "I apologize," Chad said to me. "I tend to get a little over-protective of our Miracle."

"I can understand that," I replied. "She is absolutely precious."

The man that Chad Marshall had beckoned reached us. I could see from his dark red complexion and strong, chiseled facial features that he was a Native American.

"Denby," Chad immediately introduced us, "this is Jason Avalon. Jason, this is Denby Sage, from Pine Ridge, South Dakota. Denby is the chief of the Lakota Sioux Tribe. He is a very gifted medicine man, and is highly respected by Native Americans, and by religious and spiritual leaders around the world. Denby has been here fairly often to see Miracle."

"It's good to meet you, Chief Sage," I said, shaking his outreached hand firmly.

"The pleasure is mine, Jason. I saw a strong connection between you and the white buffalo of peace," he said with admiration showing on his face.

I nodded, noticing his dancing eyes that couldn't conceal a myriad of thoughts going through his head. Distinguished lines of earthly wisdom were carved on his face. A few gray streaks ran through his black, shoulder-length hair that was tied up in a ponytail. He appeared to be about fifty years old.

"Have you ever seen Miracle before?" Denby asked.

"Well...no," I answered. *Not if you don't consider my dreams*, I thought.

"Interesting," he answered. He seemed to detect my hesitation when I answered his simple question.

"I've read about Miracle and wanted to come and see her personally," I added truthfully.

Chief Sage seemed to ponder what I had said and continued to assess me in a curious, non-threatening manner. Similarly, I returned his direct gaze. After a few seconds he nodded his head and smiled warmly.

"Tomorrow at sunrise," he explained, "we will be holding a drum ceremony here to celebrate the hope that Miracle, the sacred white buffalo, brings to all people of the world. Many members of the Lakota

Sioux Nation will be here, along with the leaders of several other Native American tribes. Tribal elders and storytellers will be sharing stories and ancient legends. It will be a special day. Would you like to join us for the celebration?"

The honor of being invited to the drum ceremony by a tribal leader and medicine man was not lost on me. Miracle was special, and the thought of visiting her again tomorrow during a Native American drum ceremony was exciting – too exciting to pass up the opportunity.

Without hesitation, I accepted Chief Denby Sage's invitation.

« Chapter 15 »

THE QUICK STOP AT the Marshall Farm to see Miracle had inspired our entire team. They were unusually fired up despite the rain that was falling steadily when we reached the football field in Janesville. I knew that I would not have to give an intense pre-game speech or do anything special to get the team fired up today. Miracle had taken care of that.

"How was the field during your pre-game warm-ups?" I asked the team during our pre-game huddle.

"Wet," Brandon Dozier answered. Everyone laughed.

"Sure it's wet. How was it when you fell on the ground?" I asked the group.

"Muddy."

"Soft!"

"Is anyone cold?" I asked, even though it was actually a relatively warm autumn night. The players were running around and staying active, so they were keeping warm. It was much more difficult for the parents and fans to keep warm while they were sitting in the bleachers or standing around on the sidelines, especially if they weren't dressed adequately for the weather conditions. Even though it was raining it was *not* a cold night, and I wanted the players to realize it.

"No, it's nice out," some players call out.

"It's fun out here!" Chris Garrett yelled.

The rest of the players got caught up in the excitement and were jumping up and down, anxious for the game to start.

"That's the important thing," I told them. "It's a great night for football, so just have a good time! Everyone will be sliding around on the wet, slippery field tonight. After practicing and playing games for a month now, you all know the plays well. The rain won't cause you to make mistakes if you concentrate on doing your jobs. Janesville has a 3-0 record just like us, but don't worry about what they do. Have confidence in yourselves, have confidence in each other, and play as hard as you can. The team that plays the smartest and makes the fewest mistakes will win tonight. When the game is over, everyone will know who has the best team. Just go out and have fun! Okay, team. Let's huddle up."

The team gathered around me. They each reached their hands into the pile, and one by one set them on top of mine.

"Now, what do we want to do?" I asked loudly.

"Have fun!" the team screamed.

"Okay, on three...1, 2, 3!"

"Have fun! Have fun! Have fun!" The team chanted in unison as they broke the huddle and ran out onto the field.

∞

Amidst all of the enthusiasm, our team kicked off to Janesville to start the game. It was a good kick-off. Janesville's kick-return player caught the ball at the fifteen-yard line and began running cautiously toward the left side of the field. He slowly picked up his pace as he felt more comfortable with his footing on the slippery turf. We could hear the sound of contact as the player's shoulder pads slammed into each other.

Jacob Kampo, one of our players on the front line on the kick-off team reached the ball carrier first. As Jacob lowered his body and leaned forward to make the tackle his feet slipped out from under him. He fell flat on his face while the ball carrier carefully maneuvered around him and headed back toward the middle of the field. By now most of the players on both teams had either been knocked to the ground, or were still blocking each other at a standstill.

We could see from the sidelines that the ball carrier had an ever-increasing, open field to work with. Only two of our players remained standing and were close enough to have a chance of tackling him before he made it into the end zone. Both of our players approached the runner at a fairly high speed considering how wet and slick the grass was. One of our players was running straight at him from the left side of the field, and the other from the right. It appeared as though they had the ball carrier surrounded.

Undeterred, the ball carrier started to pick up speed. It looked like he was going to try to run right in between our two players before they converged on him. When they noticed this they started to build up speed, too, in an effort to prevent him from getting past them.

Just as they reached him, the ball carrier suddenly stopped. Still running too fast considering the slippery conditions, our two players collided with each other harmlessly and fell onto the soft ground with a splash. It looked like they made belly flops in a swimming pool. The ball carrier deftly sidestepped them and ran the ball into the end zone for a touchdown.

Our players on the field and sidelines were totally silent. It was so quiet we could hear the rain pitter-pattering as it hit the ground and as it splattered off of the player's helmets. Even the Janesville players, coaches, and fans on the opposite side of the field were fairly muted in their celebration of their well-deserved touchdown. They appeared as surprised about the play as we were.

The team gathered around me with their heads down and their shoulders drooping.

"It's okay, guys," I assured them calmly. "That was a very good play by Janesville, but we have the rest of the game to play. We aren't going to let one play get us down. Don't give up! We are going to give Janesville every bit of effort we can for the entire game. I have absolutely no doubt that we are going to win this game tonight!"

I glanced across the field at the opposing team and coaches as our team ran back onto the field. Like us, their coaches were all bundled up with raincoats, and jacket hoods and hats to protect themselves from the heavy downpour. I pulled out the game program that was attached to my clipboard. The team rosters, including the coaching staffs, were listed for both the Janesville and Pearl Lake teams. I recognized the names of some of Janesville's coaches that I had coached against over the years. However, I noticed that they had a new head coach this year that I didn't know. I looked at the program and saw that his name was 'J. C. Donovan'.

We are in for a tough fight in this game tonight, I thought, *and if I am going to ask the team to give their best effort, then I am going to do the same.*

∞

Both teams continued to play solid, mistake-free football through the end of the first half. Janesville failed to score on the extra-point conversion after their touchdown on the opening game kick-off, so the score remained 6-0 at halftime.

The rain continued to fall steadily while our team regrouped during the halftime break. Both Janesville and Pearl Lake had stuck to conservative game plans in the first half due to the wet and slippery field conditions. Both teams ran most plays where the quarterback handed the ball directly to the running backs. Each team wisely avoided tossing the ball to the running backs, or passing the ball, because that would increase the chances of fumbling and making other general ball-handling mistakes.

Janesville was set to kick-off to us to start the second half, and I had a plan. The referees heated and dried the game ball during halftime, which meant the football would be relatively dry for a brief time in the beginning of the third quarter. Our quarterback has a very good arm and can throw a dry football a long distance accurately.

We fielded the second half kick-off safely and returned it to our thirty-yard line. The referee placed the football there, with a towel covering it to keep it as dry as possible. Once the football became wet it would stay wet for the remainder of the game.

Our team lined up on the line of scrimmage as the referee removed the towel from the football. The quarterback took the snap and quickly took several steps backward. Devon Dawkins, who was lined up on the right side of the field, ran five yards down the field, cut to the right toward the sidelines and turned to look for the quarterback to throw the ball. The quarterback made a pump fake with the football towards Devon, but did not throw it.

The Janesville defensive backs that were surrounding Devon moved toward the spot they thought the ball was going to be thrown. Devon quickly turned up field and ran by them in the opposite direction. The quarterback threw the football in a perfect arc. Devon caught the ball while running in full stride. His legs were moving so fast that it looked like his feet were barely touching the ground. With no one anywhere near him, he ran easily, untouched, into the end zone to score the tying touchdown. Janesville stopped our attempt to score on the extra point conversion, tying the score at 6-6.

The field became increasingly muddy and sloppy as the second half progressed. I was starting to feel like I was engaged in an intense chess match with Janesville's new head coach, J. C. Donovan. We were each utilizing the playing field as though it was a giant chessboard. The football players on the front lines were like pawns, either gathering together to protect the quarterback, as the pawns attempt to protect the king, or by opening paths for the more highly skilled running backs to make big plays, like the rooks, bishops, or queen in a chess match.

Whenever I made a move to mount an attack, I would inevitably have to fend off a counter-attack by the Janesville coach before I could carry out my next strategic maneuver. We were both playing offense and defense on the football field, making fluid moves one by one, similar to a chess match in an effort to put ourselves into a position where we could say, '*check*'.

For example, a few times during the game Janesville ran a play where all of the running backs ran in one direction, either to the right or to the left side of the field. The quarterback faked handing the ball to one of the backs, then turned and ran in the opposite direction. As a result our players got jammed up in the middle of the field, and the quarterback ran for big gains.

To stop this play, I gave our middle linebacker the top assignment of following the quarterback wherever he was on the field. Only after our linebacker knew for certain that the quarterback did not have the ball could he go after anyone else. The next few times Janesville called that play, our linebacker was waiting for the quarterback as he ran to the other side of the field and tackled him for losses.

On the other hand, at one point in the game we noticed that the Janesville defense was shifting to the side of the field that Chris Garrett was lined up on. They obviously knew that Chris was a very good running back and were trying to gain an advantage whenever he ran the ball by putting extra players on whatever side of the field he was on. So I positioned Chris to one side of the field, and then gave the ball to another running back that ran in the other direction, away from a majority of the defensive players. Janesville stopped making that shift in their defense after we gained huge chunks of yardage running that play a few times.

As the game progressed I was gaining an increasing amount of respect for the Janesville team and coaches, especially J. C. Donovan. Their head coach led the team very similarly to how I led ours. We were not loud, and chose to coach and teach our players quietly along the sidelines. The players in turn were not loud either and seemed determined to play solid, hard-nosed football. They did not harass the referees or taunt the opposing team's players. In fact, the coaches and players on both teams were very disciplined, and it showed in their superior performance.

The end of the contest was drawing near. The players on both sides were still enthusiastic and were continuing to exert all of the effort they could at this late stage of the game. Pearl Lake had possession of the football, which was sitting at mid-field, exactly on the fifty-yard line. We had enough time to run two more plays before the game ended.

Throughout the entire course of the game I had been working on setting up a mis-direction play, which we called a 'counter' play. At least once during each series of downs that our offense had the ball, we ran the counter play. On the counter play, our running back that was lined up on the left side of the backfield would run to the right behind the quarterback. The quarterback would turn around and hand the football to him, and the running back would continue to run to the right side of the field with the football. At the same time, Chris Garrett, who was lined up on the right side of the backfield, would take one counter-step to the right. Then Chris would swing back around in the opposite direction behind the quarterback and continue running around the left side of the field, without the football.

This did several things: First, the defense would recognize the play and start to anticipate that our running back was going to run the ball into the right side of the field, as he had already done several times in the game. Second, they would see that Chris Garrett was continually swinging back around to his left without the football, posing no threat to the defense. Eventually they just began to ignore Chris whenever we ran this play.

With one minute remaining on the time clock, once again I set up the mis-direction play. As designed, the running back on the left side of the field ran behind the quarterback, got the football, and ran to the right side for a modest gain.

The seconds on the game clock continued to tick down.

Thirty-three...Thirty-two...Thirty-one...

On the final play of the game, I called the counter play. Our quarterback took the snap and turned around to his left side with his back facing the defensive players. He reached out his hand to the running back that was running past him towards the right side of the field. The running back crouched down, clamped his arms together tight against his stomach, and lowered his shoulders as he plunged head first into the right side of the line. Simultaneously, Chris Garrett took a counter-step to the right and quickly swung back around to the left, behind the quarterback who still had his back to the opposing team.

Some of the defensive players tackled the running back that had run into the right side of the line, and others were continuing to move in his direction. By the time they realized that the quarterback had not handed the ball to the first running back, but instead had given it to Chris Garrett, Chris was running far around the left side of the field at a blazing-fast speed. Unlike the play in the football game from a few weeks ago, Chris ran by me as I stood on the sidelines, not with a look of fear in his eyes but with a smile on his face. He displayed an air of confidence as he turned the corner in complete control and galloped into the end zone. Chris was like a champion racehorse winning the Kentucky Derby. He had a big heart, played football because he loved the game, and ran gracefully as he pulled ahead of his competitors to reach the finish line first.

The final seconds ticked off the time clock:
Three...Two...One...
Chris scored the winning touchdown!
The final score:
Pearl Lake 12,
Janesville   6.

Check...and Checkmate!

∞

Both teams displayed their sportsmanship after the game and gathered in the middle of the field to shake hands and congratulate each other on a well-played and hard fought game. We met the Janesville coaches, and sincerely complimented them on a game that both teams deserved to win. I was talking to the two Janesville assistant coaches I knew, and looked around trying to find their new head coach.

We were all still bundled up to protect ourselves from the rain, which had finally slowed to a steady drizzle. I was talking to one of the Janesville coaches when he noticed their head coach approaching and promptly introduced us.

"J. C., I'd like you to meet Jason Avalon. Jason, this is our new head coach, Jessica Donovan."

I tried, probably unsuccessfully, to hide my surprise that J. C. Donovan was *Jessica* Donovan. I had never seen a football team at any level with a female coach before. Not that I was looking for it, but with everyone dressed in several layers of clothing, I certainly hadn't noticed. As well as the Janesville team played tonight, she was very good.

"Coach Donovan, it's a pleasure to meet you," I said as we shook hands. She reached her other hand around me and held my left arm in a friendly semi-embrace. I utterly melted as I absorbed the warm touch of her hand on my arm. Her penetrating blue eyes pulled me in like a tractor-beam. Even though her jacket hood was still pulled tightly around her face it couldn't conceal her radiant beauty. With her smooth skin still glistening from the rain, I felt like I was staring at the polished white-marble statue of a Greek goddess.

I tried not to stare at her, and fought to maintain my composure as I took in her stunning features. She looked so familiar. I could swear I knew her from somewhere. *Should I ask her*, I thought to myself? No. That was an old, worn-out line and there was no way I was going to use it.

"It's nice to meet you, Jason. Please call me Jessica, or Jess," she said with a smooth, confident voice and a luscious smile that was pleasantly distracting. "That was a terrific game, wasn't it?"

"It sure was," I agreed. "Your team played a great game, Jessica. They never gave up."

"I was just thinking the same thing," Jessica said. "This had to be the best-played and best-coached freshman football game I have ever seen, especially considering the wet playing field."

"You have a talented bunch of players," I said. "They handle themselves well. They have been well-coached."

"They are great kids. The coaches have worked very hard with them. I saw the same quality in your players and coaches, too, Jason."

Not yet letting go from our handshake, Jessica continued to hold my hand while retaining a firm grip on my opposite arm with her other hand. I gladly let her hold on to me as she continued to scrutinize me closely.

"Have we met before, Jason?" she asked in a soft, throaty voice, almost like a whisper. "I have the strongest feeling that we know each other from somewhere..."

« Chapter 16 »

I TALKED WITH J. C. (Jessica) Donovan for a while longer before we left the football field. She seemed almost as reluctant to leave as I was to let her go. Fortunately, before departing she gave me a clue as to where she might be later that night. Being the dedicated sheriff that I am, I definitely planned to follow up on *this* clue. *What would it hurt if I happened to bump into her again*, I asked myself? As attractive as she is, Jessica must have a lot of experience fending off unwanted suitors by now, I figured. If she ever wants to get rid of me, she certainly has the ability to do so.

∞

I met my friends at a nearby restaurant and sports bar after showering and cleaning up at the *Holiday Inn Express* in Janesville, where I was staying for the night. We had finished our meals and were still visiting at the table when I noticed Jessica Donovan and the other Janesville coaches come through the door. They were talking quietly as they entered, and I noticed Jessica discretely scan the entire restaurant and bar area. I was trying not to gawk at her, so I couldn't tell if she noticed me when her eyes quickly swept past the table where I was sitting. She and the other coaches exchanged greetings with several people as they found a table and sat down.

Jessica had a spring to her step and moved so gracefully! She removed her jacket and hood, and shook her long, flowing blond hair free as it fell below her shoulders. She was wearing a soft cotton long-sleeved white shirt and blue jeans. Her shirt was not exactly tight fitting, but it fit close enough to reveal her sleek, shapely figure. She was completely illuminated by the light above the table, which seemed to enhance her radiant beauty. Her sparkling blue eyes were so mesmerizing that not even the blue sapphire gemstones at the *Chicago Field Museum* could top them. She appeared to be surrounded by a soft white aura.

Then it suddenly struck me like a bolt of lightning. Jessica – she was the woman from my dream! When the buffalo transformed into a beautiful woman – the woman was Jessica! I thought she looked very familiar when I met her after the football game, but the lighting was so poor and she had been so bundled up to protect herself from the elements that I couldn't see her very well. Now, with her long blond hair, soft blue eyes, and exquisite body lit up by the bright table light above her, I recognized her clearly. *Not only is she the woman from my dream*, I thought, *she is the woman of my dreams*. Even though I didn't quite understand it, the realization of what had happened was both fascinating and puzzling. How could I have dreamt of Jessica so vividly before I had even met her?

Apparently my friends had been talking to me, but I hadn't noticed.

"Are you all right, Jason? You look like you've seen a ghost."

"I'm more than all right. I think I've seen an angel," I answered quietly.

"Is it the football coach that you were telling us about?" my friend asked.

"It sure is," I answered as I noticed Jessica walking toward us.

"Jason!" she said excitedly as she reached our table.

"Hi Jessica," I answered. My entire body was tingling with excitement. Jessica laughed quietly as she looked at me, as though she knew exactly how I was feeling. Maybe it was because she was feeling the same way.

"Jessica, these are my friends, Ryan and Alicia," I said. "Ryan and Alicia, this is Jessica Donovan, the toughest coach I have ever played against – and the most beautiful." After they exchanged greetings, Jessica promptly responded to my introduction.

"Why Jason!" she said, chuckling. "How flattering. You think I'm more beautiful than the other football coaches? Is that because I'm less hairy and don't chew tobacco?"

"Uh-oh," my friends groaned in sympathy for me, giving me a chance to get my foot out of my mouth.

"You don't chew tobacco?" I answered straight-faced. "Your breath is so sweet that I thought you must be chewing spearmint-flavored tobacco." Actually, when we first met I thought that her breath *was* fresh and inviting. "Well, never mind then. I take that back. I have to admit, though, you do smell much better than the guys!" Everyone laughed as Jessica prepared to leave us to re-join the other Janesville coaches.

"Jason," Jessica placed her hand on top of mine and leaned in to whisper in my ear. "I'll be very disappointed if you don't find some time tonight to come and talk to me." I felt her moist lips brush against my ear as she turned around and glided smoothly back to her table.

After Alicia and Ryan left to go home I went over to the table where Jessica and her fellow coaches were sitting. After we all visited for a while the other coaches went their own ways, leaving Jessica and me alone to talk. We talked for hours as though we had known each other forever. Aside from coaching football, we found that we had many other things in common.

Jessica was also the middle child in a close-knit family of three. She grew up in a sports-minded family, and played on her high school basketball and softball teams. Luckily, she was an avid Green Bay Packer fan, which was nothing to take for granted. The Janesville-Beloit community was located on the Wisconsin-Illinois border and was close enough to Chicago that there were many Chicago Bear fans around.

Jessica graduated from the University of Wisconsin-Madison with a business degree, and splits her time working at her office in Madison and at her home office in Janesville. As an Economic Specialist for a private company called Dynamic Solutions, Inc., Jessica works with universities and technical colleges to develop curricula that will serve the needs of various state employers. Then she matches the graduates of those programs with the employers that can best utilize their newly acquired skills. I found it to be very interesting, and respected her for the passion she had for her job.

"Jason?" Jessica asked. "You're scheduled to play Columbus in Pearl Lake next Saturday, aren't you?"

"We are," I acknowledged.

"Our Janesville team is scheduled to play against Columbus the week after that," she said. "I thought it would be a good idea for me to go to Pearl Lake next week to scout Columbus when they play you. That way I'll be better prepared when we play them the following week. Would you like to get together some time while I'm in Pearl Lake?"

"Do you mean that I would have to put up with you again after tonight?" I asked.

Jessica answered immediately with a solid punch to my left arm.

"Ouch," I chuckled, feigning pain even though I barely felt the punch.

"That's what you get," Jessica said unsympathetically. She paused, then shook her hand in an effort to get the feeling back. She stared at my arm, reached out and squeezed it firmly. "Damn, that's hard," she whispered.

"Okay," I rephrased my question. "What I should have asked was, 'Do you really want to put up with *me* after tonight?'"

"I wouldn't have asked if I didn't want to," she replied earnestly, looking at me with wide eyes.

"It would be a good time to visit," I said. "We will be celebrating our Pearl Lake Fall Festival that weekend. Our freshman football game will be starting at eleven o'clock on Saturday morning. The varsity football team plays after us at one o'clock in the afternoon. Our Mardi Gras-style parade on Saturday night is the main attraction of the Fall Festival. Plus there will be craft fairs, a farmer's market, and a carnival set up in Town Square during the weekend, so there will be a lot going on."

"Oh! That sounds like fun!" Jessica exclaimed.

"Would you like to get together after our game?" I asked. "We could do whatever you want, or you could always go on your own, if you prefer."

When Jessica asked earlier if I would like to get together while she was in town, I wasn't sure exactly how *much* time she meant. Did she just want to catch our game against Columbus and then spend some time with me briefly before getting back home to Janesville? Or was she thinking of spending a little more time together than that? I didn't want to assume anything.

"I'd love to take it all in with you if you don't mind, Jason."

"I wouldn't have asked if I didn't want to," I said with a straight face.

I caught her punch this time before it landed on my shoulder, and held her knuckled fist in my hand. She unclenched her fist slowly, interlocking her fingers with mine. It was a good fit.

"I've got plenty of room in my house," I offered. "You can stay in my guest bedroom if you'd like to stick around Saturday night."

"Thank you for the offer, Jason, but absolutely not! I'm not that kind of girl."

"I wouldn't have offered if I thought you were."

Even though I felt a deep connection to her and it seemed like we had known each other for a long time, we had actually only met a few hours ago. I didn't blame her for declining my offer. In fact, I respected her even more for it. We finalized our plans for the following week, and on the way out of the restaurant Jessica hugged me and gave me a soft, lingering kiss on the cheek.

Kissed by an angel, I thought.

« Chapter 17 »

THE MARSHALL FARM WAS bustling with activity when I got there the next morning before sunrise. Several campfires were blazing in front of the tents and teepees clustered throughout the back yard.

Chad and Gloria Marshall came to greet me and offered me a cup of steaming coffee, which I gladly accepted. They led me to a large teepee set up in the middle of the back yard, then excused themselves so they could get to their morning farm chores.

Chief Denby Sage had been sitting in the middle of a group of men and women, young and old, circled around a brightly burning fire in front of his teepee. He stood up and gave me a warm welcome. Many of the visitors, he said, were Native Americans from various tribes including the Lakota Sioux, Cheyenne, Hochunk, and Winnebago.

Denby sat back down, motioning for me to sit in the circle with the group. One of the Native Americans from the Winnebago Tribe began to talk about the 'great water'. The great water, he explained, is the Native American name for Lake Michigan. His story was about a medicine man that had used the great water, which had strong spiritual healing powers, to heal a warrior's serious injuries that he had sustained in battle. I sat contentedly, drinking my strong, rich-tasting coffee, and listened to the inspirational story.

One at a time, the people seated around the circle narrated their stories. I didn't know any stories and hadn't planned on telling any, so when it came to me I remained silent.

"Jason is new to our ceremony," Denby Sage explained to the group. "I invited him at the last minute, so he might not be prepared to say anything today." He turned to me and asked, "Jason, do you have any stories that you would like to share with the group?"

I thought for a moment, and started to shake my head. I couldn't think of any story that I could tell, but my buffalo dream from a few nights ago suddenly came to mind.

"I did have a dream recently that I thought was interesting," I answered. "Is that something you would like me to share with you?"

"Please do," Denby Sage answered, nodding his head in acknowledgement. Everyone seated around the fire encouraged me to continue.

I told the group about the black buffalo, and about how we had stood together side by side looking out over the rolling hills of the prairie. I described how at first the scene had been waves of long yellow-green prairie grass blowing gently in the wind, then changed to a green wooded area with a river winding through it, and finally changed into a snow-covered forest with the river looking cold and icy. I also described how the buffalo changed colors from black, to red, to yellow in conjunction with each change in the scenery.

I told them about the Native Americans in the dream, and described in detail the Indian leader with the tuft of red hair, the headdress with the circular bead and feather attachments that were adorned with jade, silver, and gold, and the ever-present black hawk circling overhead. I described observing what I thought was the Indians celebrating a battle victory, and then their later attempt to hold off the approaching soldiers at the icy river.

When I paused to look at the group surrounding me, I noticed Chief Denby Sage and a few others looking at me with what appeared to be intense curiosity and interest. They were totally absorbed in the story. I continued to retell my dream, and described how the buffalo finally changed colors from light yellow to snow white. Finally, after hesitating briefly, I shared with them the transformation of the white buffalo into a beautiful blond-haired woman.

"That is a fascinating story," Chief Medicine Man Denby Sage said when I finished. The others seated in the circle nodded their heads in agreement.

The sun began to rise when the groups that were seated around the other fires finished sharing their stories and legends, too. Everyone from all of the individual groups gathered around Denby Sage, and he stood up and talked to them.

"Miracle is a special buffalo," Chief Medicine Man Denby Sage said. "She offers all of mankind, of all races and colors – black, red, yellow, white – the hope of peace. Yet Miracle is suffering," he continued. "Everyone wants something from her, and it is draining her energy and her life-blood. We are here for Miracle. We pray that she will stay healthy and continue to offer the world an everlasting peace and unity. We beat our drums together in this sacred ceremony to connect us all to the earth, to the sky, and to the water – and to Miracle – the sacred white buffalo who gives us hope."

"**Boom**, boom, boom, boom... **boom**, boom, boom, boom," several Native Americans beat their drums methodically.

Whether it was from the strength of the coffee, the thunder of the beating drums, or a combination of both, I felt extremely alert as the vibration of the drums seemed to beat in time with the beat of my heart. A feeling of hope came over me as I glanced toward the barn and saw Miracle looking back at me. Her pure white hair was accentuated by the rays of the rising sun.

∞

The drum ceremony ended about two hours after sunrise, and I enjoyed it immensely. Chief Denby Sage and another Native American came up to me afterward.

Denby introduced us immediately. "Jason, this is my friend and fellow Lakota Oyate tribe member John 'Calm Heart' Yazee. Calm Heart is a holy man in our tribe. John, this is Jason Avalon."

"It is good to meet you," John 'Calm Heart' Yazee said as we shook hands.

"It's a pleasure meeting you," I said.

"What did you think of the drum ceremony, Jason?" Chief Sage asked.

"It was inspirational," I answered, "and I think Miracle liked it, too. The ceremony seemed to comfort her."

"It is very interesting to hear you say that," Chief Sage said, nodding.

"You are right in what you told me earlier," Calm Heart said to Denby. "Jason does have a deep connection with the sacred white buffalo. When you asked him about the drum ceremony, he answered from the buffalo's point of view as well as his own."

"With the bond that is evident between you and Miracle, and also the depth of the dream that you shared with us, I was wondering," Calm Heart asked curiously, "are you a Native American?"

I didn't usually find the need to tell anyone about my Native American Indian heritage, and had not mentioned it to anyone today.

"Actually," I answered, "my great-great-great grandmother was a Native American, but our family has not lived in a Native American Indian environment since that time."

"I thought so," Chief Sage said. "You showed a great understanding and sensitivity of the Native American tradition through the sharing of your dream. Your 'one-in-being' with Miracle also suggests that you may have Native American blood. What was your great-great-great grandmother's name?"

"Her name was Hantaywee," I answered.

"I know that name," Calm Heart said. "It is the Oglala Sioux name for 'Faithful'."

Yes, that sounded right. I remembered hearing my distant Native American relatives mention 'Faithful Hantaywee' in the past. I thought they were describing Hantaywee as being faithful. I didn't realize that Hantaywee was the Native American *name* for faithful.

"Do you know what tribe she was from?" Chief Sage asked.

"I have been told that she was from the Grand River clan of the Hunkpapa tribe," I answered. The medicine man and the holy man looked at each other with what appeared to be a look of excitement, but didn't say any more about it.

"We talked with some people here about your dream," Chief Sage said. "We may be able to give you some added insight into it now, if you are interested."

"I definitely am interested," I said. I was thrilled that they would take the time to share any of their knowledge that might help me to understand more about my dream.

"We would be honored to share it," Calm Heart said quietly.

We returned to the spot where we had listened to the stories earlier, and sat down again. The fire wasn't burning as brightly as it was before, so Chief Sage added a few more logs to keep it going.

"Have you read any stories similar to the one you described in your dream?" Calm Heart asked. "Did you ever talk to anyone about them?"

"No, I haven't," I answered, not sure why he had asked.

"I didn't think so," Chief Sage said. "We just wanted to ask to be sure. The stories from your dream are rarely told, even amongst Native Americans."

"You've heard stories before that are similar to my dream?" I asked.

"Let me explain," Chief Sage said. "There are aspects of your dream that have tremendous importance to Native Americans. There are also parts of the dream that we believe may have great meaning to you, even though we do not completely understand them yet.

"The dream showed your recognition of the spiritual importance of the sacred white buffalo," he continued. "When Native Americans dream of buffalo, they often dream of hunting them or praying to them in thanks for feeding their families. However, when the white people dream of buffalo, they are often fearful dreams where the buffalo are attacking them. In your dream you were standing side by side as one with the white buffalo. Together, you shared in the celebration of the victory in battle as well as the pain suffered in defeat."

"Your dream was also a clear vision of a historically accurate event that happened in the year 1832," Calm Heart added. "In fact, part of it may have taken place in the very spot that we are sitting now."

The hairs on my arms stood up straight.

"A part of what I saw in my dream actually happened?" I asked.

"It certainly did," he assured me. "Have you ever heard of Black Hawk?"

"You're not speaking generally about a black hawk – a bird?" I asked. I didn't think that was what he meant, but asked just to be sure.

"No," Calm Heart shook his head. "The Native American with the tuft of red hair that you dreamed about was named Black Hawk. Your portrayal of him was so accurate that many immediately knew whom you were describing. The black hawk that was circling over his head was a symbol that served to confirm that the Native American you saw in your dream was, in fact, Chief Black Hawk."

"Black Hawk was appointed as War Chief of the Saukenuk tribe, who had settled down in what was then called the Illinois Territory," Chief Sage added. "The Village of Saukenuk was located between the Mississippi River and the Rock River in what is now the state of Illinois.

"Black Hawk was upset by the fact that multiple treaties signed by various Native American Tribes cheated them out of their land," Chief Sage continued. "The U.S. military forced all Native Americans in the Illinois Territory, including the Saukenuk tribe, to leave their villages and to relocate west of the Mississippi River, away from their homes. As a result, Black Hawk led what was estimated to be a group of four hundred warriors in battles throughout the Illinois Territory, and then further north into the Wisconsin Territory. They traveled a path along the Rock River, only a few miles from where we now sit. The battles are commonly referred to as the 'Black Hawk War'."

Calm Heart continued to interpret my dream as it related to Black Hawk. "The United States Cavalry chased the Black Hawk Indians along the Rock River, continuing northwest to the Mississippi River on the border of Minnesota and Wisconsin. What you so vividly described in your dream was Black Hawk's last stand at the icy Mississippi River. What was left of his warriors, by that time thought to be no more than one hundred, fought the soldiers in order to give the older men, women and children enough time to cross the river to safety. This incident is widely known as the 'Bad Axe Massacre', which was fought in the city of Wisconsin Heights."

"This is unbelievable," I said, astounded. "Everything actually happened as you have described?"

"It is all a part of documented history," Chief Sage confirmed. "It is written in the history books just as we have told you, and just as you have dreamed. It has become a very meaningful Native American legend."

"Your heart tells you that it is true," Calm Heart stated knowingly.

I nodded. Deep down, I did believe that it all was true.

"You observed the events of the Black Hawk War as seen through the eyes of a sacred white buffalo,"

Chief Sage said. "Jason, one with this unique ability could be destined to become a great spiritual leader."

"I did feel a connection to Miracle in my dream," I admitted. "I sense a strong connection to her when I am here on the Marshall Farm, too."

"That is obvious from listening to your dream, and in seeing the closeness between you and Miracle when you are here," Calm Heart said.

"I don't know that it would make me a great spiritual leader," I said, expressing doubt about Chief Sage's far-reaching statement.

"You already display leadership abilities in many ways," Chief Sage explained. "You live in the white man's world and work in honorable professions serving the people as sheriff and coaching our youth. You would do well to reintroduce yourself to the Native American ways. It is not too late. You have the potential to provide spiritual guidance to Native American's, similar to what you bring to your white brethren. Would you like to get back in touch with the Native American traditions?"

I thought for a moment about what seemed to be his very deep question. I have always been aware of my Native American background. To learn more about my Indian heritage and its traditions could not only help me learn more about my family's history, but could help me gain a better overall perspective on life.

"I would like to know more about my Native American ancestry," I answered honestly, "but I don't exactly know what 'getting back in touch with the Native American traditions' means."

Both men stood quietly, apparently not very satisfied with my non-committal reply.

"Over time you may find the answer to that question," Chief Sage said. He looked at me directly, and asked one more question. "When you were telling us about your dream, I noticed that you hesitated briefly at the end. It appeared to me you might have been reluctant to mention something. Was there anything else that you would like to share with us now?"

Chief Medicine Man Denby Sage and Holy Man John 'Calm Heart' Yazee were both very perceptive. Neither of them seemed to miss a thing I said – or didn't say, in this instance.

"Actually, there *is* something I left out," I admitted. I decided to tell them about Jessica. "At the end of my dream, the white buffalo turned into a beautiful blond-haired woman. Well," I smiled again at the thought of her, "I saw her again yesterday."

"You saw her again in another dream?" Calm Heart asked.

"No." I shook my head. "I met her after our football game last night. In real life."

Chief Sage and Calm Heart looked at each other. Their interest was piqued again.

"You see things that have happened in the past, and can accurately recall the details of historic events that took place hundreds of years ago, without having been there. That is unique," Chief Sage explained. "But your dreams also contain visions that foretell what will happen in the future? That is truly rare."

« Chapter 18 »

TOM KAMINSKI WAS ALREADY at the Chicago Police Department building working on the *Field Museum* case when I telephoned him early the following Tuesday morning.

"I really appreciate your help, Jason," he said. "Having you involved in the case has kept me focused, yet calm."

"We do seem to work well together, don't we?"

"We do," he answered. "That's no surprise, is it? We've known each other since we were kids, and we always played well together in the sandbox."

"We played well on the sandy beaches, too."

"We sure did," he agreed. "We're making headway on the case, Jason."

"Do you think so?"

"Yes. As you expected," Tom said, flipping through his stack of notes once again, "Darnell Dawkins' alibi checked out. We were able to verify everything by reviewing the security cameras from McDonald's, the bank, and Shady's Bar, and by talking to witnesses."

"The witnesses were reliable?"

"Very. Between the security cameras and the witness statements, we are sure Darnell was *not* at the museum that night."

"That's good to hear," I said, slightly relieved. "If there is any hope that he will ever get his stuff together to be able to help out his ex-wife, LaRae, and son,

Devon, having any involvement in the museum case would not have helped."

"It also bears out your hunch that Darnell was not involved in the first place," Tom said. "It's good to know you can trust your gut instincts."

Could Denby Sage and Calm Heart have been right when they said I may have a unique ability to interpret past events and foresee the future? Did having good 'gut instincts' fall under the same skill-set?

We continued to pore over the facts of the robbery and run various theories by each other, before I asked, "Tom, can you do me a big favor?"

"There's still something bothering you, isn't there, Jason?"

"Yeah. I have a feeling we're missing something. We may have eliminated Darnell Dawkins as a suspect, but I believe there is still a Wisconsin connection to this thing. Not just a Wisconsin connection, but possibly even an Arrowhead County or Pearl Lake connection."

"That would surprise me," Tom said. "What makes you think that?"

"I just have a few nagging suspicions that I have been unable to put to rest," I explained. "I can't give you specific reasons why right now, but I am convinced we would be leaving stones left unturned if we did not check them out."

"Jason, I trust your instincts, too, and that's all I need to hear. We're not lawyers in a courtroom insisting on providing evidence beyond a reasonable doubt. We're not at that point yet. We're still in the fact-finding mode. Let's hear it."

"Okay," I said, knowing he was right. "First," I began, "on the Sunday after the robbery a guy from the Chicago area came through Pearl Lake. He created a ruckus at the *Pub* and ended up getting stopped for drunk driving down the road in Wautoma. His name is Richard Thomas Bonline. I know it's a stretch, but it's possible he was running away from something in Chicago. If I arrange to have his arrest file sent to you from Wautoma, would you run him through your Chicago PD files and check him out?"

"Good idea. Send them to me and we'll get on it right away."

"There's one more thing," I continued, "and this will be the tough one, Tom. I'd like to have some crime lab work done here in Pearl Lake. It needs to be done this Friday, and it has to be kept completely confidential. I'll fill you in on the details the next time I see you, but I can assure you it's related to the *Chicago Field Museum* robbery. Now, it might not pan out, but..."

"Carole Grove and her CSI team here at the Chicago PD are the best in the business," Tom interjected. "Would that be good enough?"

"I was hoping you would say that," I said. "I know it's a big imposition. Do you think there is any way that she and her crew will be able to do it?"

"I'll arrange it. Give me a few minutes to take care of the details. I'll have Carole call you when it's all worked out. You can explain everything to her when you talk to her. Jason," he added, "you are doing me a gigantic favor by helping me out with this case. Don't think I don't know it. Regardless of whether there turns out to be a Wisconsin connection or not, you have already been a big help."

"I know this is a critical case for you, Tom. When this is solved, we'll have to get together and have a big celebration," I said, optimistically.

A sense of foreboding inexplicably came over me like a blanket of dense fog.

« Chapter 19 »

OUR FRESHMAN FOOTBALL TEAM practice on Wednesday went surprisingly well. It was one of those days when everything seemed to click. The player's minds were focused on football as opposed to wandering aimlessly on video games, music, and girls – not necessarily in that order – as young teenagers are prone to do. I was done showering and dressing in the coach's office after the practice, and was feeling quite satisfied about our football team when my cell phone rang shortly after five o'clock in the evening. It was Pearl Lake resident Georgia Snead calling to complain about a neighborhood prank by some high school kids. She immediately gave me an uncannily accurate description of the perpetrators.

"It's terrible!" she complained. "There are huge pink, yellow, green, and blue fluffy balls stuck in the trees in the front yard. The place looks like a giant bubble gum machine. It's disgraceful. I've never seen such a horrendous act of vandalism in my life. I can just imagine the garbage flying into my yard and around the whole neighborhood when the wind picks up!"

I took a deep breath and tried to refrain from chuckling even though I knew it was not funny, especially to Mrs. Snead.

"Mrs. Snead, let me get this straight," I said slowly, in an effort to calm her down. "You said it appears that your neighbor's yard was 'T-P'd, or toilet-papered, sometime last night? Tuesday night?"

"I'm not sure that it's toilet paper, but it's something like that, Sheriff," she answered. "The freshman class has been working on their school float next door at Michael Ryder's house for the past month. There have been hordes of kids coming and going at all hours of the night. Harold and I don't even try to get to sleep before ten o'clock with all of the racket going on next door."

How unfortunate. Georgia Snead certainly needed her beauty sleep. Or in her case, her *crabby* sleep. She and her husband, Harold, were both probably in their mid-fifty's now. They had never had any children of their own, but that was no excuse for her being so cranky all the time.

"Did you see who did it?" I asked.

"I sure did. You couldn't miss that light blond hair from a mile away, even in the dark. It was that Garrett boy. He seemed to be the leader of the pack. I recognized Brandon Dozier, too, and there was a skinny African American boy along with them. There were a few more kids in the bunch, but I didn't recognize any of them. They should be ashamed of themselves, trashing the neighborhood like that."

I listened patiently as I looked through the large glass window of the coach's office into the boy's locker room, directly at the culprits of this heinous crime. The players had already showered-up and dressed, too. As usual, most of the players were gathered around Chris, talking and laughing quietly. Devon Dawkins was right in the midst of the throng, laughing with them. They all looked quite innocent.

It figures, I thought to myself. Leave it to me to suggest to Chris that he include Devon in the guy's activities. Maybe I should have been more specific and told him, 'Try to include Devon in your activities, but do *not* get him into any trouble.' I didn't think I needed to clarify that point.

Once again, for the most part it sounded like harmless fun, but I can understand how some homeowners get upset when their lawns and neighborhoods get trashed from T-P parties and other immature teenage pranks.

"Thank you for letting me know about the problem, Mrs. Snead," I said. "I will follow up on it right away."

"Well it had better get cleaned up because I don't want the mess getting into my yard."

"I will handle it, Mrs. Snead."

"I'm sure you will, Sheriff. Good-bye."

∞

I caught Chris, Devon, and Brandon's attention as they sat in the locker room and beckoned them into the coach's office.

"Can I talk to you for a minute?" I asked, motioning for them to sit down on the long wooden bench at the front of the small coach's office. I walked around to the front of the office desk and sat down on it, facing them.

"I just got off the phone after talking to one of Michael Ryder's neighbors. They called to complain that a bunch of guys T-P'd Ryder's yard, or something. They were very upset because of the mess it will create around the neighborhood. That's why the high school has rules against T-P'ing yards. The neighbors said they recognized the three of you as being in the group that did it. Is that true?"

All three boys had surprised expressions on their faces. They fidgeted and looked uncomfortable, but eventually nodded their heads in confirmation when the shock wore off.

"But Coach Jason..." Chris tried to explain.

I held up my hand to stop him.

"Let me finish," I said. "Do you all understand why someone would be upset with what you did?"

Devon and Brandon had their heads down, and were staring at the floor.

"Coach..." Chris repeated.

I raised my finger again to let him know I needed one minute to finish.

"At the beginning of the season we talked about establishing and maintaining our team's reputation," I reminded them. "You all agreed that you would work to make a good impression on the students of Pearl Lake High School and on the people in the Town of Pearl Lake."

"It is totally my fault," Chris persisted. "I'm the one..."

"No," Devon stopped him. "We all decorated the yard together. Coach Avalon," he sat up straight and looked at me, unwavering. "Our freshman team talks all the time about what you said. We have a lot of pride in our team. We wouldn't do anything that we think would make us look bad to anyone. Honest! Most of the decorating we did in Ryder's yard will get cleaned up by itself, and we'll do the rest."

"Decorating?" I asked. That was another way of putting it.

"We didn't really T-P their yard," Brandon piped in.

This was getting to be quite a story. I looked at each one of them closely. "Okay," I said. "You didn't really T-P their yard, but most of it will get cleaned up by itself." I shook my head. "What are you talking about?"

Devon and Brandon nodded their heads. The traces of a wry smile began to form on Chris' lips, but when he noticed the still stern look on my face he wiped it away wisely.

"Coach Jason," he said once again, calmly and patiently. "Can we show you what we mean? It's easier to show you instead of trying to explain it to you. Do you have a few minutes to take us to Ryder's house?"

∞

Rain started to fall lightly while I drove Chris, Devon, and Brandon to Ryder's house, the scene of the crime. Chris was looking up at the clouds somewhat apprehensively as we drove, as though the sky would be falling any time now.

We ran into a traffic jam as soon as we turned onto the street where the Ryder's lived. We quickly fell in line with the steady procession of vehicles that was driving slowly down the street. Most of the passengers in the cars were high school students, but there were also some parents out with their younger children checking to see what all of the fuss was about. As we approached their house we could see people sticking their heads out of their car windows to get a better look, and taking pictures of the colorful scene. Several cars were stopped and parked all along the block. A large crowd was gathered on the sidewalk in front of Ryder's yard, taking photographs and admiring the...well, decorations.

It was spectacular.

The Ryder's front yard was filled with mature oak, maple, and birch trees. That was normal. However, it appeared as though all of the trees were filled with bright, colorful foam or large, fluffy cotton balls or something similar. That's what made it fantastic.

A large banner with a drawing of the Pearl Lake High School pirate mascot was hanging from the trees on the left side of the yard. It appeared to be about ten feet tall and nearly as wide. The top of the banner was tied firmly to the trees. The bottom edge of the banner, which was hanging about one foot off of the ground, was staked to the ground with several strands of rope that held the banner in place. The drawing of the pirate in his black and red garb and pointed pirate hat, holding his sword up in the air in defiance, was an impressive sight. The larger than life-sized banner swaying in the wind made the pirate look nearly alive, and totally menacing.

Another banner about the same size was similarly hung from the trees in the middle of the yard. A drawing of a large pirate ship, sailing on a blue sea and filled with a dozen pirates of all shapes and sizes, male and female, was even more colorful and impressive than the first.

Finally, the right side of the yard was graced with a large American flag that was hanging from a flagpole sunk sturdily into the ground. A smaller black and white, skull and crossbones pirate flag was flapping in the wind underneath the American flag, and a 'Go Pirates' banner was hanging below the pirate flag.

The combination of the beautifully painted banners, the flags, and the colorful foam or cotton-like canopy covering all of the trees in the front yard made the scene absolutely incredible.

One of the bystanders looked completely awestruck.

"This is a work of art!" she exclaimed.

I had to admit, the artwork was impressive. The foam/cotton-like covering in the trees above the banners did almost look like a giant bubble gum machine, as Georgia Snead so aptly described to me on the phone earlier. I glanced over at the house next door to Ryder's house. The front window curtain was pulled aside, and Georgia was unabashedly staring out the window at the crowd.

I looked over at Chris, Brandon, and Devon, not really knowing what to say.

"It is quite a display, guys," I admitted.

Mark and Michelle Ryder, Michael's parents, worked their way through the crowd and came up to me.

"We're sorry for the commotion, Sheriff," Mark Ryder apologized. "Chris Garrett and the guys talked to Michelle and me before they decorated the yard. We both thought it sounded like a great idea and gave them our wholehearted approval. Look at it. It's a masterpiece!"

"We just didn't realize that it would generate so much attention," Michelle added.

"Chris assured us that one way or another the decorations would be completely cleaned up within a few days, so I wasn't really too concerned," Mark said. "I didn't think anyone would have a problem with it, until Georgia Snead complained to me." He turned to glance at Snead's house next door, noticed that Georgia was still looking out the window, and waved and gave her a friendly smile.   Georgia shook her head indignantly and closed the curtain, giving up her front row seat to the major entertainment in town.

I saw Michael Ryder standing with Chris, Brandon, and Devon, and caught the tail end of what he was saying to someone in the crowd.

"Devon was really the artist," Michael Ryder explained.   "Chris noticed some of Devon's artwork from school and really liked them. He asked Devon if he would want to do some drawings for the freshman class to display in our yard during the homecoming season. Devon completed the drawings on a couple of king-sized bed sheets, and handled all of the yard decorations. Chris, Brandon, and I just kind of helped him. We each had long poles that we used to push the colored filler between the tree branches.   Devon showed us what colors to put where, and this is how it turned out."

Everyone gathered around Devon, shook his hand and complimented him.

"You are a true artist, Devon!" Michelle Ryder complimented him.

"That's right," Mark Ryder said. "Nice work."

"Thank you," Devon answered modestly.

The rain started coming down faster.   Some people had brought umbrellas and started to open them up. The rest of the crowd gathered underneath the umbrellas as much as possible, trying to stay dry.

I noticed Chris looking up at the sky again. For some reason, he looked like he was relieved to see the rainfall. Almost simultaneously the crowd let out a collective, disappointed sigh.

"Oh..."

At first I didn't notice what was happening with the artistic display. As the rain fell onto the foam-like decorations, they seemed to slowly fade away. Some large pieces of the decoration fell away from the trees. As soon as they touched the wet, rain-soaked yard, they seemed to melt and completely disappear.

Chris motioned to Michael Ryder, and when he got his attention the two of them walked around to the garage on the side of the house. A minute later they reappeared carrying a stepladder. One by one, they set the ladder underneath the banners, climbed up, and easily unfastened the banners from the trees and pulled up the stakes from the ground. Then they pulled the flagpole out of the ground. Michael promptly returned the ladder to the garage while Chris rolled up the banners and flags and quietly loaded them in the back seat of my car.

In a matter of minutes, the complete display was gone. The stunning Pearl Lake pirate mascot and pirate ship banners, the American flag, pirate flag and Go Pirates banner, and the dazzling bubble gum machine canopy that had covered the entire front yard had totally disappeared. The fantastic colors were completely gone as though they had never been there at all.

"What happened to all of the colorful foam?" Mark Ryder asked Devon. Devon, Michael Ryder, and Brandon turned to look at Chris, the mastermind of it all. The entire crowd, myself included, shifted our attention to Chris. The sly smile returned to his face and he shrugged his shoulders innocently.

"Cotton candy," he announced to the onlookers. "It was cotton candy."

"What?" I asked Chris and his cohorts.

"Honest, Coach Avalon. It was Chris' idea to try to use cotton candy," Devon answered, not blaming Chris, but praising him. "He said we would not be *T-P'ing* the yard, so technically we would not be breaking any of the rules."

There was no doubt that Chris had thought through the idea thoroughly. He was smart enough to be sure that he and his teammates did not get caught on a technicality, or did not get penalized for committing a foul due to not following the rules.

Devon continued his explanation of events.

"Chris has an old cotton candy machine at home. A bunch of us spent several nights making what seemed to be a million batches of different colored cotton candy. Chris figured that the cotton candy would all get washed away as soon as it rained, and no one would even know it was there."

Everyone laughed and clapped in appreciation of the ingenious decorating idea.

"I wish that the rain would have held off for a few more days," Michelle Ryder said. "It was a lovely decoration."

"At least we took plenty of photographs," Mark said in consolation.

Eventually the crowd's cheers subsided, but the rain did not. With regretful glances back at the regular-looking front yard, the crowd reluctantly dispersed.

"Okay, you three Picasso's. It's time to go before we get water-logged," I said to Devon, Chris, and Brandon. "For the record, I'm sorry for jumping to conclusions. You are great kids, and I should have known better. I apologize. You did yourselves and the team proud today."

I received another phone call from Georgia Snead at around eight o'clock the next night.

"You didn't have to make the boys do my yard work," she stated after I said hello.

"What do you mean?"

"That Garrett boy and his buddies came here earlier this evening. They mowed my entire lawn and trimmed all of the bushes in the yard."

"Mrs. Snead, I assure you, you submitted your complaint confidentially, and I kept it that way. I did not tell Chris Garrett or the other boys that you were the person that complained, and I certainly did not put them up to doing any of your yard work. Is everything okay with your yard? Is there a problem with the work they did?"

"No, there's no problem at all. On the contrary, the yard looks very nice. They did a wonderful job, but I didn't ask them to do it. Since I didn't ask them to do it, and they did not say anything to me before they did the work, I am not going to pay them."

Even though I had not said anything to Chris, Devon, or Brandon about the Snead's making the complaint, they must have figured it out on their own, or taken an educated guess, and taken it upon themselves to make sure that the Snead yard was in tip-top shape. I was sure they did not do it for the money, and I said so.

"I'm sure the boys do not expect you to pay them, Mrs. Snead. They must have wanted to clean up your yard to make sure it was none the worse after their decorating job next door."

There was an extended silence on the phone line after my explanation. Was she expecting me to say more, or was there something else she wanted to say?

"I've made a fresh batch of chocolate chip cookies," Georgia said finally. "There are just too many for Harold and me to eat. The next time you see the boys, would you ask them to come by the house and take some with them? I wouldn't want the cookies to go to waste."

"I'm sure they would like that, Mrs. Snead. I'll let them know."

There was another brief pause.

"Harold and I have a hard time keeping up with mowing our lawn and handling some of the yard work," she said. "The boys were all so polite and did such a good job today. Do you think they would be interested in coming back during the summer months and taking care of our yard work for us? If they'd like, they could even help with shoveling our snow this winter. We would pay them nicely for their work, of course. Not just in cookies, but in cold, hard cash. Would you ask them for me?"

"Certainly, Mrs. Snead."

"Good. They do seem like very nice boys."

« Chapter 20 »

I EAGERLY AROSE FROM bed bright and early on Friday morning. The Pearl Lake Fall Festival would be kicking off later today with the carnival in the Town Square, and the boat and street parades tonight. I couldn't wait for the activities to begin.

I finished my morning workout at the fitness center with my spirits lifted at the thought of the upcoming Festival. After I was showered and dressed I made my way around town, beginning at *Katie's Place*. As always, Katie gave me a friendly peck on the cheek as I entered. She practically wrestled me to a table so she could serve me a 'healthy' breakfast consisting of a ham and cheese omelet, whole-wheat toast, and orange juice. "You've got to keep your strength up, Jason," she insisted in a motherly fashion.

After completely offsetting the benefits of my morning workout, I moved on from *Katie's Place* and walked through the Town Square. They had already begun setting up for the carnival and it was rapidly taking shape. A gigantic Ferris-Wheel was fully operational, slowly circling up and around. It appeared to be at least five stories tall as it towered over the other rides. Several work crews were busy assembling a tilt-o-whirl, merry-go-round, roller coaster, mini-golf course, miniature go-cart track, and other rides and games throughout the Town Square.

All was well at the General Store as I made my way through the store. I crossed the street to the Drake Realty Office and Antique Shop and talked with John and Barbara Drake for a while. Their spirits, like mine, were uplifted seeing the festival come to life.

Cindy Abrahms, Dan Abrahms' daughter-in-law, was busy stocking the shelves in the Pearl Lake Factory Direct Store when I walked in, awakening the sleeping doorbells.

"Good Morning, Cindy," I greeted her as I stepped inside.

"Good morning, Sheriff Jason."

Dan poked his head around the end of the aisle when he heard me walk in. Not surprisingly, he was busy arranging items on the shelves, too.

"Hello, Jason," he said. "We're just getting ready for the festival crowds. But I'm not complaining."

"Hi, Mr. Abrahms. I've never heard you complain yet, but it must be a constant battle keeping those shelves stocked."

"Oh, that's a good thing," he answered, smiling. "I enjoy it."

"It sounds like the weather is going to be beautiful all weekend, too," I said.

"I hope so. The better the weather is, the more people will come to town for all of the festivities. That will keep you busy, too, Jason."

"It will keep me on my toes," I admitted, "but everybody is usually pretty well-behaved during the festival. Even though we expect to have large crowds, most of the activities like the farm market, parades and carnival are fairly low-key."

I let Dan and Cindy Abrahms get back to their shelf-stocking duties and moved on to the Piggly-Wiggly Store next door. The store manager and girls at the cash registers were also preparing for the busy weekend. They were stocking and organizing their shelves, too.

I continued on to the Lakeshore Bank and looked for Eric Anders, the bank president. Along with Steve Dozier and Tom Kaminski, Eric is one of my best friends. In addition to being one of the 'regulars' in our friendly poker games, we often get together to golf and play in various pick-up football, basketball, and baseball games.

Eric is one of the most intelligent people I know. He is a superb statistician. I'd swear that he could recite the batting averages of major league baseball players going back one hundred years, or name the last fifty Heisman Trophy winners. Not surprisingly, he is excellent with numbers, which helps to make him a very good banker. But I don't believe that is the most important trait that makes him a superb banker. The reason why I respect him so much is because he is the most ethical person I know. Whenever I need to gather the facts about something, or need an honest, level-headed opinion, I often go to Eric.

Eric saw me walk into the bank through his glass-walled corner office.

"How are you doing today, Jason?" he called to me as he got up from his chair and came out into the main bank area by the tellers to greet me.

"Great! How is it going, Eric?"

"Couldn't be better. Are you ready for the 'boat' parade tonight?" he asked.

The boat parade marked the beginning of the Pearl Lake Fall Festival weekend activities. Pearl Lake has held the annual Fall Festival for over ten years, and it seemed to have gotten bigger and better each year. There were at least fifty boats scheduled to be in this year's parade, and each one would be decorated with a unique theme. As usual, my parents, Tom Kaminski's folks, Bob Colgate and his family, and John and Barbara Drake had each entered their boats in the parade again this year.

As in past years, the boats will all be decked out in dazzling, multi-colored lights. Most of the people that live in the houses and cottages on the lake have big bonfires blazing as they watch the boat parade. It has always been a spectacular scene and I expect that it will be tonight, too.

Traditionally, the boats gather at the Red Rock Inn pier before the parade. When they are all lined up and ready to go, a loud burst of fireworks will be set off and the boats will make their way around the lake. The boats then return to the Red Rock Inn, where they are temporarily docked, officially ending the boat parade. At that point, the Town of Pearl Lake/Pearl Lake High School Homecoming Parade, or the 'land' parade, commences, weaving its way through the town streets.

In addition to floats from each of the high school classes, led by a talented Pearl Lake High School Marching Band, there will be floats from many of the area businesses including the Arrowhead Appliance Company, the Rotary Club, the Lakeshore Bank, an antique float submitted by all of the antique shop owners in town, and several others.

"I'm as ready as ever," I answered Eric's question about the boat parade.

My sister Kimberly was working in the administrative office down the hall, and must have heard me talking with Eric. She peeked around the corner, waved, and gave me a big smile before returning to her office after I returned her wave.

I talked to Eric briefly but didn't want to tie him up too long at work, so I visited with the tellers quickly and went over to the administrative office to give Kim a good-natured, big-brotherly hard time before I made my way out of the bank.

I stopped in at the library, which was in a building adjoining the bank. Emily, the librarian, told me about the new books in stock that she knew I would enjoy reading. Then, in her unique intelligent, motherly librarian way, she pointed out books she thought I *should* read, including the latest law enforcement books and the newest crime-solving mystery novels on the current best-seller lists. She was still raving about the new library computer that Dan Abrahms had confidentially acquired. I moved on, promising Emily that I would be checking out one of her highly recommended books soon.

I crossed Highway 21 and went into the *Pearl Lake Pub*.

"Hi Sheriff Avalon," Candy said with her big friendly smile and wide brown eyes that warmed me up when I walked in.

"Good morning, Candy. How are you doing?"

"Tired," she said. "I was up way too late last night." She looked pretty perky to me. "I need my cup of coffee so I can wake up. Would you like a cup?" she asked. "I've got a fresh pot brewing."

"No, thanks. I've got to get back to the sheriff's office. I just saw you opening and wanted to say 'hi'."

"Oh, that is so sweet of you, Jason."

She was nonchalantly wiping off an area on top of the bar, and it looked like her mind was wandering elsewhere.

"Candy," I asked, "have you seen anyone new around town that looked like they might cause trouble or anything?"

Someone had mentioned to me that they saw a few shady-looking characters around town recently. It was probably just some of the carnival workers in town, I figured. They can look pretty rough sometimes, even if they are not getting into any trouble, but I thought I'd ask around town about it, just to be sure.

"No, not really," she answered, shrugging her shoulders. "Not since that guy punched Harry anyway."

I didn't think that Candy would recognize trouble if it was written on the wall in front of her, but I thought I'd ask her anyway. It didn't hurt to plant a seed in her mind to help her to recognize something that might be out of the ordinary.

"Well, let me know if you see or hear anything that doesn't seem right."

"You know I always call when we need help, Sheriff."

"I know, Candy, but it's better to try to prevent something bad from happening *before* it gets started," I explained. By the time that Candy or the other bartenders at the *Pub* called me for help, it was usually too late and the damage had already been done. "I'll probably see you around this weekend. Now remember what I said. Please keep an eye out so you notice anything unusual."

"Okay, I will. You take care, Sheriff Jason." It looked like she had already forgotten what I said.

I walked down the road to the Red Rock Inn. The Red Rock Inn was an old, large Victorian style house that the owners converted into a Bed and Breakfast Inn several years ago. I had been through the inn many times and knew that it featured several large, bright suites that were all decorated elegantly. The guest rooms and hallways were filled with beautiful, high-quality original paintings and sculptures. The guests were treated to hearty, country-style breakfasts daily. The Inn's back yard was comprised of a large sandy beach on Pearl Lake. Several sturdy chairs and umbrella-covered tables were spread throughout the beach, each with a beautiful view of the Pearl Lake lakeshore. Most of the inn's suites had beautiful views out of their large back windows overlooking the beach and lake.

Jessica Donovan had made arrangements to stay at the Inn on Saturday night. I had offered again for her to stay at my house for the night, with pure intentions, but she would have no part of that. Due to a late cancellation, she was lucky to find an opening at the Red Rock Inn during such a busy weekend in Pearl Lake. I confirmed that Jessica did, in fact, have a suite waiting for her when she got to the Red Rock Inn, and was eagerly awaiting her arrival.

∞

This year's festival began with an absolutely fantastic boat parade that got started about seven o'clock. When they returned to the Red Rock Inn, everyone in the parade told me they thought it was the best one ever. The fresh country air mixed with the smell of bonfires that were lit up all around the lake added to the ambience.

As soon as she jumped off the boat my sister Kimberly joined several of her friends that had been waiting for her, and headed to the Town Square to watch the Pearl Lake parade and to enjoy the carnival. I met Steve and Debbie Dozier, Eric Anders and his wife, Megan, at the Inn and we walked over to Main Street to watch the land parade with them there.

After settling comfortably into our spots on Main Street, we all enjoyed the parade immensely. We laughed and clapped collectively as the Pearl Lake High School Band, with each band member wearing a white glove on one hand, played Michael Jackson songs as they marched by.

The floats all seemed as colorful and well-built as ever and received appreciative cheers from the crowd as they paraded along Main Street. Each of the class floats also met with the crowd's approval. Surprisingly, the freshman float, in a major upset, won the 'Best Float of the Year' award. Their entry of a big, adorable baby blue rat sitting atop a huge apple pie with a big piece of pie stuffed in its mouth, received a thunderous applause as it passed by. Their 'pie-rat' take on the high school pirate theme was a huge hit with the student body and crowd alike. I noticed Chris Garrett, Brandon Dozier, Devon Dawkins, and a few other players on our freshman football team walking proudly alongside their award-winning float. They waved to us in acknowledgement as I clapped my hands and cheered loudly along with the rest of the crowd lining the street. The crowds at the parade this year appeared to be the biggest we had ever seen for this event over the years.

After the parade, the Dozier's, Anders', and I left our spots on Main Street and walked down the road to the Town Square to check out the carnival. While we were on our way there I received a call on my cell phone. I waved the group on, letting them know that I would catch up with them shortly. The phone call was from Carole Grove.

"Hello, Sheriff Avalon," she said. "I'm just calling to let you know that our CSI Team has finished with the work that you requested."

"Hi, Carole. That's great!" I said. "I can't thank you enough."

"You don't have to, Jason. If it helps you and Tom solve the case, it will be worth it. We certainly collected a boat-load of information."

"Now we just need to confirm that it is related to the *Chicago Field Museum* robbery," I said.

"Exactly," she agreed. "We might have gathered several pieces of the puzzle, but now it's a matter of putting the pieces together to solve it."

"It's a good start..." I said.

"...But the hard work is really just beginning," Carole finished the sentence for me.

"I know you can solve this puzzle, Carole."

"I appreciate your vote of confidence. I'll try not to let you down."

"The thought never crossed my mind."

"I'll let you and Tom know as soon as we find anything."

"Okay. Good luck, Carole."

"Good luck to you, too, Jason."

As soon as I hung up the phone it immediately began ringing again.

"Hello," I answered.

"Jason," I recognized Tom Kaminski's voice. "How is it going?" he asked.

"Actually, it's going pretty good. How are you doing, Tom?"

"Okay, other than I'm mad as hell that I'm not in Pearl Lake enjoying the Fall Festival with you," he grumbled. "I can't remember the last time I missed it. There's just so much going on here right now that I can't get away."

"That's an understatement, Tom. Try not to let it get to you. There will be many more Pearl Lake Fall Festivals in the future that you'll be able to attend."

"Yeah, I suppose you're right," he agreed, somewhat mollified.

"I just heard back from Carole," I said. "She mentioned that she had talked to you already."

"She has," he acknowledged. "That's why I'm calling. I just wanted to confirm it with you. I'm glad she was able to gather the information you wanted. Hopefully her efforts will prove to be fruitful."

"I hope so, too. Thanks again for getting her and her team here so quickly."

"Jason, you're doing it to help me solve the *Field Museum* robbery. I should be thanking you," Tom said appreciatively. "If there is anything to be learned from the information they collected, our CSI Team will find it."

"I totally agree. I have faith in them, too. Have a good night now, Tom."

"You too, Jason. Have fun at the festival."

Despite being significantly distracted by the sight of cream puffs, and the scent of barbeque beef and chicken cooking on the grills at the carnival, my gut was telling me that we were getting very close to cracking this case.

« Chapter 21 »

THE OAK LOGS WERE burning brightly in the fireplace on my back porch, helping to take the bite out of the chill in the crisp Saturday morning air. The sun was turning auburn as it rose above the Pearl Lake skyline, and the dew on the grass was shimmering in the sunlight. The leaves were beginning to show signs of the bright fall colors that would soon be emerging in full force. It had been a splendid summer. I was not ready for fall, much less winter which was right around the corner.

It was hard for me to hold down my excitement with everything going on in Pearl Lake. Our freshman football game would be starting in a few hours. The carnival in Town Square was proving to be quite popular, judging by the large crowds that were there yesterday. The Mardi Gras-style Fall Festival Parade taking place tonight was also expected to be a major draw, as in past years. Not least of all, the anticipation of spending time with Jessica contributed to my excitement.

I thought about everything that had happened over the last few weeks. Being involved in the *Chicago Field Museum* case made me glad to be the Town Sheriff in Pearl Lake. There seemed to be a lot more politics involved in the police work in Chicago and L.A. when I worked there. The city officials in those big metropolitan areas were much more visible and verbal than many of their small town counterparts, as were the news reporters and general public. Unfortunately, more often than not their involvement was more harmful than helpful to the cases they were following. I had none of those issues in Pearl Lake. On the contrary, the people in town were very supportive of my efforts and the overall efforts of the Arrowhead County Sheriff's Department.

However, I do hand out my fair share of traffic tickets – mostly for speeding. But contrary to popular opinion, they are not all to drivers with Illinois license plates. The fact of the matter is that Illinois drivers are not usually in the area all year round. If they were, they probably *would* receive the majority of tickets. It's not because they are targeted, but because many of them simply drive a lot faster than the predominantly rural, small-town Wisconsin drivers. Many of Arrowhead County's visitors are from Illinois, and they own a large share of the cottages on Pearl Lake. So I wouldn't do anything intentionally to *not* make them feel welcome and at home here. Nor would I turn my head when I see them breaking the law.

I can say with virtual certainty that in the years I have been the sheriff here, I have saved lives by removing drivers from behind the wheel that should not have been driving in the first place. That alone is enough to keep me motivated, and to want to continue serving as the Pearl Lake Town Sheriff.

∞

I had one task to complete before I could enjoy the Pearl Lake festivities. Thomas Bonline, the tough guy from Chicago that punched Harry Wilson at the *Pub,* was still being held in the Waushara County Jail in Wautoma. There was an outstanding warrant for his arrest from the state of Illinois on charges unrelated to the Wautoma DWI or the *Chicago Field Museum* robbery. I wanted to talk to him.

After making the short twenty-minute drive to Wautoma, I sat in the police interrogation room and called Tom Kaminski before Bonline was brought into the room. Tom had provided me with a copy of Bonline's arrest record as I had requested, and we quickly reviewed it together over the phone.

"Bonline is facing charges related to a drug sale in Chicago," Tom said. "He will be extradited back to the state of Illinois to face those charges after you talk to him today."

"Got it," I answered. I continued to flip through his rap sheet, which was quite extensive. "He's got quite a record, but it is mostly for minor drug-related offenses over the years."

"Right," Tom said, reading down the list. "Possession of marijuana; possession of marijuana; disturbing the peace; possession of marijuana, possession of drug-related paraphernalia, and more of the same."

"It doesn't look like he's a real good guy, but right now there is no indication that he had anything to do with the *Field Museum* robbery," I said.

"No, not yet anyway."

"I'll talk to him to find out what he has to say."

"Okay, Jason. Thanks."

"I'll talk to you later, Tom." I hung up the phone, and arranged for Bonline to be brought into the room.

∞

Thomas Bonline looked exactly like the black and white mug shot on his arrest record. He had no color to his face other than a dark, weatherworn complexion.

He hadn't shaved for a few days, which just made his face look dirty. His greasy shoulder-length black hair partially covered a black tattoo of a howling wolf that ran up the right side of his neck to the bottom of his ear. His neck was thick, and his shoulders and arms looked very muscular. He looked like a weight-lifter. I could see how from a distance Candy at the *Pub* could have mistaken him for Hector Velasquez.

Bonline had previously been read his rights by a Waushara County officer. He agreed to talk to me without insisting that a lawyer be present. I had to give him credit for that. An officer escorted him into the interrogation room, and he sat down across the metal table from me.

We assessed each other quietly before I spoke up. "Good Morning, Mr. Bonline. I'm Sheriff Avalon, from the Town of Pearl Lake. Thank you for agreeing to talk with me today. I know you don't have to, and I appreciate it," I said.

"Well," he shrugged his shoulders, "ain't got nothing better to do sitting in here, sheriff." He paused. "Is there anything you can do to get me out of this mess?"

I'm sure he was curious to find out exactly why I wanted to talk to him, but he had no reason to talk to me other than to see if I could help him in any way.

"You got yourself into this mess with the drug charges and DWI arrest, Mr. Bonline. I'm afraid you will have to get yourself out of it. I'm here to talk to you about something else."

He looked at me, waiting.

"I wanted to ask you about something that happened in Chicago last week," I said. "Have you heard anything about the *Chicago Field Museum* robbery?"

His eyes flashed immediate recognition of what I was talking about.

"Sure," he answered immediately. "Hasn't everyone? That's been all over the news!"

I nodded, waiting for him to figure out why I was asking him about it. It didn't take long.

"Oh," he said, with comprehension registering on his face. "I don't know nothing about that."

"Do you have any idea who may have been involved?" I asked.

"No, I don't."

I could see the cold, blank look return to his eyes. I'd seen that look a million times before. He had raised his defensive shield in order to protect himself. It was like he had donned a suit of armor and a steel mask to ward off any potentially damaging blows.

"Can you tell me where you were last Friday night?" I asked.

He stared into space, as though he hadn't heard me.

"It's not that tough of a question, Mr. Bonline. Where were you last Friday?"

He shrugged. "I was home all night," he answered.

"Were you with anyone?"

"No." He shook his head.

"Can anyone confirm that?"

He just looked at me. The cold, blank stare was still present.

Even if he wasn't involved in the *Field Museum* robbery, he was probably up to no good on the night it happened, I figured. He sure didn't want to talk about it, anyway.

"Mr. Bonline," I explained, "I'm not after you for any drug-related activities that you may have been mixed up in that night, or for any other trouble that you may have been getting into like you have a habit of doing. I'm only interested in knowing whether you were involved in the *Chicago Field Museum* robbery."

"I already answered that."

He certainly had clamped up. If it was this difficult getting answers to the simplest of questions, I doubted whether I would get any meaningful information from him at all. I asked him several more questions, but his answers provided absolutely no help to our investigation, or to himself, for that matter. Apparently he had determined that I wasn't going to be much help to him in his current predicament, and he was not going to go out of his way to help me in mine.

"Thank you, Mr. Bonline," I said as I wrapped up the brief discussion and stood up to leave. "In case you were wondering, the guy that you punched in the bar in Pearl Lake last week should be okay."

"I suppose he's pressing charges?"

Harry Wilson had recovered quickly from the knock on the head, and did not seem to be suffering from any lingering effects. He had no intention of filing any charges against Mr. Bonline, but Mr. Bonline didn't need to know that.

"He sustained a potentially serious head injury and received medical attention," I exaggerated slightly. "He is a seventy-plus year-old guy so we're not sure how well he will recover. As of now he is not going to press charges."

Bonline's cold, empty stare was still present as he was escorted out of the room. He didn't really care.

I talked to Tom Kaminski again briefly, and updated him on my mostly one-way conversation with Mr. Bonline, including the fact that I knew no more after talking with him than I did before. I returned to my car, pointed it east, and headed back to Pearl Lake.

The further I got from Wautoma, I found myself thinking less about Thomas Bonline and the *Chicago Field Museum* robbery, and the closer I got to Pearl Lake, the more I thought about football, the festival, and Jessica Donovan.

« Chapter 22 »

WHEN I GOT BACK to Pearl Lake I stopped for gas at the gas station next to the *Pearl Lake Pub*. It had an A & W Restaurant in the same building, so I stopped inside to get a quick breakfast.

I walked through the foyer, sidestepping several skateboards that were lying on the floor. I looked around the restaurant when I got inside, and noticed fifth-graders Nicholas Davidson, Emma Swanson, and a few of their friends eating at a table in the corner. I had seen them all around town, and as far as I knew they were all good kids.

"Hi Nicholas. Hi Emma. How are you all doing today?"

"Good," they answered collectively, somewhat apprehensively.

"That's good to hear. Are those your skateboards that are double-parked in the entryway?" I asked, pointing toward the skateboards.

They all nodded in unison.

"They could be dangerous lying there in the restaurant lobby. If someone comes into the restaurant and doesn't see them, they could trip on them," I explained. "You wouldn't want to hurt anyone, would you?"

They all shook their heads seriously.

"No," they echoed.

"Do you think you could keep your skateboards right outside there by the bike racks from now on?" I directed their attention outside, on the other side of the window where they were sitting. "That way you can keep an eye on them when you are inside, and they will be out of the way so no one coming into the restaurant can trip over them."

"Okay, Sheriff Jason," Nicholas answered. His friends all nodded in agreement.

Without any further prompting from me, they quickly sprang to their feet, ran to the foyer, grabbed their skateboards, and took them outside to the bike racks. They were back in their seats in the restaurant and chomping on their French fries in less than a minute.

"That was quick! Thank you," I said. "Are any of you planning on going to the carnival this weekend?"

"We love the carnival!" Emma Swanson said, as they all nodded in agreement. "Sure we're going!"

"Hmm..." I looked at them, reached into my back pocket, and pulled out a bunch of tickets. "I have some tickets here. Each ticket is good for five rides on any of the rides at the carnival. They're free. Would you use them if I gave them to you?"

"Yeah!" they answered excitedly.

I gave them each a handful of tickets.

"Sweet!" Nicholas exclaimed. "Thanks a lot, Sheriff Jason!"

They each politely said 'thank you', which made giving them the tickets even more satisfying. They were still chattering happily when I picked up my breakfast to eat on the run. I returned their appreciative waves as I left the restaurant, and headed to the football field.

∞

The fans were starting to pile into the stadium bleachers as our team was doing its pre-game warm-up exercises. The crowd was definitely larger than what we were used to for our typical freshman games. It was good to see, and I noticed that our players were getting fired-up as a result. My heart began beating faster when I noticed Jessica Donovan sitting in the bleachers directly behind our team. She was sitting about ten rows up, and winked at me reassuringly when I looked her way. It brought me back to the days when I was younger and my parents came to see me play. I was glad they were there, and wanted them to see me do well. Part of me felt like a kid today, too. I wanted everyone, including Jessica, to see my team play well.

The butterflies in my stomach flew away as soon as we kicked-off to Columbus to start the game. From the beginning, our team seemed to be well in control of the contest. We were ahead by a score of 16-0 at halftime. All of our players got to play quite a bit, and everyone – players, coaches, and parents alike – was happy about it.

Our Pearl Lake freshman team won the game by a final score of 22-6, but the score was not indicative of how good both teams played. It turned out to be a fundamentally sound game. Very few mistakes were made, which is good for any young, freshman-level team. It was a sign of well-coached teams, and disciplined players.

In the end, it was our team's superior talent that made the difference. Chris Garrett was developing into an exceptionally talented football player. He scored a touchdown in the game, as did Devon Dawkins, who was also continuing to improve and gain confidence. Even Brandon Dozier recovered a fumble and returned it for a touchdown. The players and home-team fans were delighted. Everyone knew how hard Brandon worked on the football field, and they were happy to see him make a great play.

As our freshman team left the football field after the game, the varsity team came running onto the field to begin their pre-game warm-ups. My friend, Bruiser, the team's head coach, stopped before he ran by me with his team.

"Great game, Jason!" he said as he gave me a high five. "That's a tough act to follow!"

"It was just a warm-up act for your big game," I replied. "I'm sure you will pick up right where we left off."

"You're damn right we will!"

"Good luck, Bruiser," I urged him on as he continued running alongside his team onto the field.

"Thanks, Jason!" he answered on the run.

Jessica came down to the front of the bleachers when I reached them. She leaned into me and kissed me gently on the cheek. The kids sitting in the stands directly behind us erupted into cheers, and the entire crowd joined in. I heard several comments from people around us.

"Ooh, Coach Jason!"

"Look! Sheriff Avalon has a girlfriend!"

"Who is that kissing Coach Jason?"

"Sorry to have put you through that," I apologized to Jessica insincerely. My face was still tingling where she kissed me.

She responded with a wide smile. I gasped at her radiant beauty that seemed to have been enhanced on this bright, sunny day. I had to remind myself that I had only seen her a few times since her mesmerizing appearance in my recent dream. The first time I saw her was in the pouring rain when she was all bundled up in protective rain gear, and the next time was later that night in a dark-lit restaurant. She was even more beautiful than I had remembered.

"Jason, it is so wonderful to see you again," she whispered into my ear as I escorted her back up into the bleachers where she had been sitting. "That was an impressive game. Congratulations!"

"Thanks, Jessica. I'm glad you came. Did you get to scout the Columbus football team enough to be prepared when you play them next week?"

"Oh, I think I've seen enough. I was slightly distracted, though," she said. Her eyes were sparkling.

I do not claim to be super-experienced with women or an expert in relationships, but I knew one thing: I felt very comfortable with Jessica, and I got the impression that she felt the same way about me. I have been in a few relationships since my college days, but this definitely seemed different. I also knew enough to understand that we would need to take the time to get to know each other.

We sat side by side as Jessica wrapped her arm around mine and contentedly watched the varsity football team until the end of the game drew near. Bruiser and his team were winning the game quite handily. Confident that a Pearl Lake victory was all but assured, I turned to Jessica and asked, "Have you checked in at the Red Rock Inn yet?"

She shook her head. "No, not yet."

"Would you like to go and get checked in now? Then we can spend some time downtown at the craft fair, or the farm market, or the carnival. We can go to the Fall Festival Parade tonight, too, if you want. I think you'd really like it. What do you think?"

"Everything sounds great! I want to do it all!" She thought for a moment, and then nodded her head. "It's a good idea to get checked in first, though. When we're done checking in, can we go to the carnival for a while, and then go watch the parade afterward? That will save the craft fair and farm market for tomorrow. Is that okay with you?"

"Sounds like a plan. Let's go."

As we stood up to leave, the crowd suddenly erupted in thunderous applause. I looked down at the football field to see what they were cheering about. It quickly became obvious that the close-knit group of high school students and parents had been playing matchmaker. Apparently, they had decided that Jessica and I would make a good couple. The cheers were for us. We waved back to the exuberant onlookers, and left the stadium hand-in-hand.

« Chapter 23 »

AFTER JESSICA CHECKED-IN at the Red Rock Inn we walked through town and went to the carnival at the Town Square. The Square was bustling with activity. Even though it was still mid-afternoon, there were already hundreds of people in what appeared to be a well-behaved crowd that was laughing and having a good time.

Jessica looked up at the gigantic Ferris-Wheel as we entered the carnival grounds.

"Let's go for a ride," she suggested, craning her neck to peer at the highest point of the ride. "It must have a terrific view of the area from the top."

"There's only one way to find out."

We boarded the Ferris-Wheel and let it take us up and around. It did, in fact, give us a fantastic 360° view of both the lake and the Town of Pearl Lake. The wide variety of multi-colored trees in the surrounding forest that covered what looked to be an infinite number of rolling hills was absolutely breathtaking. In an action that seemed totally natural, Jessica once again wrapped her arm around mine as we sat alone in the cozy compartment. We circled the air slowly and contentedly, taking in the scenic view.

As soon as we got off the Ferris-Wheel we noticed another ride right in front of us called *The Corkscrew*.

"Would you like to ride the roller coaster?" I asked.

"Okay," Jessica responded without hesitation as we walked to the back of the ride's long waiting line.

"I can see why it's named *The Corkscrew*," I said. We could see the steel-tracked roller coaster in action while we waited in line. Local advertising had touted *The Corkscrew* as being the biggest portable, traveling roller coaster in the world. It sure looked like it from where we were standing.

From a dead stop, the ride accelerated rapidly as if shot from a shotgun. It immediately went through two rapid corkscrew turns, straightened out briefly, and performed a full loop-de-loop circle. The roller coaster ride then climbed straight up into the air in a totally vertical position, came to a stop, and remained motionless for a long enough period of time to make the riders feel like they were in outer space in an anti-gravity environment. Then the force of gravity took over and the ride dropped as in a free fall, changed direction and proceeded to retrace the route in reverse until it returned to the starting point.

It finally got to be our turn after waiting in line for what seemed like hours. I laughed, and Jessica screamed all the way through the wild roller coaster ride. The entire ride from beginning to end lasted less than two minutes, even though the time we were suspended in the air at the halfway point seemed to last an eternity.

"On second thought," Jessica said, taking a deep breath after we had our feet firmly planted on the ground once again, "I think it's called *The Corkscrew* because that's exactly how my stomach feels right now!"

We both laughed as we held on to each other until our sense of balance returned. We continued walking aimlessly until we entered the carnival's midway section. We watched young kids shooting streams of water into a row of plastic clown's mouths, and observed older ones shooting BB guns at hanging pieces of paper with small stars on them. A little further down the arcade alley there were people bouncing plastic rings off of glass bottles, bouncing coins off of glass plates, and bouncing balls out of woven wooden baskets. It didn't look like anyone was having any luck. Not good luck, anyway.

As we walked by the mini-basketball court, the young, gangly teenager running the game quietly started to challenge us. It appeared as though his arms and legs had grown faster than his body could handle. *Maybe he is on loan from the circus' man-on-stilts department*, I thought.

"You can't play basketball, huh?" he jeered at us almost inaudibly as we walked by. "Are you too uncoordinated?"

We ignored him and kept walking.

"No guts, I guess," he said, speaking a little louder this time. "You must be a big spender, huh? You won't even wager a dollar to try to make two shots? You must play for the Milwaukee Bucks!" he taunted.

I chuckled ever so slightly at his derogatory 'Bucks' comment. It was the opening he was looking for. The tall kid bounced the basketball towards me, and I caught it on the second bounce. Jessica and I looked at each other. Her eyebrows were raised inquiringly, wondering if I was going to accept the challenge.

"What do you think?" I asked. "Should we play a little basketball?"

"It's up to you," she smiled.

I threw the ball back to the young antagonizer. Jessica's raised eyebrows returned to their normal position. The ball boy's shoulders drooped slightly in disappointment. I turned around, reached into my pocket, and handed him a dollar bill, the exorbitant entry fee for the game.

"Now you're talkin'. We've got a taker!" he barked out excitedly for everyone to hear. The young stilt-man had seemed quite subdued a moment ago, but was suddenly re-energized once I entered the game.

"You get two shots," he explained the game rules, "from anywhere behind this line." He pointed out a thick black line painted on top of the temporary wooden floor. The line was about twenty-one feet from the basketball hoop, similar to the 'three-point line' on a college basketball court.

"If you make both shots," he continued, "you get to pick out any one of these fine prizes." He showed us several plush stuffed animals hanging from a string, and a shelf underneath them that was loaded with shiny trinkets. "Two for two, that's all you need to do," he said, rhyming with relish as he tried to play mind games with me.

Okay. I've been playing basketball with my friends a lot lately, I thought, giving myself a pep-talk. *I've got a chance.*

I bounced the ball a few times and eyed the backboard and rim. I took a deep breath, dribbled the ball again and took the first shot.

"Ahh..." I talked to the ball as it sailed toward the hoop. "I don't know," I said doubtfully. *It might be a little off*, I thought.

"It looks good," Jessica said as her eyes followed the ball closely.

The ball barely touched the left side of the metal rim before going through the hoop. I made it! I breathed a sigh of relief. One shot down, one shot to go.

"Nice shot, Jason," Jessica said.

"Thanks."

"Jason!" The ball boy called out, having picked-up my name from Jessica. He returned the ball to me. "You're half the way there," he said half-mockingly.

I'm still in the game, I thought. *Concentrate now.* I dribbled the ball – once, twice, three times – and took my second shot. I knew the shot was going to be good as soon as the ball left my hands. It swished through the net without touching the rim.

"Winner! We've got a winner! Jason's a winner!" the boy yelled out, sweeping his arm around to direct our attention to the prizes and inviting us to choose one.

"Pick something out," I said to Jessica. "Do you see anything you like?"

"Hmm...okay." She looked over the prizes, reached down, grabbed a pair of sunglasses and tried them on.

"What do you think?" She turned to show them to me. The sunglass frames had small colorful floral designs on them. They looked good on her. They actually accentuated some of her striking features including her blond hair, full red lips, and classic cheekbones.

"Nice," I replied. "You look great in them!"

"Those sunglasses had your name on them," the ball boy said. He was staring at Jessica, obviously admiring her beauty.

I was happy to have made both shots in the game, but it was doubly satisfying to have won a prize from the taunting ball boy. I turned and began to walk away from the basketball game before Jessica stopped me.

"Hey, don't I get to play this game, too?" Jessica asked. "It's my turn now." She looked at the ball boy, who was still ogling her, and handed him a dollar bill.

I should have known. Jessica is a basketball player, too. I've seen first-hand her competitive streak on the football field, which was very similar to mine. Of course she would want to accept the challenge of this basketball game.

"Alright, Jessica! Go for it!" I said.

Jessica dribbled the basketball a few times, looked at the smitten ball boy and gave him a wink. She spun the ball in her hands, moved into position and launched her first shot. Jessica was smooth. There was no doubt the shot would go in the entire distance the ball traveled from her hands until it passed through the rim and sunk softly into the net.

I nodded at Jessica as she smiled back at me. The ball boy's mouth was agape. I wasn't sure if he was still astounded by her beauty or was surprised by her basketball skills. Probably both. He regained his composure momentarily.

"Lucky shot, lucky shot!" he proclaimed. "Everybody lucks out once in a while. It's the second shot that's the tough one."

Trying to distract her from concentrating on her next shot, he bent down and rolled the ball on the ground back to her. She deftly moved her right foot in front of the approaching ball. The ball rolled on top of her foot and continued rolling up her leg. She calmly leaned over and retrieved the basketball as it reached her knee.

"Thank you," she said, totally unfazed.

He slowly closed his mouth. Finally, he had nothing to say.

Damn, she is smooth, I thought again. *As smooth as silk!*

Jessica spun the ball around in her hands again and gracefully took her second shot. As before, it left her hand in one clean, coordinated motion and traveled to the hoop in a perfect arch. The ball hit the back of the front rim, but her shot had such a soft touch that it swirled around lightly and went through the hoop.

"Ouch! You got me again," the impressed teenager said, wincing. "Winner!" he shouted. "We've got another winner!" He held up Jessica's hand as though she were a winning prizefighter who had just won a boxing match.

"No more basketball for either of you," he whispered. "You're ringers. Your money is no good here anymore. We'll run out of prizes."

"It's your turn to pick out something now, Jason," Jessica said smiling.

"Great!" I had noticed a pair of Green Bay Packer sunglasses on the rack where Jessica had found hers. I picked them out and tried them on.

"Those are perfect for a gung-ho Packer fan like you!" she commented.

"Thank you for winning them for me," I replied. "You're my hero."

"You're my hero, too, da-r-r-r-ling," she said with as much of a brogue as she could roll off her tongue.

"Have a good day," Jessica said to the stunned ball boy as she waved good-bye to him with a sense of flair.

"That was fun," I said as we gazed at each other through our newly acquired sunglasses.

"It sure was," she chuckled. "Do you think he's sorry that he challenged us now?"

"Probably," I answered.

I turned around to look at the ball boy, and noticed that he was surrounded by a bunch of people waiting to get into the game. I think the excitement generated from Jessica and I winning had helped to draw a crowd. Towering over the rest of the group, the tall ball boy looked back at us and smiled.

"Step right up, step right up!" he barked. "We just had two winners in a row. If they can do it, you can do it! There's nothing to it! Who wants to be next?"

"On second thought, maybe he's not so sorry," I said, seeing the renewed enthusiasm for the basketball game.

"No, it doesn't look like he is too sorry, after all," Jessica agreed.

My stomach growled.

"Hey, are you hungry?" I asked.

"I'm starved," Jessica admitted. "What's cooking?"

"Let's find out."

We stopped at a hot dog stand and each got an original Coney dog with everything on it, and a pop. Pop is the term that many people from Wisconsin use for soda, which is short for soda pop, such as a Coke or Pepsi.

"Yum...this is really good!" Jessica said, obviously enjoying her carnival fare. "I was so hungry."

"It is hitting the spot, isn't it?"

I liked Jessica Donovan more and more as we got to know each other. We seemed to have a lot in common. She had a terrific sense of humor. We both played high school sports and are still somewhat active athletically. To be able to talk with someone as gorgeous as Jessica about the 'line of scrimmage' in football, or the 'hit and run' in baseball, and have her know exactly what I was talking about was a definite plus.

Jessica was very smart, too. With her finance education and experience, she was quite savvy about money and economic matters. It didn't seem like Jessica thought of me as *Quasimodo*, either. That didn't hurt.

"You know all of the perfect spots to take a girl, Jason," she said.

"Well, you are high maintenance, Jessica." We both laughed as we finished eating our Coney dogs. With the added boost of energy from the refreshments we continued to explore the carnival in the Town Square. A giant archway that marked the entrance to the mini-golf course beckoned us as we approached.

"Would you like to play a round of golf, Jason?" Jessica asked.

"Sure. Looks like fun," I answered as we passed through the archway. The sun was starting to set, and the colorful blinking lights that outlined each of the mini-golf course's holes were beginning to shine brightly.

The first several holes of the golf course turned out to be quite adventurous. We had to putt through a waterfall, putt around giant trees in the Redwood forest, putt over the peak of a mini-Mount Everest, and putt in between the moving blades of a windmill. So far, the mini-golf course was amazing, especially considering that it was temporarily set up in the Town

Square. It was colorful, challenging, well-constructed, and fun to play, and the best part was yet to come.

The next hole on the course brought us to the opening of a dark cave. The sign in front read 'Tunnel of Love'. The cave walls were made of fake rock, which looked incredibly real. It was so dark inside the cave that I could barely see anything past the entrance. There appeared to be a choice on which direction to hit the ball. Underneath the 'Tunnel of Love' sign, there was another sign marked 'Friends and Families' that had an arrow pointing to an alternate passageway around the dark cave. Apparently the alternate path was designed for those that weren't interested in entering the 'Tunnel of Love'.

Jessica read both signs. "Which way should we go?" she asked, looking at me curiously.

"It's your turn. It's up to you," I answered, wondering which direction she would take.

"Hmm..." She continued to gaze at me, unblinking, supposedly still deciding what to do. She set the golf ball down on the ground and calmly lined up to hit it in the direction of the alternate path leading around the cave, the 'Friends and Families' route. *Oh well*, I thought. We hadn't really known each other that long, so it shouldn't be too surprising if Jessica still thought of me as a friend. She slowly swung the putter back and then forward, hitting the ball solidly at a right angle directly into the main opening of the dark cave – *not* the alternate passageway.

"Oops," she said, shrugging her shoulders. "How did I do that?" she asked innocently, as though the ball went into the cave by mistake.

"Terrible shot, Jessica," I said, attempting to hide my glee.

I dropped my golf ball on the ground to take my turn. Similar to what Jessica had done, I aimed in the direction of the passageway around the cave. Jessica noticed immediately.

"If you putt the ball that way there is going to be hell to pay, Mister," she warned. Her eyebrows were furrowed together, giving her a stern look. I laughed, and wisely turned and hit my golf ball firmly in the same direction that she had hit hers. We watched it disappear into the dark entrance of the cave.

Jessica grabbed my arm as we followed our golf balls, taking a few tentative steps into the darkness of the cave. As soon as we entered the cave the front entrance door closed behind us. A black light immediately turned on and lit our way so we could see inside. After walking forward about twenty steps, we found our golf balls at the other end of the cave. The cave floor gradually descended so the balls ended up at a large spot next to the back wall, which was the lowest point in the cave. A fluorescent yellow arrow on the wall pointed down to the ground, revealing a large bright fluorescent red circle about five feet in diameter illuminated on the ground. A yellow sign on the wall read '*Golfer's Delight – Welcome to the Tunnel of Love! If Your Golf Balls are Inside the Circle - Kiss Here*'.

Our golf balls were both lying inside the red fluorescent circle. The opportunity to kiss her was too good to pass up, but I didn't want to push myself on her or take anything for granted.

"Jess, would you mind?" I asked.

"Only if you don't, Jason," she answered quietly. We stepped onto the glowing red circle. Jessica pulled me close to her, and I kissed her tenderly. The kiss quickly became more passionate as her lips parted and we both started breathing more heavily. Her lips and tongue tasted even better than I had imagined. My senses seemed to explode. I felt every part of her body touching mine, from her lips to her legs, and everything in between. Then the fireworks erupted.

Fireworks! Real fireworks started to go off inside the cave. Bright lights flashed wildly amidst a chorus of bells and whistles and loud bangs. Evidently, by stepping inside the glowing red circle on the floor and stopping to kiss, we set off the amazing fireworks and light show.

The fireworks stopped after about ten seconds. Then a spotlight turned on, directing us to an exit door on the right side of the cave. With Jessica still grasping me tightly, we exited the 'Tunnel of Love'. I was still excited, and not just from the fireworks. The last sign that we passed after leaving the dark cave read '*If You Kissed – Score a Hole in One!*'

"You are an amazing kisser, Jason," Jessica said breathlessly.

"So... are... you," I replied incoherently, trying to shake the clouds out of my head.

Jessica smirked, having rendered me speechless.

"Do you still think it was a terrible golf shot now?" she inquired coyly.

"No. It was the best shot ever."

We laughed, grabbed our golf scorecards, and each happily filled in '1'.

« Chapter 24 »

JESSICA AND I FOUND an open spot on a park bench on Main Street right in front of the Town Hall/Sheriff's Office. It was a perfect place to watch the Fall Festival Parade.

We could hear the bands playing and the crowd cheering off in the distance as the parade progressed. Starting at the Pearl Lake High School, the parade headed south from the school and was winding its way through the streets of Pearl Lake before it would finally turn back onto Main Street, passing us from right to left on its way back to the high school. The entire parade route was nearly a mile long.

Most of my friends and family were also positioned in good spots around us. Steve and Debbie Dozier and their family were just down the street from us, across the street from the Drake Realty and Antique Shop. My parents were sitting on lawn chairs nearby, and I saw Kimberly chasing around harmlessly with her friends. Chris Garrett's grandparents were sitting right between the Dozier's and us. Chris and Brandon were running up and down Main Street with Devon Dawkins and some of the other players on the football team.

This pleasant early autumn day was turning into a superb autumn night. The burnt-orange nearly full moon, still low on the horizon, was slowly shedding its orange and was turning yellow as it ascended. The stars were beginning to sparkle brightly in the clear night. We were quite comfortable wearing our jackets with the outside temperature still holding at around sixty-five degrees.

The downtown area as well as the entire parade route was jam-packed with people. After winding its way through the city streets, the Pearl Lake Fall Festival Parade finally made its way toward us as it turned onto Main Street with the New Orleans Marching Jazz Band playing the 'Star Spangled Banner'. The already excited crowd suddenly came to life as the band came into sight. Hundreds of people wearing carnival masks or fully costumed in pure Mardi-Gras fashion followed the band.

The band was playing 'When the Saints Come Marching In' as it passed us. The people in the parade were dressed as kings and queens, and princes and princesses. There were court jesters, paupers, and clowns. They wore solid colors, checkered, polka dotted and striped patterns. There were plain masks, masks of men and women, and animal masks. Many of the carnival masks and costumes were covered with fall-colored leaves, and some were decorated in brighter colors of light green, orange, yellow, and red. It was a beautiful festival to help celebrate the Wisconsin fall season.

Twenty-foot long cloth snakes and dragons, striped and dotted, light and dark, weaved their way down the street, guided by several people underneath, unseen except for their busy caterpillar-like feet. Fireworks and firecrackers went off intermittently in a chorus of snaps, crackles, and bangs.

Several floats, surrounded by costumed parader's dancing around them, began rolling by. The first float was an impressive white, gray, and light purple-colored genie sitting atop a fancy, multi-colored Arabian flying carpet. A float of a pirate, complete with a colorful parrot on his shoulder, a float of a giant steam-emitting whale, and a float of an old man smoking a pipe followed. There was also a float of a lime green long-feathered bird, a dragon float, and a unicorn float. Dozens of floats continued to pass by and each one was more spectacular than the last.

I turned to look at Jessica.

"What do you think?" I asked her.

Her mouth was open in awe. The dazzling lights from the parade were reflected in her wide-open eyes.

"Jason, I am so glad to be here with you! I'm having a great time."

"I am, too, Jessica," I said as I wrapped my arm around her, "and the parade is not too bad, either."

"Oh!" she exclaimed as she moved to punch my arm. I clamped my arm around her a little tighter, preventing her from having a full range of motion to hit me. She smiled smugly, lifted up her foot, and stomped lightly on mine.

"Ouch!" I protested, chuckling. "Jessica Donovan, you are a multi-talented woman."

"You'd be amazed at what I can do," she teased, with her eyes still sparkling.

The parade continued to work its way through Main Street, and the masked and costumed marchers were still enthusiastically dancing in the street. As a dragon float moved its way slowly by us with steam shooting out of its mouth, I glanced over at my parents and the Dozier's to my right. It looked like they were all having a good time – until I noticed Chris Garrett.

Chris and Brandon were both standing on the narrow ledge of one of the old-fashioned streetlight poles that decorated Main Street. The light pole was set on top of a concrete base, which they were standing on. The concrete base was about four feet up from the ground, which must have given them a little better vantage point to watch the parade. Chris was jumping up and down, balancing precariously on the edge of the concrete base. He was holding onto the light pole with one arm and waving his free arm in the air. For a brief second, I thought he was joining in on the dancing festivities from the parade, but I realized quickly that he was trying to get someone's attention. He finally drew the attention of his grandparents and Steve and Debbie Dozier. Brandon jumped down from the light pole as soon as he noticed Chris jumping up and down. I could see the intensity on Steve's face as he listened to Chris talking to him animatedly. Steve turned around in my direction and when he caught my eye, motioned for me to come over to them. I was already up on my feet.

Steve was pointing in the direction of the dragon float. I swung around and focused on the area he was looking at. I didn't notice anything out of order on the float or in the general direction where he was pointing.

"Something's wrong," I said to Jessica as I moved towards the Dozier's.

She had already noticed. "Go!" she said quickly.

Chris was trying to remain calm, but it looked like he was nearly in a state of shock by the time I got to him a few seconds later.

"It's okay, Chris," Steve said to him as I approached.

"That's right, Chris, it's okay," I repeated. "Here, come down from the ledge." Steve and I reached up and helped him down to the ground.

Steve immediately started to fill me in on what was going on.

"Chris said that he noticed two guys on top of that building." Chris looked up at what I now realized was the top of the Drake Realty and Antique Shop building across the street. The Drake Realty and Antique Shop was a two-story building with a flat roof and a decorative façade on the top front of the building that ran up about four feet higher than the roof.

"There were two guys on the roof," Chris explained. "One of them had a gun, and...and he...I saw him shoot the other guy!"

I looked up at the roof of the Drake building across the street again. We only had a partial view of the top of the building from where we were standing.

"Chris," I said, trying to keep him calm, "with all of the flashing lights and firecrackers going off, are you sure that you actually saw someone get shot? You're not joking around?"

"Coach Jason," he looked straight at me, "I wouldn't fool around about something like this. It looks dark up there, and there are a lot of shadows, but there was enough light that I could see the gun. I saw the gun flash when it went off and I heard it, too. The sound was mixed in with all of the firecrackers going off at the same time, but I know that I heard the gunshot. I saw the guy fall when he got shot. It didn't look good." He shook his head, obviously disturbed by what he had seen. His grandmother put her arm around him, comfortingly.

Some people around us were watching us as we talked, and a few were looking in the direction that Steve had been pointing. Apparently, they could not see that anything was wrong, either. Most of the crowd was still totally absorbed in the parade. The band was still playing, the floats were still passing by, and the masked and costumed revelers were still dancing in the street.

Chris noticed me looking up at the Drake Realty and Antique Shop building again, and understood what I was thinking. I could hardly see anything on the roof from where I was standing.

"We could see the top of the building better from where we were standing up on the ledge," he explained. "The man that got shot was standing right there," he pointed to the top right side of the Drake building. "I know what I saw."

I'd heard enough. Someone might need help. I took off running, weaving my way through the crowd and floats as I began maneuvering my way across Main Street. I grabbed the wireless radio on my belt as I was moving, and called the Arrowhead County Sheriff's Department. Cheryl answered.

"Cheryl, I've just received a report of a shooting on the roof of Drake's Realty and Antique Shop building on Main Street in Pearl Lake. I need back-up."

"Oh my God!" she said, shocked. "I'll send back-up right away. Be careful, Jason."

"Thanks, Cheryl. I will."

My radio immediately belted out in response. "Sheriff Avalon. Come in, Sheriff Avalon." I recognized the voice of our Arrowhead County Sheriff, Bill Larson, on the other end of the line.

"I heard your emergency call. Where are you?" he asked.

"Sheriff Larson, I'm crossing the street in front of Drake's Realty and Antique Shop."

The Arrowhead County Sheriff's job was an elected position. Bill Larson had been in the job for about five years now. He aggressively pushed to make sure that every law-enforcement official in the county received the best training available, and he was always supportive of me in my job as the local Pearl Lake Town Sheriff. Bill was a straight shooter, both figuratively and literally, and I liked and respected him.

"I'm right down the road from you," Sheriff Larson answered. "I'll meet you in front of Drake's right away."

I managed to weave my way through the crowd, and got to Drake's Realty and Antique Shop just as Sheriff Larson arrived. John and Barbara Drake were sitting comfortably on a bench in front of their building, enjoying the parade.

I quickly explained to them that there might be a problem on the roof of their building.

"Can we go up to the roof to check it out?" I asked.

"Of course. I certainly hope it's not something serious!" Barbara said.

They quickly led us to the inside of the Antique Shop, up the stairs to the second floor, and onto an outside deck on the back of the building. There was another set of metal stairs that led from the deck up to the roof. Sheriff Larson and I quickly ascended the stairs. It was relatively dark on the roof compared to the bright lights from the parade at street level. The streetlights did not quite reach the top of the two-story building, and the natural light generated from the moon and stars was fairly dim.

I turned on my flashlight and immediately noticed what appeared to be a body lying near the front corner of the roof, unmoving. I ran across the roof and found a middle-aged male. He was unresponsive. I checked for a pulse while Sheriff Larson called in to request an ambulance. The body was still warm.

"I can't find a pulse, Bill."

I started to perform chest compressions as Sheriff Larson stayed on the police radio to make sure the ambulance found us. I felt blood on my hands. I checked the body for wounds and instantly found a gaping hole in the middle of his chest. It appeared to be from a gunshot. I could not find signs of any other injuries in the dim light. There were no marks on the head or anywhere else on the body that I could see. The one shot to the chest appeared to have been all that was necessary.

I looked around the dark rooftop.

"Is there anyone else on the roof?" I asked Sheriff Larson, wanting to make sure that the shooter was not still up on the roof with us.

"No, but I'm going to double-check the area now," he replied, proceeding to walk around the perimeter of the roof, shining his flashlight on every shadow. I noticed him point the flashlight at the area around the back of the building before he returned.

"Nothing," he confirmed. "The area behind the building is clear, too."

I shook my head. With literally thousands of people within a four-block radius of us, the shooter could be right here in downtown Pearl Lake and still be nearly impossible to find.

Sheriff Larson checked the man's pockets for some form of identification, medical alerts, or any other information that might be helpful. They were completely empty. He had no wallet, car keys, or anything else in his pockets. There were no visible scars, tattoos, or other marks on his body that could help us identify him.

I persistently continued my efforts to revive the man. If he did not survive, it was not going to be because I did not do everything I could to save him.

John Drake, who had gone downstairs to meet the ambulance crew, led them back up onto the roof and to the body when they arrived. It seemed like it had taken an eternity for them to get here, but since an ambulance had been on hand nearby for the parade, it had actually arrived in less than five minutes.

Sheriff Larson and I updated the ambulance team as to the man's current condition and answered all of their questions as they quickly took control of the situation. We helped them lift the body onto a stretcher, carry it down the stairs, and load it into the ambulance, which was waiting in the rear parking lot in the back of the building. As usual, the ambulance attracted a crowd of curious onlookers who had been watching the parade from the front side of the building on Main Street.

A member of the ambulance crew shook her head at us, sympathetically.

"I'm sorry. You did everything you could," she said solemnly, "but it doesn't look good. We'll do the best we can for him until we get to the hospital. It appears that he has been shot through the heart."

« Chapter 25 »

Tom Kaminski was stunned as he listened on the telephone silently while I explained what had transpired over the past few hours in downtown Pearl Lake.

"I wanted to let you know what happened right away before you heard it on the news," I said. "I'm at the Pearl Lake Sheriff's Office now. We have several police officers stationed at the Drake building to be sure that no one interferes with the crime scene. The Arrowhead County Crime Unit and the Madison Crime Forensics Squad will be arriving any minute now to check out the scene."

I looked at my watch. It was 10:30 pm. The Mardi Gras Fall Festival Parade was over. The crowd had dispersed, and the atmosphere on Main Street had returned to its usual calm.

"I need to check out the immediate Pearl Lake vicinity to make sure everything is okay," I said. I thought about everything that had just happened, still struggling to come to grips with it myself.

"What the hell is going on, Jason?" Tom asked. "Was it a crime of opportunity, a crime of desperation, or what?"

"It could be anything," I replied. "It's hard to say right now, until we find out more."

"Pearl Lake is the last place I would have expected there to be a murder," Tom said. "Unfortunately, it happens even in the best of towns."

"I know you're right, Tom. There just seems to be too many loose ends with everything that has happened in Pearl Lake lately – too many to *not* be related to the *Field Museum* robbery somehow."

"What can I do to help you, Jason?"

"Nothing right now, Tom. You've got your hands full already. Let's just keep the lines of communication open. I'll continue to look for the link between the *Chicago Field Museum* robbery and what's going on in Pearl Lake. I'm sure there is one."

"With the two of us and everyone else we have working on the case, we will figure this thing out," Tom stated earnestly.

While we were talking we compared our case notes again. The Chicago Police Department was still checking out Richard Bonline's story as to his whereabouts during the weekend. Carole Grove was still diligently working on finding anything useful from the information her team collected in Pearl Lake. We had a ton of information on the *Field Museum* robbery case, but as of yet nothing tied together.

It was after midnight when I called Jessica on her cell phone. She had left me a message earlier and asked that I call her as soon as I could, no matter what time it was. The murder on Main Street had been a shock to everyone in town, and she was worried, too. Everything had happened so quickly that I didn't have a chance to talk to her before I took off running.

"Hello, Jason?" she whispered sleepily. It was good to hear her voice.

I filled in the details of what had happened since we had last been together a few hours ago, and assured her that I was doing okay under the circumstances.

Unfortunately, someone in Pearl Lake had not been so lucky.

"I'm sorry I left you stranded tonight," I apologized. "I would have rather been with you."

"You certainly know how to pay me the most flattering compliments," she laughed quietly. "First, you tell me that I smell better than a bunch of stinky coaches. Now you tell me that you would have rather been with me than chasing bad guys. Thanks a lot."

"Ahh...that didn't come out right," I said, apologetically.

"Oh, I'm sorry, Jason. I don't mean to joke about something so serious. I'm hitting you when your defenses are down and your mind is on more important things."

Even though I had known Jessica for only a week, it seemed much longer. It was good to be able to talk with her. Somehow, right now it seemed better than talking with Tom, Steve, or one of the guys.

"Jessica, it's important for me to solve this murder case. Will you give me a chance to make it up to you when the time is right?"

"You had better believe it, buddy! You sure can go to extreme lengths to dump a girl, but I'm not letting you off the hook that easily!"

"Now let me think... we started out the day with football. We went to the carnival, rode the Ferris-Wheel, and went on a wild roller coaster ride. We got to play a little basketball, we both won, and we have a few prizes to show for it. We played mini-golf, and we took in the best Mardi Gras-style parade north of New Orleans. You sure are a dull date, Jessica."

She sighed. "It was a perfect day, wasn't it, Jason? All but the very end, obviously."

"It was a great day," I agreed.

"You forgot about the 'Tunnel of Love'," she reminded me. "The lights and bells and fireworks were incredible."

"I didn't forget, and I didn't need any lights or bells going off in the tunnel. You set off enough fireworks inside of me."

"Jason," she laughed again, "you are quite a guy. I think you are very special. Are you sure that you don't have a woman somewhere that has staked a claim on you?"

"I'm sure. I only have eyes for one woman, Jessica. You'll see. But wait until you get to know me. You could be in for a huge letdown."

"Let me be the judge of that."

"Okay, fair enough," I said. Jessica was intelligent, and reasonable. She wasn't going to be dissuaded from forming her own opinion, in her own timeframe.

"What about you?" I asked. "How is it that someone has not grabbed onto a smart, beautiful woman like you?"

"Finally, a sincere compliment, although you may have slightly exaggerated. I'm not beautiful."

I chuckled.

"I suppose you're right, Jessica," I said before clarifying myself. "As far as I'm concerned, 'beautiful' is not an adequate word to describe you. You are so much more than that."

"That's nice of you to say. Jason," she continued, answering the question I had asked her earlier, "I've been in my share of relationships over the years. All I can say is that they turned out to be empty, and not very fulfilling. In the short time we have known each other,

I have felt more alive and excited than I have ever felt in my life."

I had to admit, I felt the same way. Before I had the chance to say so, Jessica said, "I don't mean to downplay what happened tonight. It was horrible."

"I swear I'm going to find out who did it."

"I know you won't let anyone get away with committing a murder in your own back yard," she said.

"In Pearl Lake," I answered, "this is more like our *front* yard."

"Yes, I suppose it is," she said. She took a deep breath and exhaled. "Okay," she added, "I've got to get my sleep so I can hit the craft fair and farmer's market in Pearl Lake tomorrow before I head back to Janesville. Don't worry, Jason. I'll be sure to think of ways you can make it up to me!"

∞

I returned to the Drake Realty and Antique Shop and checked in with the police officers on duty. Unfortunately, they confirmed that the gunshot victim had been declared dead on arrival at nearby Berlin Memorial Hospital, as we had feared.

The Arrowhead County Crime Unit and Madison Crime Forensics Squad had already arrived at the crime scene, and were examining the grounds and collecting evidence. Chelsea Collins, whom I had worked with in the crime unit for years, was taking what seemed to be hundreds of photographs of the scene. *The more, the better*, I thought. If any single photograph could lead us to the murderer, then she could take a million photographs for all I cared.

I made my way around Main Street on foot, and proceeded to check out the front and back of each building. Nothing appeared to be out of order. By now it was after two o'clock on Sunday morning. Even the *Pearl Lake Pub* and the bar in *Katie's Place* were closed for the night. Their doors were shut and locked as expected.

Finally, I made my way around the Lakeshore Bank. I had thought of the possibility that the rooftop shooting had been arranged to create a diversion so someone could break into the bank undetected. Fortunately, nothing at the bank seemed to be disturbed, and everything looked in place.

Returning to my police squad car, I slowly circled the downtown area, carefully scanning every nook and cranny with the vehicle's powerful searchlight. By the time my inspection of Pearl Lake was done, the rising sun was completely visible in the sky.

∞

At seven o'clock in the morning, I made a quick stop at *Katie's Place* and ordered a large coffee, extra-strong. Running on pure adrenaline, I returned to the Drake building. The crews were just finishing up their work when I arrived. Their initial findings included a single bullet casing from a .32 caliber gun, and a small amount of blood on the roof where the man had been shot, indicating that he had died instantly as a result of the gunshot wound.

I filed a Police Report at the Town Hall Sheriff's Office while the details of the murder were fresh in my mind. When that was done, I finally returned home for some much needed rest. All I needed was a good four to five hours of sleep, I figured, and I would be ready to resume my search for the Pearl Lake murderer.

« Chapter 26 »

THE PIERCING RING OF the telephone woke me up about two hours later.

"Hi there, Jason." It was Jennifer Erickson, an Arrowhead County Police Officer that I had worked with for many years.

"Hello, Jennifer," I answered, instantly awake.

"I'm sorry to hear about the murder in Pearl Lake. I heard that you have been up all night, but I found something that might interest you."

"Thanks. What have you got?"

"I'm a few miles south of Pearl Lake on County Road T along the Fox River. I'm looking at the rear end of a white sedan sticking out of the river. It's almost totally submerged. I know the car was not here before sundown yesterday. I just called for a tow truck to remove it from the water, but then I remembered what happened in town last night. I thought you might want to take a look around before we moved it."

"Jennifer," I perked up, "you're right! Please don't let anyone touch anything on the scene! If the tow truck driver gets there before I do, have him wait for me. Don't let him do anything. I'll be there in a few minutes."

"I figured that's what you would say, sheriff. I'll see you when you get here."

I hung up the phone, and once again was on the move.

The tow truck driver did indeed beat me to the scene. He was standing outside of his truck talking with Jennifer as I pulled up in my squad car.

Chelsea Collins and two other members of the crime unit that had also been at the crime scene on the Drake Realty and Antique Shop roof earlier this morning were already working at the river's edge. *They are right on it*, I thought to myself admiringly.

"Hello, again," Jennifer greeted me as I walked up to her as she stood along the banks of the Fox River. "Can't let you get too much sleep now, can we?"

"Who needs sleep anyway?" I answered. "I'm glad you called, Jennifer. Thanks."

She immediately brought me up to date on the present situation.

"The river is about thirty-five yards from County Road T," Jennifer explained. "You can see the path that the car took from the road straight into the river." She pointed to the county road, and swept her hand along the line of tire tracks leading directly into the river.

"The back end of the car," she continued, "which you can see protruding from the river by only a few inches, is approximately ten feet from the shore. The crime unit team found fresh footprints on the ground alongside the tire tracks about fifteen feet back from the riverbank. They figure that whoever was in the car drove it to that spot, stopped and got out, revved up the car's engine while it was in neutral, and then shifted it into drive and sent it into the river."

"The driver must not have known that it's been a fairly dry summer and fall this year," I commented.

"Maybe not," Jennifer said. "I'd say the river water level is probably five to six inches lower than it usually is at this time of year."

"That's true," I agreed. "During a typical rainfall year, the car would have been completely submerged at this spot in the river. No one would have ever seen it. Not even you with your eagle eyes, Jennifer."

Jennifer smiled at the compliment. "Tough break for the driver," she said sarcastically.

"It could be," I nodded.

The Arrowhead County Crime Unit team completed all of their preliminary work and gave the tow truck driver the go-ahead to remove the car from the water. In a matter of minutes he had the chains and hooks connected to the submerged car's back bumper. Using a heavy-duty winch that was on the back of the tow truck, he pulled the water-filled vehicle out of the river.

The crime unit crew opened up all of the car doors and let the water run out. There was no body in the front or back seat of the vehicle. I located the trunk hatch release lever on the front lower-left side of the dashboard. The back trunk popped right open when I pulled the lever. There was no body in the trunk, either.

The crime unit picked up where they had left off before the vehicle was removed from the water. They used their measuring tapes again, and began laying several numbered markers in and around the car. Chelsea Collin's camera was click-click-clicking away just as it was a few hours ago on the Drake building roof.

I peered into the trunk. Only the typical spare tire, medical emergency car kit, and a waterlogged blanket were inside. I returned to the front seat of the vehicle. There were no obvious signs of violence, or any indication that anything unlawful had taken place. A

pair of large, red felt dice, and a dream catcher
decoration were hanging from the front rear-view
mirror, still dripping wet. A lone car key was still in the
ignition. I opened the glove compartment and let the
water drain out. A soggy *Certificate of Auto Insurance*
and a *Vehicle Registration Certificate* were inside. I
carefully removed them and saw that they were still
readable. The car was registered to a Mr. Stanley Stone
in Park Ridge, Illinois, a Chicago suburb.

"Well, I'll be damned," I said to myself. "Here we
go again."

"What do you mean?" Jennifer asked.

"There was a recent robbery at the *Chicago Field
Museum*. Some of the unusual activity in Pearl Lake
lately happens to be tied to the Chicago area."

She looked at the *Vehicle Registration Certificate*
in my hands. "Stanley Stone and this vehicle are from
the Chicago area," she said. "I see what you mean."

I nodded.

I set the papers on the front seat. Chelsea Collins,
camera in tow, came over and snapped pictures of
them and the now open glove compartment. I picked
up my wireless radio from my belt pouch and called the
county dispatcher.

"Four-four-one to county dispatch."

"County Dispatch. Hi Jason, this is Kelly," she
answered. Kelly, like Cheryl, had worked as a county
dispatcher long enough to know my radio call numbers
and recognize my voice. She usually worked weekends,
and during off-shifts when Cheryl was not working.
"How are you holding up, Jason? We are all thinking
about you here in dispatch."

Out of the corner of my eye I noticed Jennifer
raise her eyebrows and shake her head at Chelsea.

Chelsea rolled her eyes in return, and nodded at Jennifer. As I walked around to the driver's side of the car, I picked up bits and pieces of what Jennifer was saying quietly to Chelsea. "Everybody loves him...so sweet... doesn't have a clue."

"What?" I asked her.

"Oh, nothing. I was just talking to Chelsea," Jennifer said, shaking her head as she resumed watching Chelsea snap more photographs inside the car.

"Thanks, Kelly," I answered. "Yeah, I'm holding up just fine. Would you please do me a favor?"

"I would love to do you a favor, Jason," she said, prompting Chelsea to roll her eyes again, and Jennifer to shake her head once more.

"I'm with Jennifer and Chelsea Collins from the crime unit at County Road T and the Fox River," I explained to Kelly. "They removed the vehicle from the river. It is registered to a Mr. Stanley Stone of Park Ridge, Illinois."

I wiped the muddy water from the bottom of the front windshield, just above the windshield wipers. Jennifer grabbed the *Vehicle Registration Certificate* that I removed from the glove compartment. Talking on her own wireless radio that was clipped to her shoulder, she gave Kelly the year, make, and model of the vehicle. Then she read the Vehicle Identification Number as listed on the certificate. As she read the numbers out loud to Kelly, I compared them to the Vehicle Identification Number listed on the dashboard, just inside the car on the other side of the windshield wipers where I had wiped off the mud. The numbers matched.

"Kelly, would you please run a complete background check on Stanley Stone, and forward it to me?" I asked.

"I'd be glad to, Jason. Is there anything else I can do for you?"

"Not right now, Kelly. Thanks. I'll see you around."

"I hope so. 'Bye, Jason."

That's all I need, I thought; another unexplained link to the Chicago area right here in the middle of Arrowhead County, nearly a stone's throw away from Pearl Lake.

« Chapter 27 »

SOME PEOPLE MAY Not think of Pearl Lake as the perfect place to live, but many of those that do live here think it's pretty close to perfect, recent murder notwithstanding. However unfairly, the murder would undoubtedly leave a black mark on the previously spotless reputation of Pearl Lake. A blemish that I hoped would fade once the murder was solved.

Unfortunately, murder is big news, especially in rural America – including rural Wisconsin. Television and radio reporters and crews had flocked to Pearl Lake to get the scoop on the 'full story' of what had happened here.

I had previously scheduled a press conference for one o'clock on Monday to update the media. After spending the rest of Sunday and Monday morning catching up on most of my lost sleep, I was ready to face them. The press conference would be held on Main Street right outside of Town Hall, with the Drake Real Estate and Antique Shop building and roof conveniently located in the background for the news cameras.

Sheriff Bill Larson, a few Arrowhead County Police Officers, and I were in the Pearl Lake Sheriff's Office preparing for the press conference. Tom Kaminski had come to Pearl Lake and was with us, too. We had been talking on the telephone frequently the past week discussing the museum robbery. We figured it was time for us to sit down together in the same room and delve into the evidence from the *Chicago Field*

Museum case, and now the Pearl Lake murder. Two events that I was becoming increasingly convinced were inexplicably linked.

"Thanks for coming, Tom. I'm glad you're here," I said.

"You know, Jason," he answered, "I needed to get away from Chicago and the museum for a while. My mind was beginning to get bogged down with everything going on. Even though I'm still working on the case, I thought a change of scenery would do me good."

"The fresh air will do you good, Tom. Maybe when we lay out all of our case files something will jump out at us that didn't when we were comparing notes over the telephone."

Sheriff Larson caught my eye across the room, and pointed at his watch.

"It's time," he said. "Are you ready to address the media?"

"Ready as ever. Let's do it," I answered.

"Are we all set to go?" I asked the rest of the group.

They nodded in agreement as we proceeded out of the Town Hall and onto Main Street, where a throng of news reporters and media had gathered. I approached the podium that had been set up for the press conference at the front of the steps of the Town Hall building. It was almost in the exact same spot that Jessica and I had been sitting together watching the Fall Festival Parade a few days earlier.

The crowd, which had been buzzing with excitement, turned quiet. As they directed their attention at me, I, in turn, swept my head slowly from left to right and assessed the crowd. Dan Abrahms,

John and Barbara Drake, Eric Anders and several other people from Pearl Lake were mixed in with the mostly unfamiliar faces of the media. The curiosity, anxiety, and need for information regarding the Main Street murder showed clearly on their faces.

"My name is Sheriff Jason Avalon," I introduced myself immediately. "First of all, I would like to express my sincere regrets to the family of Mr. Stanley Stone. The Arrowhead County Sheriff's Department and Crime Unit, along with several other area experts are working to solve this crime. We are all committed to working together until the person who is responsible for his murder is found and brought to justice."

I shared as much information as I could without revealing any confidential details that could potentially jeopardize solving the crime. I knew that the media had an insatiable desire to report the most sensational stories they could find – the more outlandish, the better. They help to raise their ratings, and the viewing public craves them. Yet I felt that everyone in Pearl Lake and Arrowhead County needed to hear as much information as possible about this shocking murder that was committed in their own hometown. Hearing the facts can often help to dispel the rumors.

When I was done addressing the media, Sheriff Bill Larson and I answered all of their questions until they were fully satisfied. The hordes of reporters then started interviewing various people from Pearl Lake. I was surprised, and humbled, by what I heard.

"Our family has lived here our whole lives," Dan Abrahm's son and daughter-in-law, Rod and Cindy, were talking to a news reporter from one of our local television stations. I caught the tail end of what Cindy was saying, "...and there is no one that we trust more than Sheriff Avalon to solve this crime."

Harry Wilson, the seventy-three year old retired electrician and recipient of the sucker punch from Richard Bonline in the *Pearl Lake Pub*, was talking to another reporter.

"I've known Jason Avalon since he was born," Harry said. "Whenever anything happened in this town that no one else could figure out, we ended up going to Jason to get answers, even when he was a kid. Damned if he didn't always figure it out. There was this time, he had to be about twelve years old, when he..." I couldn't hear the rest of what Harry was saying because a larger group of reporters flocked around him when they heard him telling his story.

Another reporter had a 'CNN' microphone stuck in the faces of a group of Pearl Lake High School students. They must have been out of school on their lunch break.

"Are you afraid that there is a killer on the loose?" the reporter asked. "Do you think Sheriff Avalon will find the killer?"

"I'm not afraid," one student answered boldly.

"Sheriff Avalon will never let the killer get away with it," a girl answered.

"...we know he will catch whoever did this," another student piped in as the rest of the group nodded in agreement.

"Very well done, Jason," Sheriff Larson complimented me back in the Sheriff's Office after the press conference had concluded and all of the individual interviews were finished.

"Good job, Jason," Tom added.

"Thanks," I answered.

I felt the pressure being involved in two murder cases, but was bolstered by the support and optimism of everyone in town. It helped stoke the fire that burned in my gut, and strengthened my resolve. I was confident that I would find the Pearl Lake murderer. I wouldn't let the people of Pearl Lake down.

∞

Tom and I spent the rest of the afternoon working on the *Chicago Field Museum* and Pearl Lake murder cases. Our case files were spread out on the desks in the office. Dozens of photographs taken at both crime scenes were posted on the bulletin boards.

We pored over every piece of evidence we had. Tom updated me on Carole Grove and the CSI team's progress, and we reviewed the names of the people of interest that we believed warranted further attention.

"The list of suspects is stacking up, along with the pile of data related to the cases," Tom said, scratching his head.

"Someone, or something, has to be tied together," I stressed. "We just need to find the connection. The answer is right here in front us. I can feel it."

"We will probably kick ourselves when we finally do see it," Tom predicted.

"Have you ever tried to think of a word that was right on the tip of your tongue?" I asked. "You knew what it was, but at that moment you just couldn't recall the word. So you put it out of your mind altogether and thought about something else. Then, after a while the word popped into your head?"

"You're absolutely right, Jason," Tom agreed. "We need to step back for a while. Let's put the case files away for now."

"Okay," I said as I gathered up the files that were spread throughout the office, and put them in one neat stack. "We can re-visit them later when our minds are refreshed."

"What's for supper?" Tom asked. I was planning on having dinner at my parent's house. Tom, likewise, was planning on spending the night at his parent's house and was having dinner with them tonight.

"My dad is putting steaks on the grill," I answered with my mouth beginning to water. "We need to take advantage of the grill as much as we can before the snow flies. How about you? What are you having for dinner?"

"Oh, some kind of stew or something. You know, the meat and potatoes kind of thing. I love my mom's home cooking. It's good comfort food, and is just what I need right now."

"Yeah, that sounds good, too," I said. "Well, enjoy the dinner. I'll talk to you soon."

"You, too," Tom said. "Call me as soon as the light bulb goes on in your head. It always does."

« Chapter 28 »

AFTER TRYING, SOMEWHAT unsuccessfully, to work off my frustrations at the fitness center early Tuesday morning, I walked across the street into *Katie's Place*. Katie kindly tried to feed me another one of her healthy omelets. Instead, I opted for a small glass of orange juice and munched on a piece of whole-wheat toast as I made my way through the restaurant.

The restaurant was quite busy for a weekday morning in late September. Everyone was still very concerned with the murder that had shattered their peaceful existence in Pearl Lake. Since I knew most of the people there, I did my best to spend some time at each table and talk with them. It was good to hear most of them express how confident they were that I would solve the murder.

Maybe no one else felt any better by the time I left *Katie's Place*, but I know I did.

I walked down the block and talked with a few people in the General Store, then crossed Main Street and stopped in to see the Drake's at their Real Estate and Antique Shop. John and Barbara were still visibly shaken from the events that transpired on the roof of their building. The antique shop was crowded with people browsing and inquiring about the goods, so the Drake's were both quite busy.

"It is absolutely horrendous to think of what happened here!" Barbara said to me with her voice trembling.

"I know it is," I agreed, "but try not to worry about it. We'll find out who did it."

"Oh, I know you will, dear." She patted my arm before rushing off to help a customer. John Drake flashed a strained smile at me as I was on my way out of the store, and I nodded back at him reassuringly.

Next door, Abrahm's Factory Direct Store was so packed with people that I had to wait a few minutes to get in the front door. Mr. Abrahm was talking with the shoppers waiting in line to check out, most with hand baskets piled full of merchandise. Murder is good for business, apparently.

"Jason will get whoever did it," I heard Mr. Abrahm say to someone in line. "Well, speak of the devil!" he announced when he saw me enter the store. "Hello, Sheriff."

"Good morning," I greeted him and the shoppers crowded in front of the checkout counter.

"Hi, Sheriff Avalon. Are you making any progress?" asked a middle-aged man who must have been from out of town.

"We're making slow but steady progress, thank you."

Many of the people came up to me and shook my hand. Others patted me on the back, offering me encouragement.

"We're all behind you, Jason," an elderly man that I knew lived on the east side of town said. "We know you can do it."

The response was the same from everyone I talked to as I continued to make my way around downtown Pearl Lake. The shoppers in Piggly-Wiggly were just as upbeat and supportive. Even the patrons in the *Pearl Lake Pub* were clear-eyed and friendly, but it was still early in the day.

The Red Rock Inn had been sold out since the Labor Day weekend, the owners told me contentedly when I stopped in. The manager at the Comfort Inn and Suites was also happy. They only had a few rooms available for the night, which was much better than usual for this time of year.

In their own way, the townsfolk in Pearl Lake were handling the shock of the murder as well as could be expected. The Drakes were the exception, since the crime hit a little too close to home for them. Yet virtually all of the shopkeepers in town seemed to be quite pleased. They had been seeing an influx of customers as a result of all the attention Pearl Lake was getting from the news stations. However, a murder would not have been my top choice as a way to attract visitors to our town.

I returned to the Sheriff's Office reinvigorated. The overwhelming support from everyone in Pearl Lake had lifted my spirits tremendously.

∞

I continued to pore over the facts of the *Field Museum* robbery and the Pearl Lake murder. There were so many loose ends already, I didn't need to add any more to the list. My mind kept going back to certain details, but I seemed to be at a standstill.

I called Chief Medicine Man Denby Sage.

"Hello?" Chief Sage answered the telephone before it even rang.

"Hi, Chief Sage. This is Jason Avalon."

Denby Sage chuckled. "Hello, Jason. I was just reaching for the telephone to call you when it started to ring."

I wasn't really surprised. Somehow, since we had met it seemed like we were on the same wavelength.

"Do you have a few minutes, Chief Sage?" I asked. "I was hoping to talk with you about something, but you said that you were about to call me, too. Is everything okay?"

"Everything is fine, Jason," he assured me. "I wanted to let you know that there is going to be a small gathering at the Marshall Farm this coming Saturday. It will just be a simple celebration for Miracle. Would you like to join us?"

I thought quickly to be sure that I didn't have anything scheduled for that day. "Thank you for inviting me. Yes, I'd like to join you."

"You can bring the white buffalo-woman, if she's interested," he said, referring to Jessica Donovan.

"I think she is all woman now," I answered, smiling. "I'll ask her."

"Good. I am glad to hear that you will be able to make it."

"Chief Sage, a few weeks ago there was a robbery at the *Chicago Field Museum*. Some Native American items in the museum were stolen. Do you think any Native Americans could possibly be involved in the robbery? By the way, this information has not been released to the public, so I would appreciate it if you would keep it confidential."

"Of course. You have my word that anything we discuss in confidence will stay that way, Jason."

"Thanks."

"I have heard about this robbery on the news, and I understand your question," he answered thoughtfully. "There are many Native American tribes and many Native American people, but both my head and my heart tell me that none are involved in this crime."

"Why do you think that?"

"There are some that have protested the public exhibition of Native American items that have historical significance," he explained. "But to my knowledge, the Native American tribes involved in the *Field Museum* exhibition agreed to the display of these items."

"The curator at the *Field Museum* said the same thing when I talked to him," I said, "but it still helps hearing it from you."

"Jason, I saw you on the news today. The murder in Pearl Lake must have been a terrible shock to your people. It is such a peaceful community. Your spirit appeared to be strong when you were on the television, but it must be very stressful for you. How are you holding up?"

"I'm doing okay, Chief Sage. It's a tough situation, but I will find out who did it."

"I have no doubt that you will," he said. "Jason, there is another reason that I wanted to talk with you at the Marshall Farm gathering on Saturday. I have been thinking about your dream that you shared during the drum ceremony. In the end, it is you who must find meaning from your own dreams, but I may be able to give you some guidance if you would be interested. It may be related to the crimes that you are working on right now."

Back at home that night, I sat out on the screened-in porch with a *Point Amber,* a beer brewed in Stevens Point, Wisconsin. I slowly began to unwind watching the setting sun as it painted the western horizon in shades of purple and red.

My mind had been occupied steadily since the night at Tom and Amy Kaminski's house, when Tom received the phone call telling him about the *Chicago Field Museum* robbery. With the downtown Pearl Lake murder added to that, my head had been absolutely spinning. This was the first time in the last few days that I really had a chance to sit and let everything that had happened sink in.

I visit regularly with my family and friends, especially Steve Dozier, Eric Anders, and Tom Kaminski, even when Tom and I aren't deeply entrenched in murder cases. I had spoken with each one of them every day since the downtown murder put Pearl Lake on the nation's map.

It was Jessica that I wanted to talk with now.

"Hello," Jessica answered my telephone call. It was funny how one word could send shivers up my spine.

"Hi, Jessica."

"Jason! It's so good to hear your voice. How are you?"

"It's good to talk to you, too. I'm doing okay. How is everything with you?"

"I'm just fine. Jason, you have been all over the news. You've been absolutely terrific! You are so good with the media."

"I'm glad you think so."

"Well, I do," she confirmed, "and you know I don't say anything that I don't mean."

"I'm starting to figure that out."

"I'm sure you are," she replied, "because that's exactly how you are yourself."

I thought about it, and had to agree.

"That's a good point," I said.

"It is, isn't it?"

"Jessica," I moved on, "I hope I didn't scare you away. Pearl Lake has always been such a safe town. Hardly any crimes are ever committed here, period, much less a murder. This is not at all typical."

"Jason, I promise you," she said deliberately, "you have enough things to worry about, and I am *not* one of them. I can't even imagine anything happening that would change the way I feel about you."

"If you tell me that I am like a brother to you, I am going to be upset."

She laughed. "Jason, I have never thought of you as a brother, nor will I."

"Whew," I breathed a sigh of relief. "I had a great time with you on Saturday. Did you really have fun, too, or did you just do everything because it's what I wanted to do?"

"Jason, I was serious when I told you it was a perfect day for me. If I had chosen what to do myself, I would have done the exact same things! Besides, everything we did we decided to do together. I didn't want to leave you that night. So enough! I won't listen to any more talk like that."

"Fair enough," I said. "Jessica, do you have plans for this coming Saturday? Would you like to do something with me?"

"I would love to, Jason," she said happily. "What do you have in mind?"

"It's a little different, so let me explain before you say yes or no. I'll understand if it's something that you would rather not do."

"Okay, explain away. I'm not worried yet."

I decided to spare Jessica the minute details of the Miracle legend, and gave her the condensed version.

"On the day that our Pearl Lake football team played against your team in Janesville a few weeks ago, we stopped to see Miracle, the white buffalo, at the Marshall Farm before the game. When we were there, I met a Native American Chief named Denby Sage. We got to talking, and he invited me to a drum ceremony that was held there at sunrise the next morning."

Jessica gasped, then laughed. "Oh, Jason. I kept you up half the night talking to you at the restaurant that Friday night. You had to get up early the next morning? I'm so sorry. Why didn't you say something?"

"Jessica, the way we hit it off I could have talked with you all night. Anyway," I continued, "I talked to Chief Sage earlier today. He invited me to another gathering at the Marshall Farm this coming Saturday. He made a special point of asking me to invite you, too."

"He did?"

"Yes. It's not a formal ceremony or anything like that this time. It's just a get-together for people who want to wish Miracle well. Native Americans believe that Miracle is a very special, sacred buffalo. If you would like to go with me, we won't have to be there at sunrise like I was the last time. The gathering starts at noon."

"Jason, I think it's great you brought your team to see Miracle at the Marshall Farm. I've read about her in the newspapers, but I've never seen her. I would love to go with you!"

We talked again about our friends and families, our work, sports, and the other things that are important to us. It seemed like the more we talked, the more we found we had in common.

Eventually we started to talk about our football teams. Both of our teams were playing their last games of the season on the upcoming Friday. Jessica was planning on getting together with her coaches in Janesville after her game on Friday. Similarly, I was planning on getting together with our coaches in Pearl Lake on Sunday, a few days after our last game. The bond we each had with our teams and coaches was another thing Jessica and I shared.

"Jason, will you have to get back home right away on Saturday after the drum ceremony? I know that you have a lot going on in Pearl Lake, but as long as you are going to be picking me up here to go to the gathering at the Marshall Farm, can you stay the night in Janesville?" Jessica asked.

"I'd really like to get away for the night if I can," I replied, "but with everything going on, I'll need to play it by ear."

"I understand. If you decide to stay in Janesville I don't want you to go to a hotel, Jason. I have plenty of room here in my condo. If you'd like you can spend the night here."

"Let's enjoy the day together, Jessica. Then we can decide what we feel like doing from there. How does that sound?"

"You're so sensible. That's a good idea."

"Great. I'll see you in a few days. Good night, Jessica."

"It's so nice talking to you. Good night, Jason. I can't wait to see you again."

« Chapter 29 »

JESSICA GREETED ME WITH a lingering kiss when I picked her up Saturday morning on the way to the gathering at the Marshall Farm. She lived in a spacious, modern condominium in Janesville that overlooked one of the city's desirable Greenbelt areas. Beyond the row of maple trees that marked the border of her back yard was a deep ravine of natural, undeveloped land that was several hundred yards wide and extended to the east and west as far as I could see – the Greenbelt. It was filled with tall green pines and other trees that were beginning to display an abundance of early autumn pastel colors.

Jessica looked as radiant as ever. I was beginning to realize that her stunning beauty was not the exception to the rule, but was, in fact, the rule. I was quite content realizing that her kisses of greeting had progressed from what started out as short pecks on my cheek to today's luscious kiss on my lips.

She looked at me with a mixture of concern and delight.

"Jason, it's so good to see you. You look good! How are you?" Her beautiful ocean-blue eyes penetrated mine like a laser beam.

I smiled, partly in response to her greeting that was loaded with feeling, and partly from my own sense of excitement at seeing her.

"It's great to see you again, too," I returned her direct gaze, and couldn't take my eyes off of her.

"Jessica, you get more beautiful every time I see you, and that's not just a line."

She smiled and kissed me tenderly in response.

"It seems like such a long time since I've seen you," she said quietly. "I've been thinking about you. I couldn't wait to talk to you about our football game yesterday. By the way, how was your game?"

"The kids played great. We won. You must have done pretty well, too, the way it sounds."

"We did," she answered. "The boys played such a good game. I'm so proud of them."

We shared the details of each of our final games of the season while we drove to the Marshall Farm. Jessica had the same level of passion for her team that I had for mine, and it showed.

"I know what you mean," I said, after Jessica talked about one of her players. "We have this one kid, Devon Dawkins, who was all quiet and kept to himself in the beginning of the season. He was loaded with natural ability, but didn't really know how to use it. By the end of the season he absolutely flourished."

"Oh, he's the quick guy that caught the long touchdown pass when you played us," Jessica recalled.

I nodded.

"I have to admit that the player I am most proud of is Chris Garrett," I said.

I told Jessica about some of the things that Chris had done during the season to bring the team together, over and above his play on the football field. Jessica, likewise, shared some stories about her team that helped to describe what made it so special to her, too.

"I'm going to miss coaching this team," I said. "They were a lot of fun."

"That's exactly how I feel about ours," Jessica said. She was quiet for a moment before she spoke again. "You know, the only team to beat us this season was Pearl Lake!" She clenched her fist as though she was going to punch me in the arm, but then reached out, pulled me into her, and kissed me.

"I would win a lot more games against other teams if that's how I'd be rewarded," I said.

"Be careful what you say," Jessica cautioned, smiling. "That could be easily arranged!"

∞

There were about fifty people gathered at the Marshall Farm when we arrived. Chad Marshall was out in the pasture feeding the animals. I returned his wave when he noticed us approach the now familiar spot by the fence in front of the barn. Chief Denby Sage was talking to a group of people that had surrounded him near the fence. His friend, John 'Calm Heart' Yazee was amongst the group.

"So, that's Miracle?" Jessica asked as she noticed the white buffalo grazing in the field alongside her mother. "She is adorable."

"That's her," I nodded, still awed at the sight of her. I looked at Jessica, and felt a connection to her that was very similar to the one I felt with Miracle. *Why not*, I thought? Jessica was in the dream, too.

Denby Sage and Calm Heart noticed us observing Miracle and immediately came over to talk to us.

"It is good to see you again, Jason," Denby said as we shook hands.

"It's good to be here again, Chief Sage."

I shook Calm Heart's hand and exchanged greetings with him, too. They were both looking at

Jessica with curiosity showing on their faces.   I introduced her to them before she began to feel too uncomfortable with them staring at her.

"Chief Sage, Calm Heart, this is Jessica Donovan. Jessica, this is Chief Medicine Man Denby Sage, and John 'Calm Heart' Yazee."

"I'm pleased to meet you," Jessica smiled warmly and shook their hands.

"The pleasure is ours," Denby said.

"You still appear to be strong in spirit, Jason. That is good to see," Denby said as he assessed me closely.

"Stubbornly persistent is probably more like it, Chief Sage," I replied.

"One with a strong spirit must have an open mind and open eyes in order to see things more clearly," Calm Heart said.

I nodded, recognizing the compliment in his statement.   He had kindly revised my 'stubbornly persistent' self-assessment to 'having a strong spirit'. I also picked up his words of caution to keep my eyes open to what is going on around me.   He understood the danger involved in trying to solve a multi-million dollar museum robbery, and now two murders. *John 'Calm Heart' Yazee, the spiritual leader, is truly a wise man, as is Chief Medicine Man Denby Sage*, I thought.

"Come sit with us," Chief Sage said, inviting us to sit around a brightly burning fire.

A large group surrounded us once again. We listened as Calm Heart retold the story of Miracle, the white buffalo, and talked of the prospect of peace that she brought to the world. Some other Native Americans in the group told stories of legends that had been passed on to them from the generations before them. Chief Sage was last to share a legend from his Lakota Sioux tribe about some of the healing powers provided by nature. He talked about various roots and plants and described the impact they have had on the world. I was fascinated by all of the stories.

Luckily, I was not called on to share my dream or any stories today. I didn't want to embarrass Jessica or make her feel uneasy by talking about something she might think was crazy. I turned to look at her sitting beside me. She was totally immersed in the story that Denby was telling.

After everyone was finished sharing their stories, we sat around a few men who were beating their drums softly, and listened to the soothing rhythm. I was relaxed and content, and it looked like Jessica was, too.

Before long some of the people started to get to their feet and move around the farm grounds. Jessica and I got up and walked over to the fence to get a closer look at Miracle. Once again, Miracle began to wander towards us. This time, her mother remained with the other buffalo by the barn.

Miracle gently pressed her nose against the fence in front of us, spouting steamed air out of her nostrils as she exhaled. I looked over at Chad Marshall, not wanting to be the source of commotion again. He was still working outside the barn filling the bins with feed, and as always, knew where Miracle was. He was smiling as he looked over at Miracle, who apparently had come over to say 'hi'. Chad gave me a cautious nod that I understood as his okay to touch Miracle through the fence. Then I realized that Miracle was not actually across the fence from me. She was standing directly in front of Jessica.

"Jason, look at her!" Jessica whispered excitedly. "She is absolutely precious. She seems so serene."

"I think she wants you to touch her," I said to Jessica intuitively.

"Oh..." she nodded, slowly reaching her hand through the fence and gently stroking the top of Miracle's head. The white buffalo snorted some more steam through her nose, contentedly, and finally turned her head towards me.

"Hi there, girl," I said soothingly. I ran my hand on the side of her head and patted her affectionately. I heard the murmur of the crowd. They were astonished to see Miracle so close, much less being touched by Jessica and me through the fence.

Miracle nodded her head a few times, as though saying, 'you are my special friends, and we share a close bond. It's good to be with you. We will be together again soon'. She slowly returned to her mother and the other buffalo by the barn.

"That was incredible!" Jessica said.

Most of the group had swarmed around us and were congratulating us on our unique experience with the sacred white buffalo.

"It appears that there is a connection between Miracle and your friend, Jessica, too," Denby Sage said as he came up to us.

"You felt a close connection with Miracle, too?" Jessica asked, looking at me curiously.

"I did," I nodded.

"The last time that Jason was here during the drum ceremony, Miracle came up to him and let him touch her," Calm Heart explained to Jessica. "She had never allowed anyone to touch her before. Today with you and Jason was the second time ever."

"That's unbelievable," Jessica said.

"It is special," Calm Heart acknowledged.

"Jason, can I talk to you?" Chief Sage asked. I suddenly recalled our conversion on the telephone a few days ago, when he mentioned he had something to share with me that might be related to the crimes I was attempting to solve.

"Would you mind?" I asked Jessica.

"Not at all. You go ahead. If he doesn't mind, I'd love to talk with Calm Heart for a minute."

"I would like that," Calm Heart gladly obliged. They immediately began talking as Denby and I returned to the fire and sat down.

"When I returned back home to South Dakota following the last drum ceremony, I talked to some members of my tribe about your dream, and about Chief Black Hawk," Denby said. "They were surprised to hear me talk about Black Hawk."

"Why were they surprised?"

"It is not often that someone brings up Chief Black Hawk. The story of Black Hawk goes back to the 1820's, nearly two hundred years ago. The fact you had a dream about Black Hawk at the same time items that once belonged to him were stolen from the *Chicago Field Museum* showed remarkable insight."

I had to admit, at the very least it was quite a coincidence.

"As I mentioned before," Denby continued, "only you can determine whether any of this means anything. The members of my tribe and I agree that there is a part of your dream that may be related to things yet to come. In seeing the events of the Black Hawk War, you saw the past. In seeing the white buffalo woman, you have seen the present. I believe that you saw something else in your dream that will relate to the future."

"Something dangerous?"

"Not necessarily. However, it could be vitally important to you."

This was all somewhat disconcerting to me. I'm used to digging deep to uncover the facts in order to solve crimes, but when it comes to the stuff of dreams and seeing into the future, I'm a little bit out of my element. *Maybe it takes more than simply uncovering the facts*, I thought, *to find out the truth*.

"Is there anything I can do to help learn the meaning of the dream?" I asked.

"It might be helpful to spend some time by yourself, when it is quiet and you will not be interrupted. Perhaps you can recreate your dream of the buffalo and Chief Black Hawk. Then try to focus on the individual details of the crimes that you are attempting to solve. Think of the details one by one. Do *not* think of them in the order of when they occurred. Just think of them randomly as they come to mind. Something might come to you then."

"Thank you for telling me this, Chief Sage," I said appreciatively.

"I hope it proves to be helpful to you," Denby said.

Somehow, I had a strong feeling that one way or another it would turn out to be very helpful.

I was still absorbed in everything he had said, but when I looked at him I could tell that he was not finished.

"There is one more thing I would like to share with you," he said. "It may be something that will have tremendous meaning to you. You told Calm Heart and me on the day of the drum ceremony that your great-

great-great grandmother, Hantaywee, was a member of the Grand River clan of the Hunkpapa tribe."

I nodded in confirmation.

He looked at me to be sure he had my complete attention. I sensed that what he was about to tell me would have an impact on me for the rest of my life.

"A great Native American chief and holy man was also from that clan during the same time period," Denby explained. "It is also said that he had a very loving and loyal wife who was called Hantaywee. His name was Chief Sitting Bull."

« Chapter 30 »

"Do you know what that means, Jason?" Jessica asked me later when I told her what Denby had said. "You could be a direct descendant of Chief Sitting Bull."

"It's hard to believe," I admitted.

"Did you know anything about this before?"

"No, not at all," I answered. "I've always known that my great-great-great grandmother was a Native American named Hantaywee, but if she was the wife of Chief Sitting Bull, one of the most legendary Native Americans in history, why didn't my family pass that fact on to me? They must have known."

"It does seem unusual," Jessica agreed. "Wouldn't it have been much more likely that you would have heard that your great-great-great *grandfather* was Chief Sitting Bull?"

"I would have thought so," I answered. "I will certainly delve into it further when I get a chance."

"I would love to hear what you find out," Jessica said. "I think it's fascinating."

Calm Heart hadn't said anything to Jessica about my dream, or at least the part in which she played a starring role. I was glad about that. I didn't want her to be upset when she found out I had a dream about her before we even met. I was still a little unsure what to think about it myself.

"What did Chief Sage talk to you about?" Jessica asked, curiously.

"He told me about Chief Black Hawk. He thought the information might have something to do with the crimes I'm working on right now."

"Does it?"

"I don't know yet, but I have a feeling it will when I get it all figured out." I didn't want to give her too much information relating to the crimes. What she didn't know couldn't hurt her.

Quite a few people were still hanging around the Marshall Farm, and Jessica and I remained huddled by the warm fire visiting with them. We could have stayed for hours listening to the Native American legends and stories, but after about an hour most of the group began to get up, and slowly started to leave. Many had traveled from out of state and probably wanted to get started on their trips back home.

"Now that I'm in the spirit of things, let's go for a ride on the 'Chief Black Hawk Trail'," Jessica suggested.

"That's a great idea," I agreed. Jessica was sharp. There was no specific trail named after Chief Black Hawk, but she knew that he and his war party had been chased by a group of soldiers along the Rock River, close to where we were sitting.

We left the farm and Miracle, and headed west, stopping briefly at a local bar called the Anchor Inn in Newville. Newville has an approximate population of 1,835 cows, and 17 people – not including the patrons inside the Anchor Inn. The place was packed. We each had pop, even though a majority of the large afternoon crowd was drinking *Miller Lite*, the famous Milwaukee-brewed beer. We sat at a table by a window overlooking the Rock River as it rushed by.   The Newville Bridge towered over us as we looked out the window to the east. The bridge crossed the river just south of the point where it flowed into Lake Koshkonong, one of the largest, fresh water inland lakes in Wisconsin.

After we finished our drinks, we drove west a few miles to Edgerton, and turned north onto Highway 51 to continue our journey.

"Jessica, I know of a great restaurant nearby," I hinted, as my stomach told me it was starting to get hungry. "Have you ever heard of Halverson's?"

"Halverson's? Sure, it's up by Stoughton. They have great food, and I'm starved! Let's go there for dinner."

"Great. That's where we'll go."

We continued on the highway another twenty miles until we arrived at Halverson's, which was located on the southwest shore of Lake Kegonsa. We walked onto the wooden slat dock in front of the restaurant, and instead of turning left, which would have taken us out onto the pier over the lake, we turned right, which took us through the front door and into the restaurant.

After we had been seated at a table, Jessica pointed to the back of her menu.

"Look at this," she said curiously.

I turned my menu around, and saw that there was a brief history of the restaurant and the area. It described how the first white settlers came to Lake Kegonsa, which is the Indian name for 'Lake of Many Fishes', in 1831. Coincidentally, the area first began to develop after the Black Hawk War in 1832.

"That's interesting," I said.

"It is, isn't it?"

"I hadn't even heard of Chief Black Hawk before," I said. "Within the last few days, I've had a dream about him and the Black Hawk War, and learned of his exploits that brought him and members of his tribe into Wisconsin and up along the Rock River. Now here we are in a restaurant in territory that was settled right after the Black Hawk War ended."

"It's almost as though you were meant to learn of Black Hawk," Jessica said, thoughtfully. "It seems like he is trying to tell you something."

I hadn't thought about it before, but Jessica could be onto something. A chill ran up my spine. I thought back to Calm Heart's suggestion to me this morning. 'Keep your mind open', he had said.

"Maybe Black Hawk is trying to tell me something, Jessica. I just need to be able to hear it."

We sat by the front window and took in the picturesque view of the lake as the sun set for the evening. My medium rare filet mignon and glass of red wine were hitting the spot, and Jessica raved about her grilled bass and white wine. I was very relaxed, and was quite happy being with Jessica. Even though I was in a stressful situation being wrapped up in two, high visibility murder cases, I was having another terrific day with her.

"This was the perfect place for us to come," Jessica said. She reached under the table and squeezed my hand. "Jason, I can't tell you enough what a wonderful time I'm having." She held my hand instead of slugging my arm. *Another sign of progress*, I thought.

"Remember last week when I said that you were a dull date?" I asked. I squeezed her hand in an effort to prevent her from using it to punch me. "Well, I'm going to have to take that back."

She smiled, turning her head to look out at the beautiful view of Lake Kegonsa.

"Does that mean you're not going to throw me back in?" she asked, referring to the instances when fishermen throw fish that are not worth keeping back into the water after they catch them.

"Oh, you're a keeper, Jess."

There may be a lot of fish in the sea, I thought, *but if I can help it, I am not going to let this one get away.*

"You are so sweet," she said.

She rose slightly from her chair, so as not to cause too much attention in the restaurant, leaned over the table and kissed me.

"I've had a great time with you today, too," I said.

"The day is not over yet, Jason!" she said, smiling.

∞

After dinner, we couldn't get back to Jessica's place in Janesville soon enough for me. I had a very difficult time keeping the speedometer to within five miles an hour over the speed limit on the drive back. The last thing I needed right now was a speeding ticket. With all of the media attention on me and the Town of Pearl Lake, that would not have gone over too well.

Maybe it was just my imagination, but when we first saw each other on the wet and rainy football field after the Pearl Lake/Janesville freshman football game, I felt an unusually close bond with Jessica. After being so physically close to her on our journey up the 'Chief Black Hawk Trail', at the restaurant, and now in the car on the way back to Janesville, that bond had become even closer. Actually, the more I thought about it, the bond between us may have begun on another level of consciousness going back to when I first laid eyes on her in the vivid dream with the buffalo.

Jessica was sitting close to me as I tried to keep my concentration on the road, and my hands on the steering wheel. With her head lying comfortably on my shoulder, and her hand resting provocatively on my leg, the sexual tension between us had built up to the point where it was palpable.

Jessica gave me a record-fast grand tour of her condominium when we finally arrived. She left a trail of clothes, flinging them off piece by piece like a trail of breadcrumbs for me to follow. I flung my shoes next to hers lying in the hallway, and tripped on my pants as I yanked them off and put them on top of hers hanging on the doorknob of the open bedroom door. I pulled my shirt over my head and threw it by hers lying on the floor next to the bed.

She was sprawled on the bed, nearly naked, and totally alluring. She was lying quietly as though she had been waiting for me there for hours. I kissed her gently, beginning just below her navel and working my way slowly up her sleek body to her white bikini-top bra. I continued past her firm breasts as she sighed pleasurably. I kissed her neck, and cheeks, and ears. Her thick blonde eyebrows were irresistible so I kissed them, too, then slowly moved back downward, kissing her nose and cheeks again. She was breathing more heavily now. Her tongue was moving slowly over her parted lips, keeping them moist and luscious. By the time our lips met we were both in a state of ecstasy.

Jessica slid her hands to my chest, and moved me away from her at arm's length. Her watery blue eyes were opened wide and were looking deeply into mine as though inviting me to come along for a swim.

"Jason," she said softly. I looked back at her and saw the deep intensity in her eyes. "This is not some wild fling, and I am not a one-night stand. I'm here with you tonight because I care deeply for you. If you do not feel the same way about me, do the honorable thing and stop now. You will hurt me if you don't."

"Jess," I glanced at her hands on my chest. "It is you who has my heart in your hands," I answered honestly, returning her direct gaze.

Satisfied that I had understood what she was saying and had responded sincerely, she slowly relaxed her arms and lowered me back on top of her. Our lips met again. She wrapped her arms around me and pulled me closer. We kissed passionately, and returned, together, to the land of bliss.

∞

It was just before midnight when Jessica, out of breath and gasping for air, called out, "Enough!"

"Are you okay?" I asked.

"Okay?" she laughed. "I have never been better. Oh, my god! I didn't know it could feel so good. I'm exhausted, Jason. My whole body is tingling."

"I can take care of that," I answered, laughing quietly.

"All right, tiger," Jessica smiled. "I don't have an ounce of energy left. I need to sleep."

"If you go to sleep, then I need to take a shower because you are too beautiful to resist."

"Oh, thank you," she said, both for the compliment and for honoring her plea for rest. "You had better make it a cold shower, Jason," she chuckled.

A cold shower it was. Every muscle in my body was tired, and the activity that caused it was worth every second. However, I needed a cold shower just to make sure that all of my body parts were still there and functioning properly. After I was reasonably sure, I returned to bed.

Breathing softly, Jessica reached out her hand to me contentedly and guided me back into bed next to her. We fell asleep in each other's arms.

« Chapter 31 »

THE WEATHER WAS COLD and blustery on Sunday morning, but I was warm and content waking up with Jessica's arms wrapped around me tightly. We both had smiles on our faces when we got out of bed. After I washed up, retrieved my scattered clothes and got dressed, Jessica pointed me to the kitchen.

"You have a lot of spent energy to replace, Jason," she said. "Why don't you find something for us to eat? Go ahead and start without me. I'm going to take a quick shower and will be there in a minute."

I stirred up a few eggs and made an omelet with some ham and mushrooms that I found in the refrigerator. I gathered some fresh fruit that I found on her countertop, put them in a bowl and set it on the kitchen table, and poured two glasses of orange juice. Jessica came into the kitchen wearing comfortable-looking pajamas, with her blond hair piled neatly on top of her head. She looked as fresh and radiant as ever.

She grabbed a few plates from the cupboard as I divided the omelet in two and set each half on a plate. Everything seemed so natural, as though we had been together for a long time.

"Mmm...this tastes good," Jessica said after taking a bite of the omelet.

I smiled.

"I'm glad you like it," I said, feeling relaxed and comfortable in her presence.

We talked freely and easily, knowing that the last twenty-four hours had been incredible for both of us. Jessica was fully aware of the critical cases that I was absorbed in, and understood what I had to do.

"You need to get back to Pearl Lake, don't you?" she asked.

I nodded in reply.

Instead of begging me to stay, or making it difficult for me to leave, Jessica encouraged me to take care of the business at hand.

"Jason, I have no doubt that you will catch whoever did it. I have so much faith in you."

"I'm glad to hear that. I feel like I'm getting closer to breaking the case wide open. When you say you're sure I will catch whoever did it, I know you mean it. That means a lot to me."

"Well, you know where you can find me, Jason. If it takes too long, I know where I can find you. So go figure this thing out, and catch the bad guys!"

Jessica's can-do attitude raised my spirit and made me want to solve the crimes even more. Not that I needed any more incentive than I already had. I would not let a Pearl Lake murder go unsolved. If it turned out to be linked in any way to the museum robbery, as I suspected, then I would solve that case, too.

After a warm embrace and a lingering kiss that guaranteed I wouldn't forget her anytime soon, Jessica sent me on my way back to Pearl Lake and to the challenges that awaited me there.

∞

My car got whipped around as I drove north directly against the blustering wind. I had to grip the steering wheel tightly to keep the car from being pushed all over the road. Fall was definitely upon us, and today's weather was a reminder that winter was not far away.

I thought about my dream of Black Hawk and Miracle, the snow-white buffalo. Denby Sage had recommended I take some time to ponder each of the details of the events that have taken place over the past few weeks. He knew that I was racking my brain trying to find links to everything that had happened. Denby suggested that I try to look at each fact of the cases, and each detail in my dream, as separate events. I concentrated on keeping the car on the highway, listened to the steady rhythmic hum of the tires as they gripped the road, and thought back to the beginning of all the turmoil.

It all started with the phone call Tom Kaminski received at his house on the night the team visited the *Chicago Field Museum*. I recalled returning to the scene of the crime with Tom early that morning while he filled me in on the details of what had happened. I recalled the items in the museum that had been stolen, including the museum's once-permanent showcase gem, the yellow crystal of topaz. I thought about the Indian headdresses and other items from the Native American exhibition. I remembered the jewelry from the special exhibition, Marilyn Monroe's pearl necklace, the royal jewel and broach collection from around the world, and the *La Peregrina* necklace.

I recreated the conversations I had with the various people I thought may be involved in the crime: the museum guards, including *Kenny the guard*, Darnell Dawkins, Richard Bonline, Jack Trader, and a few others in Pearl Lake that had ties to Chicago. I replayed in my mind the details of the dream that I had about Miracle, Black Hawk, and the beautiful white buffalo woman, who in my mind was Jessica.

Finally, I recollected the events of the Pearl Lake murder. I thought about the shadowy figures that Chris Garrett saw on top of the Drake building roof, which led us to the dead body of Stanley Stone, who once again was from the Chicago area. I thought, admiringly, of the work done by the Madison Crime Forensics Squad and the Arrowhead County Crime Unit, first on the rooftop of the Drake building, and then at the Fox River after Mr. Stone's vehicle was recovered. I recalled the plethora of photographs that Chelsea Collins took at both of the crime scenes.

I got back to Pearl Lake and pulled my car into the parking space downtown in front of the Town Hall and Sheriff's Office. I was still quite relaxed and relatively content after being with Jessica. I did not come up with any enlightening answers to any of my questions during the drive back to Pearl Lake, but then I did not expect to. At least my mind was not muddled up with an overabundance of information when I entered the Sheriff's Office.   I had followed Denby Sage's advice and simply reviewed the facts of the cases without necessarily trying to tie each of them together. I felt completely rested and alert.

I sat down at my desk with a cup of coffee from the fresh-brewed pot I had just made. I thought of Jessica.   She was beautiful and intelligent, and I enjoyed being with her. My mind lingered on her, and I was in no hurry to push the pleasant memories out of my head. I recalled my recent memories of Jessica, working backwards in time from the amazing night and day we spent together yesterday, to the fun we had at the Fall Festival parade and carnival, to the football game in Janesville when we met, and further back to my dream in which she had transformed from a white buffalo into an exquisite woman.

I remembered when the buffalo and I had looked out together over the rolling hills. We saw the red haired warrior, Black Hawk, with his impressive headdress, and the feathered, multi-colored circular attachment that fell on his shoulders. It looked familiar. *I have seen that before somewhere else, besides in my dream*, I thought to myself. Could it have been when we walked through the *Chicago Field Museum's* Native American exhibition? No, that wasn't it. I knew I had seen it before, but not in the museum. I could see it clearly in my mind.

Dice. The picture of dice popped into my head. *What do dice have to do with it,* I asked myself?

Suddenly, it hit me.

Tom Kaminski had given me photographs of the items stolen from the *Chicago Field Museum.* I opened my desk drawer and pulled them out. Then I grabbed the large pile of photographs that Chelsea Collins had taken. I sorted through them until I came to the ones that were taken of Stanley Stone's vehicle after it was retrieved from the river. I set aside the photographs of the outside of the vehicle and the contents of the trunk. Finally, I came to the pictures that were taken inside the vehicle.

There it was. The picture of the red felt dice and what looked to be a dream catcher decoration hanging on the rear view mirror. I set the picture of the decoration in front of me on the desk. The decoration may still have been soggy from having recently been removed from the river, but it was not an ordinary dream catcher. It was an Indian headdress with three white and black feathers, and two circles of bright, colorful feathers and bejeweled adornments attached to it.

I looked again at the pictures from the *Chicago Field Museum* Native American exhibition, and pulled out a photograph of one of the headdresses that was stolen. I laid the photograph on the desk next to the photograph of the dream catcher decoration taken inside Stanley Stone's vehicle. They were identical. Even with the red felt dice partially covering the headdress in the vehicle, I was certain that the headdresses in both pictures were one and the same!

This was the first physical evidence that had turned up from the museum since the robbery. More importantly, it linked Stanley Stone to the museum crime. The headdress was a key piece of evidence that could potentially take us one step closer to solving both the museum robbery and the Pearl Lake murder.

My thoughts turned to some of the conversations I had had with various people in the Pearl Lake area since the museum robbery. For one reason or another, some of the things they said raised red flags of caution in the back of my mind. I needed to follow up on them. I was anxious to talk to Tom Kaminski, and breathed a sigh of relief when he immediately answered the telephone when I called.

"Hi Tom," I said. "I have some updated information for you. Do you have a minute?"

"I sure do. What do you have?"

I explained what I discovered.

"Jason, this could be the break we have been waiting for!"

"It could be, but we still have a lot of dots to connect before we have the full picture," I said cautiously.

"It's still a major breakthrough, Jason!" Tom said excitedly. "It's good timing, because I just got a piece of news that you will like hearing, too. With what you just told me, it's going to mean a lot more."

"What's that?"

"Stanley Stone worked for an electrical contracting firm two years ago. It was the same firm that the *Chicago Field Museum* hired to update their security system. We checked their work records. Mr. Stone was part of the crew that did the work on the security system at the museum."

I nodded to myself. It was all starting to come together now.

"Stanley Stone switched jobs about a year ago," Tom continued. "That's why it took us a while to find the connection."

"That's great detective work, Tom!"

"Perry Williams deserves all of the credit," Tom said. "He is the one that uncovered it."

"You are humble, as always. This could mean that Mr. Stone was killed because of his involvement, to whatever degree, with the museum."

"Now, let me get this straight," Tom repeated the information for clarification. "Stanley Stone, who worked on the *Chicago Field Museum's* security system a few years ago, was found murdered in Pearl Lake, of all places. His car was dumped, we assume by the murderer, in the Fox River. When his car was retrieved from the river, it was discovered that a Native American headdress stolen from the museum in the robbery was in the vehicle." He hesitated. "Do you think that someone could be framing him?"

"No, not really," I answered. "Stanley Stone had in-depth knowledge of the museum and its security system. I believe he was involved in the robbery. To the best of our knowledge, the robbers have been very cautious about not letting any of the loot get out of their hands. Stone's killer must not have known that the Native American headdress from the robbery was inside the vehicle. He certainly would have removed it if he had."

"Yes, he would have," Tom said.

"The most important thing right now is that we find whoever killed Mr. Stone."

"Right," Tom agreed. "His killer is very likely to be the person behind the whole museum robbery. Murdering Stanley Stone in Pearl Lake surrounded by thousands of people was an extremely bold move. The murderer must think we are getting closer to finding him. He could be getting desperate now. Maybe we are closer to solving these crimes than we think, Jason."

"I think we are close, Tom – extremely close. I have an idea that might shake things up a little bit, but I'll need your help. How soon can you get here?"

I talked to Tom again about my suspicions that there was an individual, or individuals, in the Pearl Lake area that were involved in the crimes. I explained to him what I wanted to do.

"Even though it might only have a slight chance of succeeding, it would be taking a big risk," I cautioned. "But there are steps we can take to minimize the risks."

"If it leads us to the killer, then I think it's an option we should seriously consider," Tom stated.

"Then I have to get moving to set up everything."

"I need to make some calls, too," Tom said. "I'll arrange to get a search warrant for Mr. Stone's house. With the evidence we have, I wouldn't expect there to be any problems with that. I should be able to get to Pearl Lake around one o'clock this afternoon. Will that be okay?"

"That will work," I replied. "Remember, our poker game is on for tonight at six o'clock at my place. Bruiser, Bob Colgate, and Steve Dozier should all be there. It would be great if you could join us again, too."

"If everything goes according to plan, I'll be there. Our poker games are always fun, and I'm sure this one will be as entertaining as ever! I've got to run. I'll see you in a few hours."

"Okay. See you later, Tom."

"Jason," he added, "that was a great job in discovering that the dream catcher decoration from Stanley Stone's vehicle was actually the Native American headdress missing from the museum. You said all along that the answer was right in front of us. I still can't believe you figured it out. I'm going to start calling you 'Mr. Instinct'."

"Thanks, Tom, but we have a lot of work ahead of us yet."

My 'instinct' was telling me that tremendous danger still lurked around the corner.

« Chapter 32 »

I HUNG UP THE TELEPHONE after talking with Tom, and immediately called Steve Dozier.

"Hello," Steve's wife, Debbie, answered the telephone.

"Good morning, Debbie. How are you today?"

"Oh, good morning, Jason. I'm doing just fine. How are you?"

"I'm hanging in there," I said. "Is the old work horse available?"

"If you're talking about Thurston, he's still in the barn," Debbie answered. Thurston was one of their pet horses. "But if you are talking about Steve," Debbie continued, giggling, "he's right here."

"I guess I'll have to talk to Steve then," I replied, smiling to myself. "Thanks, Debbie."

I could hear her in the background telling Steve that I was on the line as she handed him the phone.

"Hello, Jason."

"Hi, Steve. Would you mind if I stopped over to pay you a quick visit? I'd like to talk to you about something, but I'd rather not talk about it on the telephone."

"Of course you can. Is everything alright?"

"Yeah, everything is okay, Steve. I'll be there in a few minutes. I'll explain everything to you when I get there."

All was quiet at the Dozier corral when I arrived. Steve opened the front door before I had a chance to knock. He led me into the kitchen where Debbie was busy baking what smelled like apple pie.

"Something smells pretty good in here," I said to Debbie.

"Oh, it's just a few apple pies," she answered modestly.

"*Just* apple pies," I exclaimed. "Debbie, you make absolutely the best apple pies in Arrowhead County. I believe you have quite a few Blue Ribbons for taking First Place at the County Fairs over the years to prove it!"

"That's very nice of you to say, Jason. They should be ready to come out of the oven in a few minutes. They will probably still be too hot to eat for a while, though. If you would like, I can pack you a piece to bring home with you."

"I won't argue with you, Debbie. That would be great!"

Steve noticed me looking around and listening, trying to determine whether anyone else was in the house. He realized that I was checking to make sure that no one else would hear our conversation.

"Bart and Andrew are out on the combine," he said. Combines are large harvesting machines that can cut, head, thresh, and clean corn and other grain in one operation as they are driven through the fields.

Modern farming had advanced quite a bit from the old days. Crops used to be harvested one stage at a time. They used to be cut first. Then they were threshed to separate the seed or grain from the plant. Finally, during the last stage they were cleaned. Now a combine can do everything all at once, and do it several times faster than the previous farming methods.

However, combines can cost several hundred thousand dollars; far more than the average American home costs today. It made me appreciate Steve's ability to manage the costs involved in investing in combines and other modern farm machinery. It helped him survive the ups and downs that come with the business, and was part of what made him a successful, profitable farmer.

"We still have over forty percent of our corn crop standing in the fields," Steve explained, "so we need to keep getting it in whenever we get a chance."

"I understand," I said. "You have to take advantage of the good, dry weather while it's here."

"That's for sure."

"Is Brandon home?" I asked.

"No. He is over at Chris Garrett's house with the guys playing video games. My dad is out in the barn with his special helper, Sara," he said, referring to their eight-year-old daughter. "They are futzing around with some piece of farm equipment or another."

I smiled and turned to look at Debbie.

"How is Brandon doing?" I asked.

"He was quite shaken up by what happened during the parade even though he wasn't the one who saw it," Debbie answered. "He settled down after you talked to him, though. Brandon really trusts you, Jason."

"Actually, that's why I'm here. I wanted to talk to you about something in relation to the murder," I said, satisfied that I would be talking to Steve and Debbie in confidence. "I think I know who is responsible for committing the crimes."

"That's great!" Steve said.

I shook my head.

"Not yet. I can't prove it." I sighed, looking at them closely to gauge their reaction to what I was about to tell them. "I would like to try something, but I need your okay first. In order to carry it out I would need your absolute trust. I won't do it unless I have it."

Without revealing any confidential aspects of the cases, I carefully explained what I wanted to do. I spelled out all of the specific details of my plan, and brought up all of the possibilities of what could happen as a result of seeing it through. They asked me several questions to make sure they understood everything. In the end, they gave me their shared vote of approval.

"You've got our full support," Steve said as Debbie nodded in agreement.

"Jason," she said, "I'm sure that you would never do anything that would put us in danger. If you think this will help catch the Pearl Lake murderer, then we will do what we can to help."

She had already placed the dreaded 'Pearl Lake murderer' label on the crime, which strengthened my resolve. I didn't want to hear anyone say those words again.

"We have complete confidence in you, Jason," Steve said. "It's a carefully thought out plan. I hope it works!"

"Then let's give it a try," I said. "I know this will be a big hassle for you. I can't thank you enough."

"As Debbie said, Jason," Steve added, "if this will help you catch a killer, then we're behind you all the way."

I stayed for a while longer as we talked about more enjoyable subjects such as the weather, this year's corn crop, and football. Luckily, the apple pies had come out of the oven and had cooled off enough for me to have some right away. Debbie insisted that I try a piece while it was still fresh. I was more than glad to oblige.

"Yum..." I audibly expressed my pleasure as I finished the last bite, while Steve and Debbie chuckled. "It was delicious, as always, Debbie. Thank you."

"Any time, Jason. It's always nice to see you enjoy my apple pie."

"I'll need to run one hundred miles on the treadmill to work it off, but it was worth it," I said. I turned to look at Steve. "We have a lot of work to do to get prepared. I'll be back here around three o'clock this afternoon to pick you up. That should give you enough time to get everything ready on your end. We should be just in time to get to the *Pearl Lake Pub* to catch the 3:15 p.m. Packer game kick-off. Remember, the poker game at my house will start around seven o'clock tonight."

"I'll be ready," Steve said.

Debbie displayed a brave smile that couldn't quite hide her apprehension as I left. I was looking to trap a murderer, after all, and animals, as well as humans, can be very dangerous when they are cornered or trapped. But my plan was a solid one, and I was confident it would be carried out safely without the Dozier's or anyone else getting hurt. I had better not be wrong. The lives of my closest friends were at stake.

« Chapter 33 »

"HI, STEVE. HI, SHERIFF Jason," Candy greeted Steve Dozier and me with a wide smile from behind the bar at the *Pearl Lake Pub* as we entered. She was wearing a very low cut sweater, and a necklace with a large heart-shaped gold pendant that rested smack dab between her breasts. I didn't mean to look, but with her breasts spilling over the top of her sweater and her shiny gold pendant flashing like a lighthouse beacon, it seemed that all of nature's forces were directing one's attention to that specific location. *She really does have nice eyes and a pretty smile*, I thought, as I redirected my focus on them.

Steve and I exchanged greetings with Candy and the other familiar faces in the bar. It looked like the regular crowd was all there. I waved at Harry Wilson, firmly planted in his usual spot at the other end of the bar.

I looked around the bar and quickly assessed the crowd. There were a few dozen patrons interspersed throughout the bar and at the few tables on the right side of the bar.

John and Barbara Drake were eating at one of the tables. I didn't want to interrupt them, but John noticed me when I walked in and beckoned me to their table.

"Hello John, Barbara," I greeted them both. "Don't let me disturb you while you're eating."

"Nonsense," Barbara said. "It's always good to see you, Jason. We usually stay home to watch the

Packer games, but John likes the prime rib sandwiches here so we thought we would stop in for a bite to eat and watch the game for a while."

"How are you doing?" John asked me, in between bites.

"Good," I answered. "How about you?"

"We're both doing much better," John answered. "The shock of the murder has worn off a little, but it's still scary to think of what happened on our property while we were right out front at the time."

"You, and about a thousand other people," I added.

Barbara and John both appeared to be doing better than when I last saw them, when they were still visibly shaken up. It was obvious that they were anxious for the murder to be solved, as were the rest of the people in Pearl Lake and the surrounding area. As long as the crime remained unsolved there would always be a sense of insecurity amongst the Pearl Lake residents.

"Enjoy the game, and your sandwiches," I said as I moved back towards the bar.

They each nodded in appreciation, and continued eating.

Dan Abrahm's son, Rod, and his wife, Cindy, were sitting at the bar with a group of people from Pearl Lake. They were all wearing their green and gold Packer jerseys and sweatshirts, and were watching the television, ready for the game to begin.

Steve and I talked to them briefly, then worked our way to a few empty seats at the bar next to Jack Trader and a few of his friends from the area.

"Howdy, Sheriff," Jack piped up when he saw me. "What brings you out today? We don't usually see you in here during Packer games."

"Hello, Jack. A little change of scenery is good once in a while, isn't it?"

"I'd think you could find a little better scenery than here," Jack said sarcastically, just as Candy leaned over the bar and asked what we would like to drink.

Steve turned to me. "The scenery looks pretty good to me," he said quietly.

Unfortunately, Candy picked up on what Jack had said.

"Yeah, what are we doing in Pearl Lake anyway?" she complained as she returned with our drinks.

Jack jumped on the bandwagon. "We could be someplace nice, like Florida or Arizona where the weather is warm all the time."

"It's so boring here," Candy griped. "Nothing ever happens in Pearl Lake."

"That's for sure," Jack agreed. "When it does, it turns out to be a murd..." he caught himself before finishing the sentence, realizing that it might not be a good comment to make with me sitting right next to him.

I thought of the many good things about Pearl Lake: friendly people, neighbors that looked out for each other, four seasons that each brought plenty of activities like hunting, fishing, swimming, water skiing, snowmobiling, and even some pretty good downhill snow skiing nearby. There were also talented local theatre troupes that performed throughout the year, and music festivals and art fairs held in the summertime. *There are no hurricanes, either*, I thought, thinking of Florida.

"Pearl Lake is perfect for someone like me who prefers living in a small town, and who hunts and fishes and enjoys the four seasons," I said simply.

Steve nodded in agreement. "Jack, you lived in Chicago over forty years, didn't you?" he asked. "You could have gone anywhere, or even stayed in Chicago. How come you moved here?"

"I have to admit," Jack answered begrudgingly, "it was getting pretty rough living in Chicago. The crime and traffic and everything were getting to be pretty bad."

I knew by talking to Tom Kaminski that Jack had gotten into some minor scrapes with the law over the years when he lived in Chicago. Tom and I had checked his record as a part of our current crime investigations. The incidents Jack had been involved in were mainly disorderly conduct charges from a few fights he had gotten into. Other than that, the most serious offense was a possession of stolen property charge, 'the stuff just fell off the back of a truck' kind of thing.

It was probably a good move by Jack to get out of Chicago when he did, before he could get into any more serious trouble. Although it's possible that he could have been getting into trouble here in Pearl Lake, unnoticed. I'd keep my eye on him.

"Well, we hardly ever have any crime in Pearl Lake, and we sure don't have any traffic," Candy said.

"No, I don't have to worry about any of that now," Jack admitted, "and there is plenty of carpenter work and other odd jobs around town to keep me busy."

At least for the time being, Jack looked convinced that Pearl Lake wasn't so bad, after all. He had quieted down anyway, so Steve and I continued talking and watching the football game, and Candy went about her business lifting the spirits of the people in the bar, and serving them, too.

The *Pearl Lake Pub* turned out to be a pretty happy place over the next few hours. The Green Bay Packers had a comfortable lead over the Tampa Bay Buccaneers at half time, and the crowd was content.

Steve jumped when his cell phone began ringing.

"Hello," he answered. After listening for a few seconds, a worried expression appeared on his face. "Is he okay?"

Jack Trader, Candy, and everyone within hearing distance listened with curiosity as he talked.

"What happened?" Steve's voice trailed off as he stood up from his seat and walked out of the pub so he could continue to talk in private without disturbing anyone.

He returned to the bar a moment later with a look of relief on his face, and sat back down next to me.

"Is everything all right?" I asked.

"I guess so," he answered, breathing a sigh of relief. "That was Debbie. Her brother, Tim, was in a car accident. She said he's doing okay, but he fractured his leg and is scheduled to go into surgery tomorrow to get it repaired. It's a routine surgery, so his doctor said there is very little risk of any complications. They live in Appleton, and he is in a hospital there. Our families are both pretty close so Debbie would like to go there tomorrow to be with his family."

"Do you know what kind of surgery he's going to have?" I asked.

"It sounds like his fibula and other bones between his knee and ankle were pretty much shattered," he explained. "I didn't get all of the details, but the doctor is going to put a temporary rod in his leg to keep it stable and to help it heal. Tim said that with rehab, there is a very good chance that his leg will totally heal and return to normal."

"That's good news, anyway," I said.

"It could have been worse, I suppose," Steve admitted.

"Is there anything I can do to help?"

"No thanks, Jason. I think all of the necessary arrangements have been made. I talked with Debbie and my dad about it on the phone. Our family is going to Appleton to visit Tim and his family. Debbie hasn't seen him and his family for several months, so even though this isn't the best of circumstances she wanted to go."

"What about the farm chores?"

"We've got it all figured out. Bart, Andrew, Brandon and I need to get up a little earlier than usual to get the cows milked. I'll stay behind to finish feeding all of the animals while the rest of the family goes to visit Tim and his family. There are enough chores to do in the barn that I'll have plenty to keep me busy. Luckily, school is going to be closed tomorrow for a Teacher's Conference, so the kids won't be missing any school time."

"How long will Debbie and the family be in Appleton?" I asked.

"They'll stay long enough to be sure that the surgery went well and Tim is okay. They don't keep anyone in hospitals very long any more. According to the doctor, Tim will probably get released from the hospital tomorrow. If all goes well, Debbie and the family will get back home sometime tomorrow night."

"You're sure you'll be okay for the day?" I asked.

"Oh, it's no sweat. I can handle it," Steve said, unconcerned.

"Is everything okay here?" Candy asked as she returned to our side of the bar.

Jack Trader answered, filling her in on the story. "Steve's brother-in-law broke his leg. He's okay, but he'll need surgery to repair the damage. Debbie and the rest of the family are going to visit him in Appleton tomorrow while Steve stays back to take care of the farm."

"Oh, that's good," Candy said. "I mean," she clarified, "are your drinks okay? Would you like anything else to drink?"

Steve and I looked at each other and chuckled.

"No thanks, Candy," I answered. "We have to get going now."

"Besides, it looks like the Packers don't need our help anymore," Steve said, apparently believing that rooting for the Packers while watching them on TV had a positive impact on their performance. The football game was nearly over, and the Packers were still winning by a wide margin.

"Okay. Thank you so much for stopping in. It was nice seeing you both again," Candy said as Steve and I stood up to leave.

"Eye Candy..." Steve's voice trailed off. "Oops. Freudian slip," he whispered to me. "*Bye*, Candy," he said. "Have a good night."

"Good night, Candy," I said, smiling. "It was good to see you again, too."

« Chapter 34 »

"HERE WE ARE AGAIN, boys," Bruiser said contentedly as he dealt the cards around the table.

Bruiser, Bob Colgate, Steve Dozier, Tom Kaminski, and I sat comfortably at the table on my screened-in porch. The glass windows were closed, covering the screens and helping to keep the fall's ever-descending temperatures outside. The fire was blazing in the porch fireplace, and the dry wood was crackling softly as it burned, warming the room comfortably.

"I was running low on money, so it's about time that we played cards again," Tom taunted us.

"You'll have to wait for another night," Steve responded. "I'm feeling lucky tonight."

We laughed as each of us in turn chimed in to convince the others that we were going to be the winner at the end of the night. We all knew that our poker games were very low-stake events. If any one of us ended up winning or losing twenty bucks by the time we were done playing, that would be a lot.

"You guys had a great season," Bruiser said to Steve, Bob and me.

"It was a good group of kids," Steve answered. "They were fun to coach."

"You did a good job coaching the linemen, Steve," Bruiser said. "They seemed to control the line of scrimmage during the games I saw."

"We stuck to teaching the fundamentals and the kids did a good job with it. They were a very coach-able bunch," Steve said.

"It looked like it," Bruiser agreed, as he retrieved the pile of poker chips from the middle of the table after winning the first card game. "The fundamentals you taught them will come in handy when they play on our varsity team."

"We had some talent to work with," I added. "Jacob and Matt both really improved this season. Steve, I think that Brandon developed more than any of our linemen this year."

"Yes," Steve chuckled. "I would swear that he gained ten pounds during the season."

"You know what I mean. I don't mean developed *size-wise*, I mean *talent-wise*. He played well this year."

"Thanks. He had a lot of fun playing this year," Steve said. "Bob, you had some defensive players that really had a good season. Eli O'Connell really came along this year, didn't he?"

"When we opened up the clam, we found a pearl," Bob answered, agreeing that Eli's performance was a pleasant surprise. "Coming in such a small package, he made quite a few good plays."

"Jason," Steve said, "I'd have to say that your boy, Chris Garrett, was the most valuable player on the team this year."

I smiled. "We had a lot of good players this season," I said. "Brandon did a great job on the line, Eli made quite an impact on defense, and Devon Dawkins was impressive in the last half of the season."

"Yes, he was," Steve agreed, "but Chris had an outstanding year. He made so many spectacular plays it was unbelievable. He really helped pull the team together off the field, too."

It was good to hear that the other coaches recognized all of the things Chris had done to help the team this season. He was a good kid, and everyone knew that I was proud of him.

"Tom, it's good that you could get up to Pearl Lake considering everything you have going on in Chicago," Steve said.

Tom laughed. "Why? Just so you can take my money?" he asked good-naturedly as he watched Steve rake in his newly acquired poker chips from his winning hand. "No, really," Tom said seriously, "it's good to get away from Chicago for a while. It helps clear my head a little bit, if nothing else."

"It must be all of this fresh Wisconsin dairy-air," Bruiser suggested.

"That's for sure," Tom laughed. "The fresh air, and the good company, of course."

"Aw...that is such a nice thing to say," Steve ribbed him. "It doesn't get any better than this, does it?" Steve commented, looking out the windows as the lights from the houses around the lake reflected on the water.

"I'm glad you had the card game tonight, Jason," Bruiser said. "I was afraid you wouldn't have it with everything going on with the *Chicago Field Museum* robbery and the Pearl Lake murder."

"We've been putting in quite a few long days and nights, so it helps to take a break once in a while," I answered. "Even when we're not officially working, we still have our minds on the cases. Don't you think so, Tom?"

"That's true," Tom agreed.

"How are your cases going anyway?" Bob asked.

"Pretty good, although it can be a tedious process sometimes," Tom answered, shaking his head. "Everyone always wants major crimes like the *Field Museum* robbery solved immediately. Unfortunately, it doesn't usually work out that way. There is so much information to check out that it just takes time."

"How about the Pearl Lake murder, Jason?" Bob inquired. "The gossip around town is that someone witnessed the shooting."

"There is someone, but I really can't say who. We're hopeful he can help in the case, though," I said before looking over at Steve. "Steve, we're lucky you could make it tonight, too."

"What do you have going on, Steve?" Tom Kaminski asked.

"It's nothing as dramatic as what you and Jason are going through," Steve answered. "Debbie's brother, Tim, was in a car accident and is going to have surgery on his leg tomorrow. Our family is going to Appleton for the day to visit him in the hospital. Everyone except me. I'm going to stay home to mind the farm. Tim should be okay, but Debbie and the family wanted to go to be with their family."

"They're just going for the day?" Tom asked.

"Yeah, they're going to get an early start tomorrow morning, spend the day in Appleton with Tim and his family, and get back to Pearl Lake tomorrow night. We can't afford for them to be away too long. There's still a lot of work to do on the farm."

"I'm sorry to hear about the accident," Bruiser said. "I'm sure Debbie's brother and his family will be glad to see your family, though."

"They will," Steve answered. "By the way," he added as he scooped up the poker chips from another winning hand, "thank you for helping with the gas money for their trip." The rest of us groaned after involuntarily contributing to his travel fund.

"Hey, what's going on with you tonight, Jason?" Bruiser asked, looking at me with a sly grin on his face.

"What?" I asked.

"Are you down tonight?" Tom continued with the line of questioning, referring to my losses from the card game.

I looked at the dwindling stack of poker chips in front of me, and it finally dawned on me what they were getting at.

"You don't ever lose when we play cards, Jason. What's wrong with you?" Bruiser asked, rubbing it in.

"Come on. Isn't it obvious?" I answered. "I have to let you win once in a while or you won't ever come back to play cards again."

"No, that's not it," Steve said, persisting. "What happened to your favorite phrase 'Lucky in cards – unlucky in love'? By god, I think your luck may have changed, Jason! Which means our luck might have changed, too, guys. I think Jason may have found true love, and now he is *unlucky* at cards."

They all joined in with a mixture of disbelief, encouragement, and sympathy regarding the possibility that I may have met a woman that could put up with me. But I didn't disagree with Steve's assessment.

"Hey, I've only known Jessica for a few weeks. That barely gives her enough time to get tired of looking at my ugly mug, much less enough time to signify that we've reached a *true love* stage," I insisted, although I had to admit that my explanation didn't sound too convincing.

"Right. Your ugly mug, Jason?" Bruiser quipped. "Give me a break. Then why do all the women think you've stepped right out of '*GQ*' whenever they see you?" The rest of the group around the table all nodded their heads, registering their agreement.

I didn't know what they were talking about, but I rephrased the saying to myself as I thought of Jessica Donovan: '*Unlucky* in cards – *lucky* in love'.

That has a ring to it, I thought. Yeah, I can definitely live with that.

« Chapter 35 »

I WAS STAKED OUT inside Dozier's barn the next morning, as planned. Standing just inside the big, open square front barn door, I was plugging my nose, holding my breath, and doing everything I could to prevent the ripe smell of fresh manure from permeating my nostrils. Even though the odor was so intense that my eyes were watering, I had a clear view of the entire driveway, from the road to the barn.

Arrowhead County Sheriff Bill Larson looked at me out of the corner of one of the windows on Dozier's house. The window was directly across the driveway from the spot where I was stationed inside the barn, about thirty yards away from him. He raised his hand slightly, acknowledging our visual contact.

"Test one," I spoke softly into the wireless transmitter that was clipped onto my coat collar.

"Got you, one," I heard Bill reply clearly through the tiny receiver in my ear as he backed up from the window, out of sight.

"Acknowledge, one," I heard Tom Kaminski respond through my earpiece.

We each, in turn, spoke into our transmitters and replied to each other to verify that our communication system was working.

I turned around and looked at Tom standing at the back of the barn by the back door. I chuckled to myself as I watched him quietly jumping up and down in place in an effort to keep warm. Even though it may have been a little warmer inside the barn where Tom and I were stationed, the outside temperature was around 39°, so to say it was freezing would not be much of an exaggeration. All of the farmers I know around town, the Dozier's included, breathe in the air in their barns and claim that it is the cleanest, purest, most invigorating air on earth. Maybe that's true, but standing inside the barn and seeing and smelling the steaming piles of fresh cow dung plopped everywhere, I would have to respectfully disagree.

I could think of many other scents such as wood burning in a fireplace, anything cooking on a grill, cream puffs and food at the carnival, leather on a fresh-oiled baseball glove, or the fresh, alluring scent of Jessica Donovan, that I would prefer over this 'stimulating' barnyard air. Standing amidst the farm-fresh fertilizer now, it was difficult to imagine smelling anything else.

The Dozier family had departed in their car around eight o'clock in the morning. However, unlike the announced plan that called for Steve to stay behind and tend the farm while the rest of the family was away, he gladly joined them in the car and left with them on the trip to Appleton. Several plainclothes police officers driving in two unmarked police vehicles met them when they were safely on the main road a few blocks from their house and were sure they had not been followed. From there the officers escorted them on their way to Appleton.

I had no proof, but I needed to follow up on my suspicion that there was an individual, or individuals, in Pearl Lake that were involved in the *Field Museum* robbery and Pearl Lake murder. I was lucky that Tom Kaminski and Bill Larson and the Arrowhead County Sheriff's Department trusted my instincts, even though

I had no solid evidence to support them this time around.

With their backing and the complete trust of the Dozier's, I was able to implement my plan to attempt to get the killer to reveal himself. Debbie's brother's unfortunate injury and upcoming surgery created an opportunity, and I took it. I had Steve innocently spread the word at the *Pearl Lake Pub* and around town that the rest of his family would be leaving the farm for a day, while he supposedly remained behind by himself to mind the farm. I knew it was a long-shot, but there was a chance that it could give the killer an incentive to make another move. Since he had made a few bold moves already, it was possible that he might do so again. It began with the brazen break-in and robbery at the *Chicago Field Museum*, and continued with the potentially related murder of a former *Field Museum* worker right here in downtown Pearl Lake.

My theory, which I had shared with Tom Kaminski and Bill Larson, was that the museum robbery and the Pearl Lake murder were both committed by someone from the Arrowhead County area, if not from Pearl Lake itself. The murderer did not plan on killing anyone during the museum robbery, but after the guard died later unexpectedly, either the murderer, or one of his cohorts became desperate in an attempt to keep from getting caught. When Stanley Stone, who I believed was one of the museum robbers, panicked and threatened to go to the authorities, the murderer killed him, too. There were just too many links to the Pearl Lake area for me to think that all of these events were purely coincidental.

Even though we did not tell the news media that someone witnessed the Pearl Lake shooting, I had heard the word going around town that there was a witness.   The person that was most frequently mentioned as the one to have seen it was...Steve Dozier. I had noticed that many of the people watching the parade around us saw Steve pointing to the rooftop when he was repeating to me what Chris had told him seconds before. Not once did I hear anyone say it was Chris Garrett that had witnessed the shooting. Based on these factors, boosted by the perpetuation of the rumors that Steve had witnessed the shooting, I thought it was very possible that the killer might take the bait.

It was logical, I believed, to think that if the murderer killed one of his cohorts to keep from getting caught, he might consider doing the same to Steve Dozier. It was a terrible, frightening thought, but it was plausible.

I'm involved in another chess match – another game of wits, I thought. But this time around, the theoretical chessboard was the Dozier farm instead of the Janesville football field as it was a few weeks ago. However, unlike the football game against Janesville, this was not a game. The stakes were much higher. This was a life or death situation.

I looked over at Dozier's house for what seemed like the five hundredth time this morning. There were no lights, sounds, or signs of activity coming from inside the house. Everything appeared normal as I glanced around the perimeter of the yard. There was a modicum of activity inside the barn. The lights were turned on, the cows were mooing, and occasionally, I could hear Thurston and the other horses whinnying in their stalls. The old radio inside the barn was barking out a rap song. It sounded like the radio was going to shatter into tiny pieces from the reverberations of each note of the bass guitar. Obviously, the Dozier boys won out on what station the radio was turned to since it was not playing the oldies music that Steve preferred. I walked quietly to the radio and turned the volume dial to an audible level that would not damage my eardrums, or those of the poor animals in the barn. They probably preferred country music anyway.

Everything outside the barn looked and sounded like it was supposed to, with Steve supposedly working in the barn all by himself, while the rest of the Dozier family was miles away – if the news that was spread around town were to be believed.

Another hour passed...

...then two hours...

There was no activity whatsoever on the farm. I turned around and looked at Tom at the back of the barn. Apparently, his body had adjusted to the cold temperature since he was no longer jumping up and down. He was leaning against a wooden support beam, looking out one of the back barn windows.

Sheriff Larson pulled back the edge of the window curtain slightly. Once again, he patiently acknowledged me with a brief wave of the hand.

What was I thinking? Yeah, the plan was one hell of a long-shot. In order to believe it would work I had made quite a few assumptions: that the murderer had ties to Pearl Lake in the first place; that he heard the word going around town that Steve Dozier had witnessed the shooting that took place on top of the Drake building; that the murderer would have heard, and believed, the rumor spread around town that except for Steve, the Dozier's would be out of town today; and finally, that the murderer would actually consider going after Steve if he was going to be at home alone. As every minute ticked off the clock, I thought I must be crazy to think that such a plan had even the remotest possibility of succeeding.

I knew all along that the odds the plan would work were very slim. *But why not try it*, I thought? At least I'm taking action in an attempt to make something positive happen. It was better than sitting around waiting for the killer to make his next move. After all, he had already killed two people. In his mind, what was one more, even though the target happened to be a well-respected, hard-working farmer?

My earpiece receiver crackled faintly with the sound of interference before I recognized Cheryl's voice from the county dispatch office.

"Base to four-four-one," she said softly. "Come in four-four-one."

"Four-four-one," I replied immediately.

"Just passing on confirmation that the package has arrived safely at its destination. Repeat – the package has arrived safely at its destination."

"Ten-four," I responded with relief. "Thank you, Cheryl."

"You're welcome. Good luck, Sheriff."

The Dozier family had arrived safely in Appleton, and were out of harm's way for the time-being. It was one less thing to worry about.

"That's good news," I spoke quietly into the transmitter.

Sheriff Larson pulled the window curtain open again and gave me the thumbs-up sign. "Ten-four," he acknowledged. "Now that we know the family is safe, with plenty of distance between us, we can concentrate all of our efforts right here on the Dozier Farm."

I turned around and looked at Tom standing at the back of the barn.

"Ten-four," Tom confirmed.

If something were going to happen here today, I would have thought it would have happened by now. Doubt crept back into my mind. The Dozier's were scheduled to get back home sometime in the early evening. If the killer was going to make a move it was likely to be well before then, I figured. The more time that passed, the less likelihood that my grand plan was going to come to fruition.

I peered out the barn door and gazed up at the mostly cloudy gray sky. Hundreds, if not thousands, of geese were flying by. They were flying low in the sky in several groups of v-shaped formations on their journey south. I sighed. It was another sign of the impending winter.

I tried not to stare too long at the geese that had filled the skies, as captivating as they were. I didn't want to become distracted from what I was here to do, although the geese generated more activity than anything else on the farm so far today.

The 'honk, honk, honking' of the geese echoed in the air as they continued to fly by, strangely accompanying the rap music still playing on the radio. They had the same beat, I chuckled to myself as I orchestrated the sounds together...

"I'm walking in the hood..." the radio rapped out, and the geese joined in, "honk-honk-honk, honk, honk."

"Doing what I should..." the radio rapped, and the geese reprised, "honk-honk-honk, honk, honk."

I shook my head and reprimanded myself. It was getting to be a long day. If my plan was going to have any chance of succeeding, I was going to have to keep my head in the game, not in the clouds.

I walked quickly to the radio, and turned the dial until I found a classic rock station.

Another hour went by...

I looked at my wristwatch. It read twelve o'clock on the button. I gazed out the barn door again. The sun, no longer totally obscured by the flock of geese flying overhead, was partially peeking through the still thick, cumulous clouds that covered the sky. The sun was nearly at its highest point in the sky, confirming that it was high noon for those of us small town country folk who were accustomed to utilizing the sun to tell the time.

I'm not going to give up, I thought to myself. Sheriff Bill Larson had backed me completely on this endeavor. Tom Kaminski trusted me. Steve Dozier and his entire family went way out of their way to support me in what could very well turn out to be a wild goose chase. I owed it to myself and to all of them to see this plan through to the very end. If nothing panned out, it wouldn't be for lack of trying.

Suddenly a vehicle turned in to the Dozier driveway and stopped momentarily at the edge of the road. I wasn't sure if it was just going to back up and turn around, but after pausing briefly it continued to slowly drive further into the driveway.

"Heads up," I spoke into the transmitter to alert Tom and Bill. "There is a vehicle coming in the driveway."

"Ten-four," Tom acknowledged.

"I see it," Bill confirmed.

I recognized the dark blue Cadillac as it got closer. I was not surprised, but I was disappointed. Very disappointed.

The car came to a stop mid-way between the barn and the house. Tom, Bill and I held our positions. There was still a small pile of corn about a foot high on the ground between the parked Cadillac and the open barn door.

Bob Colgate got out of the driver's side door and stood warily as he assessed the property. He glanced over at the house, which was still dark and quiet inside. He turned and looked inside the barn, directly at the area where I was standing motionlessly. I had backed up a few feet behind an unoccupied horse stall and was looking back at him through a narrow gap between the boards in the stall. I was sure he could not see me from where he was standing.

Cautiously, Bob stood still and continued to look into the barn as the animals stirred harmlessly. The lights inside the barn were still turned on, and a classic rock ballad was playing on the radio. Bob was looking and listening to determine whether anyone was inside the barn. Or more specifically, whether *Steve Dozier* was alone inside the barn, as he expected.

Bob quickly walked around the front of the car and opened up the passenger side door. "You can get out of the car now," he said to the passenger.

He reached inside and guided Chris Garrett out of the vehicle.

« Chapter 36 »

BOB COLGATE PLACED ONE hand on Chris's shoulder and held him firmly in place as they stood outside the Cadillac. Bob's other hand remained buried deep inside his jacket pocket.

"What's going on?" Chris asked Bob. "You told me that Brandon was here by himself and needed my help."

"Just stay right there and shut up!" Bob answered harshly.

Chris stood motionless, but I could see that he was alert. His eyes moved from the house to the barn and around the entire farmyard assessing his complete surroundings.

It was all starting to come together in my mind now. After the murderer shot Stanley Stone, he must have immediately looked down onto the street and seen Chris Garrett looking back up at him. Sadly, the murderer was Bob Colgate, and he wasn't going to take any more chances. He was going to make sure that anyone with even a remote possibility of identifying him as the rooftop shooter would not get the chance to do so. Obviously, it didn't matter to him who the witnesses were, or whether he knew them or not.

Bringing Chris Garrett to the Dozier farm was a clear act of desperation by Bob. It was a shocking confirmation of how deeply he had gotten himself into this mess. He had crossed the line from legal to illegal, from friend to foe, and from good to bad – or from good to evil. He was here to take care of Steve Dozier and

Chris Garrett, and I knew I had to take immediate action. I was convinced that Bob would take whatever measures he felt he needed to keep from getting caught. I was not going to let him take control of the situation.

"I've got to stop this," I spoke softly into my transmitter to Tom and Sheriff Larson.

"Hold on! I'll be right there," Sheriff Larson replied.

"Wait for me!" Tom called out.

This is not part of the plan, I thought to myself as I moved away from the empty stall inside the barn. If anything, I expected the murderer to come snoop around to see if he could find Steve Dozier on the property, alone and vulnerable. I did not expect him to show up with Chris in tow.

I slowly walked through the open front barn door, keeping my arms at my sides, in plain sight. I did not want to startle Bob, or to put Chris in any greater danger than he was in already.

How stupid could I have been, I asked myself? Based on the fact that Steve, and not Chris, was the only one rumored to have seen the shooting, I focused my efforts on protecting Steve and his family, making sure they were safe and out of the way. If Chris had looked up and seen the shooter on the roof, wasn't it equally as likely that the shooter may have looked down and seen Chris, too? Obviously, that's exactly what had happened. That's why Bob Colgate was here.

"What are you doing, Bob?" I asked, fighting to remain calm as I walked out of the barn.

Bob was totally surprised to see me standing at the entrance to the barn. His eyes darted nervously from the house to the barn and back again to me.

Obviously, Bob had heard the rumors that Steve Dozier and I had spread around town. He was expecting to find Steve in the barn, and no one else.

Quickly recovering from the initial shock, Bob took a few steps straight towards me. He stepped over the pile of corn with Chris still in his grasp, and removed his hand from his jacket pocket. It held a black .32 caliber handgun, the same caliber weapon that was used in the Pearl Lake rooftop murder.

I would much prefer to be shot with a tranquilizer dart like the ones used on the guards at the Chicago Field Museum, I thought, wishfully. But it didn't look like Bob would be open to much discussion on the topic at the moment.

Unfortunately, I was right.

Bob did not seem to be affected at all by finding me on the farm. He had a firm grip on the gun, which was pointed with a steady aim directly at Chris' head.

"Bob," I said quietly in an effort to keep him calm. "The game is over. Don't you see that?"

"I don't look good in orange," he said with a twisted smile on his face.

Whether he ended up wearing prison garb or not was the least of my concerns. I reached for the gun in my shoulder holster, making no effort to conceal the movement. I needed to get Bob's attention away from Chris. I wanted him to see me go for my gun.

He did. With a cold, steely look on his face, Bob pointed his gun straight at me. Without hesitation from about fifteen yards away, he pulled the trigger. The flash of searing pain as the bullet thudded into my chest was simultaneous with the flash of the gun. The entire right side of my body exploded in pain. My back actually hurt more than my chest, if that was possible.

The gunshot hit me with what felt like the force of a three hundred pound lineman. It spun me around as though I was not following the proper blocking techniques that I taught our football team. *Always coaching*, I thought to myself, ridiculously. *How do you coach against a bullet shot at you from fifteen yards away?*

I found myself facing the barn. My left arm was leaning unsteadily against the side of the barn. I turned my head around and looked over my right shoulder until I located Bob out of the corner of my eye. He still had a firm hold of Chris' shoulder with one hand, and on the .32 in his other hand, still aimed at me.

I needed to keep Bob's attention on me.

"Chris!" I called out firmly. It felt like someone had punched me in the stomach and had knocked the wind out of me. Gasping for air, I spoke to Chris as loudly as I could. "Run the counter play! Go!"

Chris was still frozen in shock after seeing me get shot, but he quickly understood what I wanted him to do. In a blaze of speed, he took one step to his right, in front of Bob, and quickly spun around to his left, pulling free from Bob's grip on his shoulder. It was a flawlessly executed counter move, just as we had practiced all season long. I smiled painfully with pride as I watched Chris sprint toward the Dozier house.

The second gunshot that whizzed past me was confirmation that Bob's attention was still focused on me. He had realized quickly that I was more of a threat to him than Chris. *Good*, I thought. *Good? What was I thinking?*

I felt as much as heard the steady stream of bullets whir by my ears as they hit the side of the barn in front of me. The wooden fragments pelted my face.

I couldn't seem to get my breath back. My legs felt like wet noodles, and could hardly hold me up any longer. I leaned more heavily against the barn for support.

The next few shots hit the barn inches from my ear, flinging another batch of wooden splinters into my face.

I jerked my head back reflexively from the flying debris and noticed the uneven pattern of bullet holes on the side of the barn. Fresh, deep red blood was splattered everywhere. Damn! My blood. It was amazing how vivid it was on top of the now well-faded coat of red paint on the barn. *Steve and the boys are definitely going to have to re-paint it now*, I thought regretfully.

Several connect-the-dot bullet holes directed my attention to a square metal box attached to the side of the barn, just within arm's reach. It was also covered with streaks of wet, bright red blood. There was a large yellow push-button on the metal box. My legs were giving way as I raised my left arm. My entire body felt weak.

Summoning all of the strength I had, I reached up and pushed the button.

The grain auger motor instantly lurched to a start behind me. I turned around to face Bob, but my legs could no longer hold me up. The last volley of bullets followed me on the way down, missing my head by inches as I slowly sank to the ground. I sat there, helplessly, leaning awkwardly against the barn.

Still standing on the small pile of corn directly on top of the grain auger, Bob was thrown off balance as the motor kicked into gear. He threw his arms up in the air trying to regain his balance. The gun flew from his hands.

Everything happened in a matter of seconds. Even though it may not have looked like it, Sheriff Larson knew that I could take care of myself. His main job right now was to make sure that nothing happened to Chris, and that's what he did. I watched as he briskly ushered Chris across the yard and safely into the house. He returned with his gun drawn, and cautiously approached Bob.

Tom Kaminski was just running out through the front barn door from his stakeout spot at the back of the barn. He paused briefly to assess the situation, then rushed to me when he saw me sitting down propped against the barn, covered in blood.

Bob's arms were now flailing, and his leg jerked as it was being tugged from beneath him. It was as though a shark was biting him and was attempting to pull him underwater to finish him off – albeit in a pool of corn kernels instead of water.

The first rotation of the powerful auger blade chopped off Bob's foot just above the ankle. It made a sickening crunch that sounded like a giant nutcracker. He let out a blood-curdling scream as the rapidly rotating blade swung around again and severed his leg below the knee.

Tom Kaminski looked above my head. He noticed the push-button for the auger through the splattered blood, and mercifully pushed it to turn it off. Everything became eerily silent. The grain auger was quiet, and Bob's screams ceased as the shock set in.

Sheriff Larson quickly kicked Bob's gun out of the way, and began tending to him as he talked to the Arrowhead County dispatcher on his transmitter to request ambulances. It was obvious that Bob Colgate had come here to kill Steve, and would have killed

Chris, too, and whomever else he had to in order to keep from getting caught. None of that mattered to Sheriff Larson now. His job was to protect people, not to hurt them, regardless of whether they were murderers or not, and he was carrying out his job.

Tom ripped off his jacket and pressed part of it firmly against the bullet wound on my chest. Then he wisely wrapped the rest of it around my right shoulder to my back, where he bunched it up, held it on the wound on my back, and leaned my body back in place against the barn to help hold the jacket/bandage in place.

"How are you doing?" he asked.

What a question, I thought, grateful that he was there. I mustered up as much of a smile as I could, and nodded weakly in response.

"Hold on," he said. "Help is on the way."

"Chris?" I inquired, barely audibly.

Tom called out to Sheriff Larson. "Is Chris alright?"

"Yeah, Chris is okay. He's safe inside the house. He wasn't hurt," Bill answered as he continued to administer aid to Bob Colgate. I was tremendously relieved to hear that Chris was safe.

"You're going to be okay, Jason," Tom said firmly. "You're too strong to let this get you."

I was glad he thought so, because I wasn't feeling quite so strong at the moment. I must have lost quite a bit of blood. I was sweating profusely, but then suddenly got so cold that it felt like the sweat was freezing to my body in a January blizzard. I was extremely tired, and started to feel very faint.

Then everything went black.

« Chapter 37 »

I VAGUELY REMEMBER WAKING up. Jessica was standing over me with tears flowing down her face, like water slowly meandering down a stream. Her hands were firmly wrapped around mine, and it seemed as though I was absorbing her warmth, if not her energy.

Even though the room was dark, I noticed that my entire family surrounded her. My brother and sister, Dave and Kimberly, and my dad and mom were sitting on chairs spread throughout the room. Tom Kaminski was perched on the window ledge on the side of the room.

Jessica smiled through her tears when she saw my eyes open. I tried to say something to her, but neither my mouth nor my brain seemed to be functioning properly. Even though the rest of my body was comfortably numb, when she kissed me the touch of her lips on mine sent a tingling sensation through me with the power of all five senses combined. Maybe it was all just a dream. My eyelids were too heavy to keep open, so I closed them and drifted back to sleep.

∞

It was my sense of smell that woke me up to the fresh powdery fragrance of sandalwood and jasmine a few hours later. The scent was musky, wholesome and clean. It was Jess. I opened my eyes and saw her sitting beside me, illuminated by rays of golden sunlight pouring into the room from the open window, rewarding my sense of sight with an enchanting vision.

The light added a polished look to her smooth ivory skin. *She is an angel, and I am surely in heaven*, I thought.

Jessica lifted my hand, gently placed it against her soft cheek, and moved it to her lips and kissed it. She then brought it to her heart and firmly held it there, awakening my sense of touch – the tingling, satisfying sense of touch.

"How are you doing, tough guy?" she asked after a few moments, confirming that my sense of hearing was intact.

I took a long, deep breath of fresh air and savored the *Essence of Jess*. She was so beautiful that she took my breath away when I gazed at her. I took a chance and continued to look at her, anyway.

"How could I be anything less than great with you here by my side?" I answered hoarsely. My throat was extremely parched and my tongue was still not in sync with my brain. "Is my family here?" I asked, glancing around the room.

"Not right now," she answered. "They were all here most of the night, and when you regained consciousness briefly around midnight. The doctor said you were past the most critical stage and the chances were very good that you would pull through. He said you just needed rest and sent them home to get some sleep, too. I called them a few minutes ago to let them know you were starting to wake up again. I'm sure they will be back in a few minutes."

"Have you been here all night?" I asked.

"U-huh," she nodded, "but I fell asleep a few times. I didn't do a very good job watching over you, did I?"

"I'm still here, aren't I?" I replied, smiling. "I knew you were here with me. Somehow, it felt like you were passing your energy on to me, like a battery charger re-charging my batteries."

"Hmm..." she nodded silently.

"I would rather have you by my side through all of this than anyone else," I said.

"That is so nice of you to say, Jason, but look at me!" she exclaimed. Tears welled up in her eyes. "I was so worried about you. I must be an absolute mess."

"You are the most beautiful woman I have ever laid eyes on, especially now."

"You must not be seeing things too clearly yet," she suggested. "The doctors said they have you on some pretty potent painkillers."

"That's easy for you to say," I said, chuckling quietly at the 'pretty potent painkillers' tongue twister. *Say that three times quickly*, I thought. "Actually, I'm seeing things surprisingly clear – crystal clear. I already know how I feel about you, Jessica. Even with the pain medication. You'll see."

∞

Tom Kaminski and my entire family returned to the hospital room a few minutes later. They were happy to see that I was awake, and were relieved that I seemed to be okay. After we talked quietly for a while, Tom apparently could see that I was lucid enough to fill me in on the details of what had happened after I lost consciousness at the Dozier Farm.

"It didn't take long for the two ambulances to arrive after Sheriff Larson called in," Tom explained. "Bob Colgate and you were both brought here to the Berlin Memorial Hospital yesterday after the incident.

They flew Bob to a Milwaukee hospital shortly after he got here. His left leg was severed just below the knee. The doctors in Milwaukee were considering performing reattachment surgery, but there was just too much damage to the leg. They were not able to do it. Otherwise, it sounds like he is going to make it. He'll survive, but I'm sure it will be a tough road to recovery for him."

"Especially in prison," Kimberly said, "where he belongs."

Everyone nodded in agreement.

"It was touch and go with you for a while. You lost so much blood," Tom said. "Once they gave you some blood your vital signs improved quickly. Even though you were wearing a bullet-proof vest, unfortunately the .32 caliber bullet just missed it. It struck you in the upper right chest near your shoulder, within an inch of the edge of your bullet-proof vest. The bullet passed through your body and out your back. The worst damage was caused by the exit wound. The bullet fractured your scapula, or shoulder blade, which is the flat bone on the upper back."

I listened quietly, taking it all in.

"After you were stabilized," Tom continued, "the doctors removed some bone fragments and repaired some of the muscle tissue in your back. Fortunately, they expect you to make a full recovery."

"You had quite a guardian angel," my father said to me as he nodded his head at Jessica. "She has hardly left your side since she got here yesterday afternoon."

"Well, I'm glad she's here," my mother said with a grateful smile on her face as she winked at Jessica. "She is all Jason has been talking about lately."

Everyone in the room nodded their heads in unison. Jessica turned to look at me, attempting to stifle the surprised expression on her face.

"I really didn't think I talked about her that much," I said innocently as I shook my head and shrugged my shoulders. "Ahh," I winced in pain at the slight movement of my right shoulder.

"Try not to move around so much," Jessica said softly as she placed her hand gently on the middle of my chest. "You need to give yourself a chance to start healing."

Right on cue, a tall, solid-looking, stern-faced nurse entered the room.

"Good morning," she said, solemnly, as she marched directly to my bedside. She quickly signed on to a computer terminal that was located on a bedside table, and absorbed the information that was displayed on the screen. Her strong fingers typed rapidly on the keyboard. The computer beeped so many times that I started to think she was playing a computer game. Before long she turned and checked out the readings on a separate monitor that had cords hooked up to my arms and chest. Judging from her sturdy physique, I figured that her nursing job must be just a part-time gig. Her full time job had to be pouring concrete with a construction crew or something like that. I didn't want to mess with her. Apparently reading my mind, she revealed a barely perceptible smile. As I looked at her, I noticed that the smile showed more in her eyes than on her face or lips. She flashed a lightning-fast wink at me.

"I'm glad to see you are still with us, Jason," she said quietly. "We weren't sure you were going to make it for a while there. You certainly are a fighter. How are you feeling?"

"Better, thank you."

The nurse looked at me closely, and nodded. She seemed to detect that I was still very tired. She glanced around the room, and the tough construction woman expression returned to her face.

"Okay," she announced firmly, "it's time to let our hero here get some rest. You can come back to see him again later."

Looks can be deceiving, I thought. Maybe it was better that she was a nurse. She was right. I was still feeling pretty drained. My eyelids were getting very heavy again. I closed my eyes, and felt Jessica's warm, sweet kiss on my lips. I fell back to sleep with a content smile on my face.

« Chapter 38 »

THE WORD ABOUT THE shooting at the Dozier farm on Monday spread quickly throughout the area. The news media flocked to Pearl Lake in droves, anxious to report the full *Showdown at the Dozier Corral* story, as they had dubbed it. *How quaint*, I thought. After slowly dwindling over the past two weeks, the attention on Pearl Lake had become intense again, much to the delight of the business owners in town. The stores and restaurants were crowded with customers, and the hotels and inns were fully booked. Everyone in Arrowhead County was relieved that the 'Pearl Lake murderer' had been caught.

It was Friday morning, just four days after the shooting. Hundreds of news reporters, television cameras, and onlookers surrounded me on Main Street in front of the Town Hall as I addressed the media – against doctor's advice.

"The alleged suspect, who we believe is responsible for the murder of Mr. Stanley Stone during the Fall Festival Parade in Pearl Lake, has been arrested and is in police custody," I announced. "His name is Mr. Robert Andrew Colgate."

Even though almost everyone had already heard the name of the culprit, there was an audible gasp from the crowd. They were still coming to grips with the harsh reality that someone from the area had committed such a cold, brutal murder in Pearl Lake.

"There are several aspects of this case that each seemed to take on a life of their own. They all eventually tie together and I will do my best to describe them to you." I paused momentarily, and took a deep breath as I looked back at the reporters and townsfolk that filled Main Street.

"Bob Colgate is currently the president and owner of Badger Finance Company, which is located a few miles away in Fond du Lac, Wisconsin," I explained. "Evidently, Mr. Colgate's business had not been doing very well lately and he began running into financial difficulties. Having been successful in business for many years, he had become accustomed to a high standard of living. Whether he became desperate, or greedy, or a combination of both, we believe the financial struggles pushed him to commit a daring robbery, which led to murder.

"Bob Colgate and the murder victim, Stanley Stone, were both originally from the Chicago area. As it turns out, they were old high school buddies. Bob Colgate knew that Stanley Stone had worked on the *Chicago Field Museum's* security system a few years ago. After talking with Stanley Stone a few times, Mr. Colgate came up with an idea that could potentially solve all of his financial problems at once. He decided to break into the museum.

"The total insured value of all the items that were stolen from the *Chicago Field Museum* ran into the hundreds of millions of dollars," I explained. "The news of the museum robbery had spread around the world instantly, and the stolen property became extremely hot. We do not believe Mr. Colgate had close connections to individuals or organizations where he could fence the goods. He found out that it was going to be very difficult to unload them quickly. Under the circumstances, the most he could have expected to receive on the black market was anywhere from five percent to twenty percent of the total insured value of the stolen property. That would have put a sellable value of the stolen merchandise in the range of $10 million to $40 million. Obviously, that is still a large sum of money. As far as Mr. Colgate was concerned, it was well worth the effort. After all, he had planned on waltzing into the museum and cleaning the place out in a matter of minutes without leaving a shred of evidence behind. That is, other than leaving a few guards with no more than headaches from the effects of being shot by tranquilizer darts.

"That was the plan," I continued. "Unfortunately, one of the museum guards died as a result of getting shot with a tranquilizer dart. That's when the major trouble ensued. Stanley Stone and Mr. Colgate's assistant at the finance company, who has also been implicated in the crime, both panicked with the realization that if they were caught they could be charged with murder. Stanley Stone was having a hard time sitting tight as Bob Colgate requested. Mr. Stone, still living in Chicago, needed to talk to Bob Colgate, but he didn't want to talk to him on the telephone. So Bob arranged for them to meet at a 'safe' location on the roof of the Drake Antique and Realty Shop in Pearl Lake during the Fall Festival Parade. They would be surrounded by thousands of people watching the parade. What could be safer than that, Stanley Stone figured? He was wrong."

I looked again at the crowd as they stood in stunned silence. They appeared to be listening intently, so I continued to describe what happened.

"When Bob Colgate talked to Stanley Stone on the Drake building roof, Stanley told Bob he was considering turning himself in to the authorities. He pleaded with Bob to do the same. Bob could see that Stanley was frightened to the point of panic. Bob Colgate had absolutely no intention of surrendering, but he knew that if Stanley Stone did, it would only be a matter of time before Stanley led the authorities to him. Bob was not ready for that to happen, so he shot and killed Mr. Stone."

The television cameras swung around to film the crowd that had gathered on Main Street to hear what had happened. Their eyes were focused on me as they stood quietly, still interested in hearing the rest of the details of the crime.

"Mr. Colgate," I continued, "did not think that he could be seen by anyone on the roof. However, after he shot Mr. Stone, he looked down on the street and noticed that some people, whose names cannot be released at this time, were looking up towards him on the roof. It was fairly dark on top of the roof, so Bob Colgate could not tell for sure whether they, or anyone else in the crowd, had actually seen him. If they did, he didn't know exactly how much they saw.

"After a few days of not hearing anything from the authorities or in the news about any potential suspects, his fears started to ease slightly. Yet he continued to hear persistent rumors that someone from town had witnessed the shooting. He just couldn't ignore the rumors, so when the opportunity presented itself, he decided to eliminate the possibility of the potential witness talking to the police."

I continued the press conference, explaining briefly what had happened on the Dozier Farm. Even though the news of the shooting was widespread, I hoped that Chris and Steve's names would stay relatively anonymous. Unfortunately, with all of the news reporters constantly in search of the inside scoop on such a sensational story, keeping their names anonymous, at least locally, would not likely happen.

Even with my arm held stationary in a sling, I noticed that I was beginning to involuntarily wince in pain from the bullet wound. Maybe it had been a little too soon to stop taking the pain medication. It was time to bring the press conference to a close.

"After he heard all of the evidence that had been gathered against him, Bob Colgate made a full confession to the authorities," I said, with the strength of my voice slowly fading. "Over the next several days you will hear more details of the crimes. In the meantime I wanted to let you know that the murderer is off the streets. I am confident that he will be brought to justice for the crimes he has committed.

"I would like to thank our Arrowhead County Sheriff, Bill Larson, the Arrowhead County Crime Unit and Sheriff's Department personnel, and the Madison Crime Forensics Squad for their tremendous support. Without the help of Detective Tom Kaminski and the Chicago PD, and Carole Grove and the Chicago CSI Team, this case would not have been solved," I turned around to look at Tom, "and I most certainly would not be here today to tell the story. Thank you, Tom."

Tom's freckled face turned crimson red, nearly matching his bright red hair. I had so few opportunities to embarrass him in public that I couldn't pass this one up. Despite his embarrassment, he nodded appreciatively to me in response.

Some people in the crowd came up to me after I was done speaking. They shook my one good hand, patted me on my injury-free shoulder, and congratulated me for my part in capturing the criminals. I could see some of the news reporters interviewing people from Pearl Lake to get their opinions about what had happened. Mr. Abrahm, God bless him, was saying to a reporter, "We are lucky to have Jason Avalon as our sheriff. Pearl Lake couldn't be in better hands. The way he solved this murder was absolutely incredible."

I smiled and thought, *I'm the lucky one – lucky to be alive, and lucky to live in Pearl Lake.*

« Chapter 39 »

FRIDAY AFTERNOON WAS SUNNY, calm, and peaceful. My house was filled with family and friends that had gathered together after the recent shocking events in Pearl Lake. Steve Dozier, Tom Kaminski, Eric Anders and I were sitting on the porch. As usual, the fireplace was crackling as it sent out waves of relaxing warmth throughout the house.

It was near the peak of the autumn season as far as fall colors go. I looked out the large porch windows at the panorama of Pearl Lake shimmering in the sunlight, and the surrounding rolling hills splashed in a cornucopia of colors. It looked like an artist had flung a paintbrush with multiple colors against a canvas and dabbed the colors into the scenery. The trees displayed the most vibrant greens, reds, yellows, oranges and purples imaginable.

The large French doors that led from the house to the porch were open, creating a wide-open living area from the porch to the kitchen and living room. My parents were sitting at the kitchen table talking with Debbie Dozier, Chris Garrett's grandparents, and Amy Kaminski with her daughter, Elizabeth, sitting on her lap. The table was covered with greeting cards, cookies, cakes and other dishes that were brought to the house by my neighbors, friends, and others from the Pearl Lake community. So many people stopped by to wish me well that there were too many to count.

My brother, Dave, and his wife, Barb, were gathered around the couch visiting with Jim 'Bruiser' Johnson, and LaRae Dawkins.

My sister Kimberly and one of her girlfriends were in the living room talking conspiratorially with Jessica. I watched as Kimberly reached over and gave Jessica a big hug. They were laughing and crying at the same time. When the three of them turned towards me and saw me looking at them, they turned back around with their arms around each other and giggled. *I will never understand women*, I thought. I smiled. It made me appreciate, admire, and love the women in my life all the more.

Chris, Brandon Dozier, Devon Dawkins, and my brother's two girls were sprawled out on the floor in the corner of the living room. They were all laughing as they played video games on multiple hand-held electronic devices.

I inhaled deeply, savoring the fresh autumn air as it filled my lungs. I was glad to be surrounded by the people I cared about the most. There were no guarantees in life, and I reminded myself to appreciate every moment I had with my family and friends.

Steve Dozier was looking at me curiously as we sat on the porch looking out the windows at Pearl Lake.

"I meant to ask you," he said. "How did you know that Stanley Stone was involved in the *Chicago Field Museum* robbery?"

"When Arrowhead County Police Officer Jennifer Erickson found his car in the river the day after the shooting, we came across a Native American headdress that linked Mr. Stone to the robbery," I answered.

"How in the world did you tie Bob Colgate to any of this?" Eric Anders chimed in. "I don't see anything that would have even remotely pointed you to him."

"I had been uneasy with some of the things that Bob said right from the time the museum robbery took place," I explained. "It didn't really hit me until later. First of all, he was constantly trying to get specific information about the robbery – way beyond what I thought was the curious stage. He kept asking how the guards were doing, and if we had any suspects. Even though I was telling him all along that I couldn't really talk about it, he kept prying."

"That wasn't really much to go on," Tom Kaminski added, "but I think that's when your gut instincts kicked-in. You mentioned to me a few times that you heard some comments from people in town that you thought meant more than they seemed to on the surface."

"You're right, Tom," I said. "For instance, that next day following the museum robbery, right after our football game against North Chicago, Bob mentioned he heard on the news that the museum guards had been shot with tranquilizer darts."

"But we never released to the media the fact that the museum guards were shot with *tranquilizer* guns," Tom Kaminski stated. "We said that they were shot, period. We never specified that they were hit by tranquilizer darts."

"That was a key piece of information, when it sunk in," I said. "At the time, I didn't know exactly what information you released to the media, Tom. It must have been over a week later when I confirmed it with you. There was no way Bob could have known that fact on the day following the robbery, unless he had been involved."

"So, at that point," Eric clarified, "you knew that the *Chicago Field Museum* robbery and the Pearl Lake murder were connected."

"I was ninety-nine percent sure, but I had no proof."

"It wasn't enough," Tom explained. "Jason told me later that the Arrowhead County district attorney told him he needed irrefutable evidence against Bob Colgate to make a strong case to convict him in a court of law. Luckily, Jason was already working on that."

"That's where Carole Grove and the Chicago Police Department CSI Team came in," I said. "When we got to the museum immediately after the robbery, Tom wisely asked the officers on the scene to expand the perimeter of the crime scene all the way around the building and out to the lake. The officers had initially cordoned off only the areas immediately surrounding the front and back entrances to the museum. Tom's decision to expand the area of the crime scene to the water turned out to be a smart move. Carole and her team found water spots on the pier right next to the museum. They were able to lift some wet footprints from inside the museum, as well as from the pier."

"We came to the conclusion that the burglars arrived and left the museum via boat, not by car or van as was previously assumed," Tom said.

"There were multiple traffic cameras in the blocks surrounding the museum. None of them picked up any vehicles at the time, other than the police vehicles and ambulances when they arrived," I added.

Tom looked at me, and continued. "That's when you asked me if Carole Grove could come to Pearl Lake, confidentially, to do some work on the case. By that time, Jason believed that Bob Colgate was the person we were after, but he didn't tell me or anyone else about his suspicions because we were both Bob's friends."

"I did not want to jump to conclusions or say anything if it turned out *not* to be true," I explained. "I knew how it might look to the media and to the public. With both Tom and I being Bob's friends, there are people who would automatically assume that we had something to do with the crimes, even though we didn't. We needed to have enough evidence to prove that we had absolutely no involvement in the crimes; none whatsoever."

"Unfortunately, that's true," Tom said. "It's guilt by association."

"I can understand that," Eric said, as Tom and Steve nodded.

"Suspecting that Bob was involved, I asked Carole Grove to come to Pearl Lake on the night of the Fall Festival Boat Parade," I continued. "I know how fast rumors can get started. If the word got out that someone from the Pearl Lake area was suspected of being involved in the *Field Museum* robbery, the news would have spread like wildfire, especially in a small town like Pearl Lake. I felt more comfortable asking Carole to come up here to collect evidence on Bob's boat, rather than asking our Arrowhead County Crime Unit to do it. I thought it would help minimize the risk of Bob finding out that he was being investigated."

"Bob Colgate has a nice, big boat," Tom continued. "You told me later that you believed there was a good chance it was his boat that was used to carry out the museum robbery."

"I did," I confirmed, "and it turned out to be true. Bob was conveniently in Chicago with the team for our football game that weekend. Evidently, he had arranged for his assistant at Badger Finance Company to take his boat to Sheboygan, put it in Lake Michigan, and drive it to Chicago. Bob and his old friend Stanley Stone met him there."

"You couldn't prove it, though," Tom stated.

"No," I replied, "but I knew that Bob had his boat entered in the Pearl Lake parade again this year, as usual. I figured he would probably leave it unattended with the rest of the boats for a short time after the boat parade finished. Bob did, in fact, leave his boat at the Red Rock Inn dock while he went downtown with everyone else to watch the 'land' parade. Since the boat had been docked and left unattended on a public pier, we were able to legally obtain evidence without having to get a search warrant. That left Carole and her CSI Team open to complete their work."

"That was a pretty shrewd move," Steve Dozier said. "Did they find anything?"

"They were able to photograph some footprint impressions on the boat," Tom answered, "but we had a major challenge. The footprints were barely perceptible when we looked at the photographs."

"Tom always tells me how good Carole Grove is. This next piece of evidence shows it," I said. "At the time, neither the footprints obtained at the *Chicago Field Museum,* nor the footprints taken on Bob's boat were substantial enough to prove that they were in any way related. However, Carole and her team had been working on a new three-dimensional technology that they thought could help in the case. They used the footprint photographs to make 3-D impressions of the traction patterns on the bottom of the shoes.

"Carole worked with the 3-D impressions tirelessly. Finally this past Tuesday, the day after the shooting at Dozier's farm, she figured it out. Utilizing their new 3-D technology, Carole was able to provide a positive match of the footprints from the pier outside of the museum, the footprints from inside the museum, and the footprints taken on Bob's boat after the 'boat' parade. By the way, the final footprint match was provided using Bob Colgate's shoe that was cut off along with his foot by the grain auger."

"Eew," Steve groaned.

"Ish," Eric said simultaneously, grimacing.

"Too much information," Tom informed me.

"Sorry," I nodded. "I guess it was."

"We have another significant piece of evidence now, too," Tom added. "The Arrowhead County Crime Unit performed a ballistics test on Bob Colgate's gun. The bullet that killed Stanley Stone, and the bullet that went through your chest, Jason," Tom pointed to my still sore but healing chest, "were both shot from that gun."

We sat silently on the porch, contemplating the recent events. I looked over at Eric, noticing that his eyebrows were furrowed and he was still deep in thought. He started to shake his head slightly as he looked back at me. I smiled and nodded back. Eric was extremely sharp – the sky-high *I.Q.* kind of smart. He realized there was still a missing piece to the puzzle.

"You have the evidence against Bob Colgate *now*," Eric said, "but you didn't get it until this Monday, or until Tuesday in the case of the footprint match. It's still very possible that you wouldn't have obtained the key evidence against him if he hadn't shown up at Dozier's farm. How did you get him to go there?"

Tom helped me out, and explained. "Jason, Steve, and I all spent some time talking to people around town. We wanted to find out exactly what the rumors were regarding there being a witness to the Pearl Lake shooting. Several people told us that they heard specifically that 'Steve Dozier' had seen the shooting. Other than that, all we heard was that 'somebody from town' may have witnessed the shooting."

"Everyone we talked to," Steve confirmed, "said they either heard generally that 'someone' saw it, or that 'I', Steve, was the one who saw it."

"The only specific name anyone ever mentioned was Steve's," Tom said. "By then the word was already out so there was really nothing we could do about it."

"Other than to try to take control of the situation," I added. "Bob Colgate was beginning to develop a pattern. When Stanley Stone became a threat, Bob killed him. Bob certainly heard the rumors spreading around town that someone, or Steve Dozier, may have witnessed the shooting. If Bob Colgate saw Steve as a threat, unfortunately, I believed that Bob would try to kill him, too."

Steve shuddered again at the thought, similar to how he and Debbie had reacted when I first explained the situation to them nearly a week ago in their kitchen.

"With Steve and his family's help, we led Bob Colgate to believe that Steve would be home alone at the farm during the day on Monday," I said.

"Ah-hah!" Eric nodded, immediately comprehending.

"But I actually left with my family, too," Steve said.

"It turned out to be an opportunity that Bob Colgate couldn't pass up," I said. "Up until that point, I had been holding on to a glimmer of hope that Bob Colgate wasn't the culprit. Seeing his car pull into Dozier's driveway confirmed my suspicions. In a way, I was also relieved. After waiting in Dozier's barn for several hours, I was beginning to think he wasn't going to take the bait. I wanted to finish this nasty business once and for all, for the Town of Pearl Lake, and especially for the Dozier family."

"Bob Colgate had Chris Garrett with him when he showed up at the farm?" Eric asked.

"I didn't expect that," I admitted, shaking my head. "Chris had never been mentioned as having witnessed the shooting. Once I saw Bob get Chris out of the car, I was not willing to put Chris' life in jeopardy any longer than it had been already. That's why I decided to immediately walk out of the barn and talk to Bob."

"He shot you without a second thought," Tom said, still having a hard time believing it.

"Everything happened so fast," I said. "All I knew was that I had been shot. I didn't really know where or how bad I was hit. It just felt like I had been kicked by a mule. The shot spun me around towards the barn, and Bob just kept shooting. I wanted to make sure that Chris did not get hurt, and when I saw Sheriff Larson get him into the house I knew he would be okay."

Eric, Steve, and Tom were all listening closely as I filled them in on the details of what had happened, so I continued.

"My gun was still in my shoulder holster, but after I got shot I didn't think I'd be able to reach it. I knew my legs were not going to hold me up very much longer. I remember the splinters of the barn spraying onto my face and all around me from the constant barrage of gunshots. When I saw the button to start the grain auger right there, within arms-reach, I didn't think, I just reacted. I pushed the button and hoped to hell that the auger was still working, and that Bob was standing close enough to it that it would at least throw him off balance."

"That it did," Tom said. "I ran to the front of the barn as fast as I could after I heard the first shot. It couldn't have taken me much more than five seconds to reach you. I turned off the auger when I got there. Chris was safely in the house, and Sheriff Larson was tending to Bob. You were down, and I just did what I could to help you. The whole scene was pretty nasty, but I would have to say, Jason, your move to push the start button to the grain auger most likely saved your life."

"No, Tom," I said. "I think you saved my life by working to stop the bleeding. I don't know if I could have made it without your help."

Tom blushed. "Well, that's what friends are for," he said. "Besides, it's the least I could do for someone who solved the *Chicago Field Museum* robbery/murder case for me. This was the biggest case I've ever had in my life. The Chicago PD and the *Field Museum* staff are very happy to have the case wrapped up."

I was glad the Pearl Lake murder had been solved, too. I didn't want that hanging over me or over the people in town.

"There were a lot of people that worked to make it happen," I said.

"We all know that you were the one responsible for solving this case, Jason," Tom said, "and it wasn't an easy one."

Steve and Eric nodded their heads in agreement.

"Were all of the stolen gems, jewelry, and necklaces and everything from the museum recovered?" Eric asked.

"Every piece of it," Tom answered satisfactorily.

"Where did you find them?" Eric asked.

"It was all in Bob's safe at the Badger Finance Company office," Tom answered.

"Well, all of it except for Chief Blackhawk's headdress, which we found in Stanley Stone's vehicle," I clarified, smiling, "and the rest of the stolen Native American artifacts, which we found in Mr. Stone's residence."

"That's right," Tom agreed. "We were lucky you made that connection to the museum when you saw the headdress in his car. Everybody who saw it thought it was just another typical dream catcher decoration hanging on the rearview mirror."

It helps to pay attention to your dreams, I thought.

« Chapter 40 »

THE FRONT DOORBELL RANG. My dad went to the door and opened it, and stood there for a while talking to the bell-ringer. I couldn't see who it was from where I was sitting on the back porch.

Before long my dad escorted Chief Medicine Man Denby Sage and Holy Man John 'Calm Heart' Yazee into the house. Despite Denby's hand motion for me to remain seated, I stood up to greet them.

"Chief Sage, Calm Heart, it's good to see you again," I said sincerely, as they nodded in response.

"Hi Jason. I hope we are not intruding," Calm Heart said.

"Absolutely not," I said. "You are both always welcome in my home."

Jessica joined us on the porch and stood by my side.

"Hi, Chief Sage. Hello, Calm Heart," she welcomed them warmly. "It's a pleasure to see you both again."

"Hello, Jessica," said Calm Heart.

"It is good to see you, too, Jessica, Buffalo Woman," Chief Sage said.

Denby and I both looked at Jessica. I was sure Denby could tell from the look on her face that she had not heard the 'Buffalo Woman' description before, and did not exactly know what it meant. She still returned our gazes with a calm, confident smile.

"It is the ultimate compliment, Jessica," Calm Heart said. "You will understand when Jason has a chance to tell you the full story. It is one that you will find very fascinating, I'm sure."

"I'm sure I will," Jessica replied. "I know Jason will share it with me when he has a chance. I definitely want to hear all about it, though." She turned and looked at me. I could tell from her intense facial expression that she meant sooner, rather than later.

"Jason, congratulations on recovering the gems and Native American items that were stolen from the *Chicago Field Museum*," Denby said.

"You must be very happy to have solved the *Field Museum* robbery case, and the Pearl Lake murder case, too," Calm Heart added.

"*Happy* might not be the right word for it, but I am glad it's all over," I answered. I was glad that the crimes had been solved, but two people had been killed – and I was nearly the third. It all just hit a little too close to home.

"I'm glad to see that you are recovering well from the shooting," Calm Heart said.

"I'm feeling a lot better than I did a few days ago, that's for sure."

"When I heard about the shooting, I had a strong feeling that you would be okay," Denby said matter-of-factly.

"Thank you, Chief Sage. I appreciate that, but I have a feeling that you didn't come here all the way from South Dakota to tell me that," I said, grinning.

"You are right, Jason. We did come to wish you well, but that is not the only reason we came to see you today."

Looking at their faces, I was not overly concerned, but their visit had definitely piqued my curiosity. I waited patiently for Denby to explain.

"I am glad that you are here, too, Jessica, because you are very much involved," he said to her with a comforting smile on his face. "I wanted to tell you about a dream I had last night. I believe both of you will find it very interesting."

"Oh?" Jessica said curiously, looking at Denby, Calm Heart, and back to me.

The house grew silent. Everyone in the kitchen, family room, porch, and spread throughout the house was listening intently. They were all looking at Jessica and me to see our reaction to what Denby had said. Denby noticed, too. He glanced briefly out the porch windows at the sandy beach leading to Pearl Lake.

"Would you like to get some fresh air?" he asked, giving us an opportunity to hear what he had to say in private. His calm smile was reassuring, and I was still not worried about hearing the dream that he had come to share with us. Jessica and I exchanged glances. Her cheeks were flush with excitement in anticipation of hearing about the dream.

"That sounds like a good idea," I answered. Jessica and I led Denby and Calm Heart out the porch door and onto the beach. We sat, contentedly, on my picnic table, hearing the waves rush rhythmically onto the sandy shore.

Denby didn't keep us waiting.

"I had a dream," he began. "I could see everything clearly, as though I was there in real life. It was a good dream."

Jessica and I were watching him, listening closely.

"I was walking in the wilderness, over hills and plains. I came to a small, peaceful town that was surrounded by rich, green meadows, fertile farmlands, and abundant rivers and streams. I arrived at a house on the outskirts of town. Jason and Jessica, you were both there."

Jessica and I looked at each other, excitedly, waiting for Denby to continue.

"You were playing with a young boy and a young girl. They both had light, curly blond hair. You and the children looked healthy, and happy. It was clear that you were very close and had a deep affection for each another."

Jessica reached over to me and wrapped her arm around mine. It felt good to have her close to me.

"Miracle was standing nearby, and was watching over you and the children," Denby said.

Jessica and I both smiled. I felt we had a special connection to Miracle. I think Jessica sensed it, too, especially after Miracle came to her on the Marshall Farm. I also believed that Miracle somehow had a role in bringing us together.

"In my dream," Denby continued, "Miracle was still a young buffalo. She was bigger than she is today, but her hair was still pure white – as clean and white as freshly fallen snow. It was obvious that Miracle is a special buffalo!

"You were playing catch with the children, and were throwing a baseball back and forth. There were two wolves off in the distance, watching the boy and girl very closely. The wolves were odd-looking creatures. One had long red, straggly hair and eerie green eyes. The other had shiny jet-black hair and shifty brown eyes. At one point while you were playing, the girl walked away to retrieve the baseball near some trees. The wolves crept up close to her, stopping on the other side of the trees. The girl did not see the wolves, but Miracle and the little boy both saw them immediately, and they realized that the girl could be in great danger."

Jessica gasped, clamping my arm tighter.

"Then something powerful happened," Denby said, looking at us closely. "I saw a ball of light rise from Miracle, and another ball of light rise from the little boy. The two balls of light joined, and became one larger, more powerful ball of light. The light moved very quickly to the little girl, and surrounded her in what seemed to be a protective shield. As I looked closer, I could see two other figures standing beside the girl inside the shield of light, one on each side of her, helping to protect her. I could tell by the style of clothing and the lone eagle feathers on each of their heads that they were Lakota Sioux Indians. The wolves immediately turned around and ran away until they were out of sight. Now seeing the retreating wolves, and fully aware of the Lakota Sioux Indians and protective shield around her, the little girl calmly picked up the ball and smiled in appreciation at Miracle and the boy. She knew that they had protected her. As she walked back to you and Jessica, the shield of light and Lakota Sioux Indians surrounding her slowly disappeared. When you were done playing baseball, I saw you walking back to the house. All of you, including Miracle, were together as one, and were happy and content." Denby took a deep breath. "That is how the dream ended."

Denby remained seated, giving us time to contemplate the dream.

"That was a beautiful dream," Jessica said after a few seconds. "Thank you for sharing it with us. I'm still not exactly sure what it means. Is it saying that

Jason and I will be together? Were the two children ours?"

"There is deep meaning to the dream," Calm Heart answered, "but you cannot take everything in it literally. Denby saw the two of you together in the future. It cannot be said for certain whether you will remain friends, will continue to grow closer, or will even be joined together in marriage. That has yet to be determined. The same goes for the children in the dream. It is not known whether they are your children, or not. You are both coaches. It is possible the dream is simply portraying that type of relationship with the children."

I thought about what Chief Sage had said. It made sense, but one thing about the dream bothered me.

"It was a good dream," I said. "It lifted my spirits when I heard it, except for the part about the wolves. Was it a warning?"

"The wolves could represent great danger," Calm Heart admitted, "but they also revealed signs that are very encouraging."

Chief Sage nodded in agreement.

"No matter who the boy and girl in the dream were," he explained, "it is clear they had a close connection to Miracle, just like the one you and Jessica have with her. The possibilities of what that could mean are very exciting."

"The part of the dream about the Lakota Sioux Indians and protective shield around the girl was absolutely magical," Jessica said.

"That was certainly an aspect of the dream that was very revealing," Chief Sage said. "It showed that the boy and girl had unique strengths that may have been aided by Miracle. They displayed extraordinary abilities that were used to protect each other, and that most likely can be used to help others. Just as important, they were able to summon Native American spirits to come to their aid. The boy and girl were very special."

Jessica and I looked at each other again. Even though we did not say anything, we were both probably thinking the same thing – that the boy and girl in the dream would turn out to be our children.

"Now, about the wolves," Chief Sage added. "We all face uncertainties in our lives. It is how we prepare for them, and how we choose to handle them when they arise, that matter the most. Jessica and Jason, if you have children, do not let the fear of the wolves prevent you from encouraging them to reach for their dreams. My dream tells me of the likelihood that their accomplishments will be far beyond what you could ever imagine."

He glanced at Calm Heart, and then turned his attention back to Jessica and me.

"I believe the most important message from the dream is to recognize the close bond you both have with Miracle," Chief Sage stressed. "She is a sacred white buffalo, and is a great Native American legend. You can trust her. If you need help or find yourselves in danger, listen to her. Miracle will lead you to safety, and will protect and guide you at times when you expect it the least, but need it the most."

THE END

My special thank you to Barb Callaghan for performing the unenviable task of reviewing the first draft of the manuscript and completing the line item editing. Her direct comments, honest opinions, and unending encouragement were invaluable to me in completing the book.

I would also like to extend my sincere appreciation to Denise Kelly for taking my ideas and wild imagination and making them come alive on the book cover.

ABOUT THE AUTHOR

J D Griesbach lives in Menasha, Wisconsin, where he was born and raised. He bleeds green and gold in testament to his love of the Green Bay Packers.

Like many authors, J D depends on the reviews and word-of-mouth referrals of his readers. If you enjoyed reading Pearl Lake, please consider leaving a review on Amazon.com and Goodreads.com.

www.jdgriesbachauthor.com

Feel free to contact J D at:
jdgriesbach.author@yahoo.com